Open Doors:
Fractured Fairy Tales

Edited by
Elisabeth Hirsch

Illustrated by
Candiss West

Compiled by
Wayman Publishing

Open Doors: Fractured Fairy Tales

waymanpublishing.com
P. O. Box 160693
Clearfield, UT
84016

Open Doors: Fractured Fairy Tales

ISBN-13: 978-1480157187

ISBN-10: 148015718X

Printed in the United States of America.

Table of Contents

The Three Little Pigs: A Lesson in Modern Economics and Green Living
Sarah Clark Monagle

Once upon a time, there were three little pigs who left their mommy and daddy to see the world. There are other stories about other pigs, and these pigs thought themselves quite knowledgeable when it came to housing. They were confident and happy pigs, but, as their fun summer came to an end and autumn descended, the three pigs realized that they would need to find real homes and stop crashing on their friends' couches.

The pigs knew that they must get to work on their housing or they would be left homeless or, worse, back at their parents' house. The laziest of the pigs, Little Pig, grabbed a giant armful of straw and declared, "I'm good. I'll make something out of this." And off he went.

The other pigs scoffed at his lack of planning, but the laziest pig was content. The other two pigs went on their way.

The second pig noted that he needed a bigger, sturdier house—wood, perhaps. For that, he would need lumber and supplies. This required a quick trip to Mr. Wolf's Bank.

In no time, the pig had his loan and was building his wooden house.

"Clunk, clunk, clunk!" He nailed all of the lumber together into a strong wooden home.

But the third pig did not like the house. It was too small.

"Your house is not good enough!" he exclaimed. It needs to be bigger, more impressive, and in a better neighborhood. The only problem was that the oldest pig had just left his parents' house and had no money to finance his dream home. Fortunately for him, Mr. Wolf, the banker, explained that mortgage rates were at an all-time low, and he granted the pig an adjustable rate mortgage to build his dream mansion.

The third pig's mansion was beautiful, and the other pigs came by to admire it. It had granite countertops, stainless steel appliances, and a Jacuzzi. What the other pigs didn't know about the pig's impressive brick mansion was that he had already begun to default on his hefty mortgage payments, and Mr. Wolf was about to come calling.

The pig enjoyed almost six months in his mansion before Mr. Wolf's Bank foreclosed on it, and he was evicted. It seems the pig had fallen victim to the housing boom and the mortgage crisis all in one. He took one last look at his brick house and, suitcases in hand, took the long walk of shame back to his parents' house.

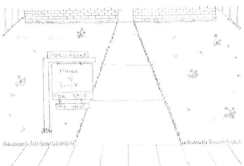

Meanwhile, the second pig had been living a more modest, middle class life in his wooden house. Unfortunately, the pig was laid off from his job at the Piggly Wiggly.

Unable to pay his bills, the pig fell behind on his loan

payments. Soon, Mr. Wolf was calling, and the small wooden house had a sign out front that said, "BANK OWNED."

Now two pigs were back at home with their parents. No one had heard from the youngest pig since he set off with the pile of straw. One day, annoyed by the noises and smells of four adult pigs living under one roof, they set out to look for Little Pig.

They found him on a hill with a line of people waiting to see him. Out front was a sign that said, "Eco Houses—designed by Little Pig." Little Pig sat on the ground surrounded by a circle of big rocks just taller than his head. The roof of his stone home was made of thatched straw, the straw he had carried with him the day he left.

Little Pig saw his family standing there and got up right away. "What do you think?" he asked. Not waiting for an answer, he told them, "These houses are all the rage! Back to the basics—that's where it's at."

Little Pig, being generous and eco-friendly (and also quite wealthy by this time) built an Eco House for each of his family members, mortgage free. And they lived happy, eco-friendly, debt-free lives ever after.

© Sarah Clark Monagle 2012

About the Author

Sarah Clark Monagle is an educator, mother, writer, photographer and brain tumor survivor. Her work has been published in many poetry reviews and photography sites, and she is a regular contributor to the Chicken Soup for the Soul series. You can follow her at www.sarahmonagle.wordpress.com

Much Ado About a 'Do
B.J. Lee

When Rapunzel the fair
had let down her long hair,
Goldilocks, shocked,
stood stock-still to stare.

Finally Goldi called,
"Hey you up there,
what product is giving you
such great hair care?"

Rapunzel said,
"If I were freed from this lair,
I'd show you my tricks
and give *your* hair some flair."

But Goldilocks told her,
"No way! You'll stay where
the princes can't see your hair.
No, I won't share!"

9

Rapunzel cried,
"Goldilocks, I do declare,
your selfishness fills me
with deepest despair.

You must be aware
there are princes to spare.
I hope, down the road,
you run into a bear!"

About the Author

B.J. lives on a barrier island in Florida with her poet husband (Malcolm Deeley) and toy poodles, JoJo and Clementine. She spends most of her spare time writing poetry, rhyming picture books, and a young adult novel. B.J. has had two of her poems nominated for The Rhysling Award which appear in The Rhysling Anthology 2011 and 2012. She's also been published in In the Garden of the Crow, and And the Crowd Goes Wild. She has over 40 poems published/forthcoming in such magazines as Highlights for Children and The SCBWI Bulletin and has won/placed in contests/awards including runner up in the 2011 SCBWI Magazine Merit Awards for poetry.

www.childrensauthorbjlee.com.

Nursery Rhyme Re-Mix
Steven Kaminsky

"Again?" I said as the Boobster handed me the same story we had been reading for what seemed like forever. I had given the Boobster two new books for her birthday. I tried to stroke her ego, pointing out the bright yellow words, *For Children 4 and Up*, on the front covers. That was two weeks ago. The books were gathering dust.

"I like this story," said the Boobster. "This is the one I want you to read."

"You see," I said. "That's the problem right there. It's always about you. Did it ever occur to you that I might want to read a different story?"

The Boobster kicked off the covers and jumped out of the bed. "Where are you going?"

"I'm going to ask Mommy to read me the story."

Mommy? Story time was *my* time and it was going to stay that way.

"Okay, Okay you win. We'll read this story again."

When the Boobster got back in the bed I tightly tucked her in, to discourage another escape attempt, before I suggested a compromise.

"Hey, I got a good idea that will make both of us happy. We'll do the same story, look at the same pictures, but I'll spice it up a little so it's fun for me too."

"The same story?"

"Isn't that what I said?"

She thought it over and warily gave me permission to get started.

"Once upon a time—"

"That's not what it says!"

"I told you that I'm going to spice it up. That means it's going to be the same story but with different words.

11

Trust me; you're going to like it."

She didn't say 'Yes' but she didn't say 'No' either. I took that to mean that I could start again.

It was shortly after sunset. The Cat had waited until the Farmer, carrying a full bucket of milk, walked through the gate of the white picket fence surrounding the farmhouse, before entering the barn. He went straight to the Cow's stall to lap up the milk that had escaped the Farmer's bucket. The Cow was looking out of the stall window and seemed oblivious to the Cat foraging beside her udder.

When there was no milk left to be found, the Cat said, "Yo Cow, what's up?"

"MoOo0on," said the Cow.

The Cat was walking away but came to a sudden halt when the Cow asked, "How come you're walking away? I thought that cats were supposed to be curious?"

Careful . . . thought the Cat. When he had been a kitten, his mother had told him over and over: "Curiosity kills." Nevertheless, he turned around and said, "What's so curious about a cow saying 'mooo'. Isn't that what you're supposed to say?"

"Not mooo," said the Cow, "MoOo0on."

"Moon?" said the Cat. "Oh, I get it. When I asked you 'what's up', you thought I was asking you if the moon had risen yet. That's not what I meant. It's just the way us cool cats say, "What's new."

"I know that, Mr. Cool Cat, and my answer is still the moOo0on."

"What are you talking about? There's nothing new about the moon."

"That's what you think, Cat. To me the moOo0on is always new. It's never the same two nights in a row. I always discover something unique and wonderful that

I've never seen before."

"Well, isn't that interesting," said the Cat sarcastically, "A cow that likes the moon."

"Not like," said the Cow. "I love the moOoOon. I love it so much that I even dream about it when I sleep."

"You dream of looking at the moon?"

"No," said the Cow. "In my dream, I start running as fast as I can, then I leap into the sky and I jump over the moOoOon."

"That's your dream? To jump over the moon? Can't be done."

"But that's the beauty of dreams," said the Cow. "They're not limited to the laws of the natural world. Anything is possible. In fact, if you wish hard enough, some dreams do come true."

"Yeah, right. Keep wishing."

"Don't you have any dreams, Cat?"

"Of course I have dreams. I dream of eating gourmet cat food out of a platinum bowl with lots of smoking hot pussy cats who can't keep their paws off me. But I don't dream of crazy things that can't be done, like jumping over the moon." The Cat started walking out of the barn. "I better get back to the farmhouse before I get locked out for the night. See you tomorrow."

"Sweet dreams," said the Cow.

"You were wrong, Dad," interrupted the Boobster. "You don't know me."

Huh, where was this coming from? "Of course I know you. I'm your father."

"You said that you know me and that I would like your story, but you don't know me cuz I don't like it. Can you read it the right way now?"

"You can't like it or not like it until you hear the whole

13

story. I just got started. There's more to tell."

"More," she whined in disbelief. "Well, how am I s'pposed to know when you're finished?"

"Simple. When I'm finished I'll say 'The End.' Now where was I?"

"The Cat and Cow went to sleep at the end of the story."

"It's not the end because . . ."

The next night, as soon as the farmer left the barn with the full bucket of milk, the Cat streaked to the Cow's stall and ignoring the spilled milk said, "Cow, we got to talk!"

"Mooo," said the Cow.

"Again with the moon," said the Cat impatiently.

"Not moOoOon," said the Cow. "I said, 'Mooo', that's the way us cool cows say, 'What's up'?"

The Cat wondered if the Cow was mocking him but her big brown cow eyes were filled with sincerity.

"I'll tell you what's up," said the Cat. "This afternoon; the Farmer's Wife set the table with her fancy table cloth, the fine china and the good silverware. Now guests are arriving and one of them brought a fiddle."

"Sounds like they're having a shin-dig," said the Cow. "What's the big deal?"

"Well . . ." the Cat hesitated. He didn't like to open himself up, as in a college comparative anatomy lab. It made him feel vulnerable. "I have a dream that I didn't tell you about yesterday. I've loved the fiddle from the first time I heard one played. But it was more than enjoying the music. I could feel it in my gut. It was like I had a fiddle inside me, vibrating in sympathy with every note the fiddler played. As if the fiddle and me were connected by some invisible umbilical cord and—"

14

The Cat hissed and arched his back when he heard derogatory laughter. He leapt onto the windowsill and saw the Dog rolling on the ground, kicking his legs in the air in a fit of hysteria.

"I knew the Cow was a lunatic, but I didn't know you were a Krazy Kat," said the Dog. "Of course you feel the music in your gut. What do you think they make fiddle strings of?"

The Cat and the Cow looked at the Dog in silence. They were both feeling like one of the sheep: Sheepish.

"You're awful quiet," said the Dog to the Cow. "Cat got your tongue?"

"What a clever little doggy," said the Cow. "Don't you have any dreams?"

"You must be green . . . if you don't know my dream. . . . Need another clue . . .? I just gave it to you."

"He wants to be a poet," said the Cat.

"Not a poet," growled the Dog. "Do poets wear heavy, 24K, diamond studded dog collars? Do they 'corn row' their fur? I want to be a rapper like my idol Snoop Dog. I can bust a rhyme with the best of them. I really love rapping. Check this out: "Hey diddle, diddle. The Cat playin' the fiddle? That's crazy: Fo'shizzle!"

The Dog was howling with laughter and he couldn't go on. He started trotting towards the sty and managed to say over his shoulder, "I gotta tell this to the pigs. They're going to eat it up."

"Wait a minute," interrupted the Boobster. "I saw Snoop Dog on MTV. He's not a dog. He's a people."

"I know that," I said. "What am I, stupid?"

"Not you, stupid: The Dog. The Dog thinks Snoop Dog is a dog."

"Who cares what the Dog thinks? It's not important."

"But the Dog thinks he can rap because he thinks Snoop Dog is a real dog. It's the best part of the story," she explained.

"Forget about the dog," I barked. "Can you just stop talking and pay attention to the rest of the story?"

"Fo'shizzle," she giggled . . . as I continued.

"Well, that's just great," said the Cat. "By tomorrow, I'll be the laughing stock of the farm."

"Or you can be the envy of the farm," said the Cow, "If you play the fiddle tonight. Didn't you say one of the guests brought a fiddle?"

"Yeah, I did," said the Cat. "But how can I get the fiddle to try it?"

"Simple," said the Cow. "The music won't start up until after dinner, so you'll get your chance while they're eating."

"Hmmm," thought the Cat. "That does sound like a good plan. Oh, who am I kidding? I'm a Cat. I can't play a fiddle. It's just a crazy dream."

"Stop thinking so much," said the Cow. "What's your gut telling you?"

"It's saying I can do it."

"Then listen to your gut. I know you can do it. This is the best chance you'll ever have."

The cat was purring and his front paws were alternatively going up and down: extending and retracting his claws.

"Don't sit there purring," said the Cow. "Follow your gut before it's too late . . . while they're still eating. Go! Go now."

The Cat took off towards the farmhouse like his tail was on fire. He slid under the white picket fence and jumped through the sitting room window.

Now that the Cat was gone, the Cow wondered if encouraging the Cat was the right thing to do. After all, cats can't fiddle.

She stopped fretting when a stream of music poured out of the same window, the Cat went through, and washed over the Cow like a soft, spring rain. Her hooves were rhythmically stomping the ground as she danced out of the barn. She stopped, closed her eyes, and tried to imagine the cat fiddling but she couldn't conjure the image. This had to be seen; to be believed.

She started to trot towards the farmhouse and realized that in order to look in the window, she would have to jump over the white picket fence. She started to run. The closer she got to the fence, the higher it seemed to get. She was unaware that she was running in perfect syncopation with the music. The faster the fiddler played, the faster she ran. Faster than she had ever ran before. When she reached the fence, she pushed off her hind legs and felt a wave of music swell beneath her, lifting her up and over the . . ."

"How much longer?" groaned the Boobster.

"How much longer?" I was exasperated. "I can't believe you're asking me that now when the story is really starting to take off."

"Does that mean you're almost finished?"

I had reached the end of my rope but fortuitously found a *rule*.

"Listen to me, there's a new rule: You can't talk until you hear me say, 'The End'. Understood?"

"Yeah . . . dish and spoon?"

The Dish and the Spoon were side by side after being separated for months.

"I missed you," said the Dish.

"I missed you too," said the Spoon. "It was hard being without you especially when the other silverware made fun of me for loving you. They said, 'Stick with your own kind. Those dishes aren't even American. They're from China. That's why they're so disgustingly round'."

"Does it bother you that I'm round?"

"Are you kidding me?" asked the Spoon. "Your roundness was what attracted me in the first place. Round is so sexy, so exotic. But the reason I fell in love with you is because your roundness isn't just superficial, like the other dishes. You're also round on the inside, where you hold the hot soup. That's where it really counts, on the inside."

"You're so sweet to say that," said the Dish. "I wish the other dishes could see you like I do. I love the way the light reflects off your rim, especially after you've been polished. And you're a soup spoon; not like the teaspoons or tablespoons. When I'm filled with hot soup, and you're dipped inside me, only you know how much soup to take out so that I can't wait for you to come back for more; again and again. Sometimes I think I'm going to chip or crack, it feels so good. Oh, why can't the others see that we were made for each other?"

18

"Society will never accept our love," said the Spoon. "They'll always put you with the other dishes in the cupboard and me with the other silverware in the drawer. They even keep us separated in the dish washer."

"They should call it the dish and the silverware washer," said the Dish.

"Let's run away," said the Spoon. "If we run away, we would never have to be apart. Let's go now, before the music stops and they sit down to eat."

"You're dreaming," said the Dish. "We can't even walk, let alone run away. It's wonderful, but it's only a dream."

The Spoon wasn't easily discouraged. Maybe if he wished hard enough. . . . He was eying the open window as the best escape route when, in the clear night sky, he noticed something moving over the moon and felt a surge of electricity race up his handle.

"We can run away, it's not impossible," said the Spoon. "Quick. Look through the window and tell me what you see."

"I see a beautiful, romantic moon that will be back here tomorrow, just like us."

"No!" said the Spoon, "look closer . . . tell me what you see."

The Dish gasped.

"Yes, yes! You see it, don't you?"

"But that's impossible," said the Dish. "Is that a—"

"Are we there yet?" asked the Boobster.

"We're not in the car; we're in your bed reading a story. What do you mean, 'are we there yet'?"

"The end of the story," said the Boobster. "Are we there yet?"

"Hey, you broke the rule!" I was hyperventilating. "Did

you hear me say, 'The End'?"

"That's not a real rule. You just made it up. How much longer?"

"About two minutes."

"Is that a long time?"

"No. . . Unless you keep interrupting me."

"C'mon into the dining room everyone, it's time to eat," said the Farmer's Wife.

The guests were seated and complimented the Farmer's Wife on her fancy tablecloth, fine china and good silverware. The Farmer was a very stoic man, so when he stood up, all the bantering came to a stop.

"How come ever 'body but me get to eat soup tonight?"

"Heavens, what are you talking 'bout Pa?"

"Seems to me," said the Farmer, "that there's a soup dish and soup spoon in front of ever 'one 'cept me."

The Farmer's Wife glanced at the settings before each guest and when she got to the Farmer's seat she saw that, indeed, there was no soup dish or spoon.

"That's strange," she said, almost to herself.

"Ain't nothing strange about it, Ma. You were busy and just plain old ferget."

"That's not what I'm talking about." She slowly looked around the table again, nodding her head as she came to each guest.

"It is strange," she said staring at the Fiddler. The guests looked at the Fiddler hoping to see what was spooking the woman so bad.

The Farmer cautiously asked her, "What's so strange, Ma?"

She swallowed hard, took a deep breath and said, "If we're all sitting down at this here table . . . who's in the

sitting room playing the fiddle?"
"The End"

I closed the book and stared at the cover. I imagined my name under the title as the author of the 'new and improved' edition. The sound of a sniffle broke my reverie.

"Maybe you didn't hear me. I said 'The End'. You can talk now."

Another sniffle; then two snorts.

I turned toward the Boobster and saw that her eyes were wet and her lower lip was trembling.

"Umm . . . wasn't that a good story?"

"No," she sobbed. "It was stupid. I'm not even sleepy."

"Okay, okay," I said, "No reason to get upset. You want me to read you the story the regular way?"

She nodded, so I opened the book and began to read.

Hey, diddle, diddle,
The Cat and the fiddle,
The Cow jumped over the moon;
The little Dog laughed
To see such sport,
And the Dish ran away with the Spoon.

My story was stupid? Whoever wrote this story must have been tripping. Maybe it makes more sense when you're four years old.

I know. I'll ask the Boobster to tell me what this 'smart' story means so when we read it again tomorrow, maybe I'll be able to enjoy it too.

Or maybe not . . . when I turned to ask; she was already asleep.

I lay there not moving. The only sound: her soft, rhythmic breathing. When there's love; life feels timeless and a moment can last forever.

Yet I felt the sad chill of an insight. No more improvisation: re-writes or forced variety. The school is waiting for her. It won't be long before she can read the stories; by herself. . .

. . . without me.

About the Author
Steven is the former director of Pediatric Dentistry at Jamaica Hospital and Bronx Lebanon Hospital. He plans on writing a textbook on pediatric dentistry using creative non-fiction. He also has decided to write a memoir with the theme on 'Parental Alienation Syndrome'. [He really doesn't want to write this, however, he has been 'chosen'.]

Hey Diddle Diddle
Variation by Fran Fischer

Hey diddle diddle,
The Cat and the fiddle,
The Cow jumped over the moon,
The little Dog laughed to see such a spree
and they enjoyed their LSD!

About the Author
Humorous writer and editor, Fran Fischer can make anyone laugh. As her 74th birthday present she flew in the same anti-gravity plane that the astronauts train in! She walks with a cane, but did one-handed pushups and flew like Superman—WHAT A BLAST that must have been!

http://www.fishducky.blogspot.com/

Danny and his Magic Beans
Siv Maria Ottem

Now, Danny was a good looking lad but not very nice. That does not mean he did not have friends. In fact he had a lot of friends. They followed him everywhere, and every day after school they would go over to his big house and play with all the latest videogames that money could buy. If there was something that Danny wanted all he had to do was ask and his mother would get it for him. You see Danny and his mother were very rich and everyone treated them like royalty. Yes, Danny was spoiled but it wasn't really his fault. His widowed mother was always busy making lots of money. Instead of giving him time, she gave him things, and that made Danny happy enough. The more things Danny had, the more he wanted and the meaner he got.

At first no one seemed to notice how rude he was becoming. He had no father, his mother was busy and his friends didn't care as long as they got to play with his things. When he started to bully the poor kids at school the teachers turned a blind eye. After all, his mother was a sad widow. But more importantly, she gave a lot of money to the town and the school. No matter how mean Danny got, no one said or did a thing.

One day Danny wanted to see what a naked bird looked like so he plucked off all the feathers on his mother's pet parrot. When his mother came home and saw what Danny had done, she gave out a large sigh. "What good is a naked parrot that cannot talk? You will have to go into town and trade it for another!"

Danny, who was bored anyways, took the frightened parrot in a cage and headed off towards town. On his way he ran into an old man carrying a small golden bag. As curious as he was greedy, Danny stopped the old man, tilted his head and asked, "What's in the bag old man?"

To which the old man replied, "Tell me what you have in your cage young man and I will tell you what I have in my bag." Danny lifted the cage in front of the old man's face and with a proud smile said, "This is what a naked parrot looks like. I took off all the feathers myself, but now the stupid thing won't talk so I am off to trade it for another."

"You don't say!" said the old man while he opened his bag and let the boy look inside. "What you see here lad are magic beans." Danny's eyes grew wide, and he squealed with delight as he looked at the one thing in the world that he suddenly wanted more than anything. The old man took pity on the bird and knowing what kind of magic the beans processed he made a proposition that the young boy could not resist.

"I will trade you three of my magic beans for your parrot."

"What kind of magic will these beans do?" Danny asked as he made the trade. The old man just smiled

25

and walked away repeating to the bird, "He will see. . . . He will see. . . ."

Danny ran home and showed his mother the magic beans. She looked at them and started to laugh. "Those are just regular beans, you silly boy! There is no such thing as magic." Then she tossed the beans out the window, gave him a new video game to play, and sent him to his room. It didn't take long before Danny forgot all about the beans.

The next morning Danny woke up to the sound of scratching outside his window. Angry, he got out of bed and pushed aside his curtains to see what was making that dreadful noise. He rubbed his eyes, and stared in wonder as his jaw dropped. There, outside his window, where his mother had thrown the magic beans, was now a gigantic strange tree. He stuck his head out the window and saw that the tree reached right up into the sky and past the clouds with no end in sight. "Awesome!" he said, and then he tested his weight on one of the branches before crawling out of the window and onto the tree. He was in a hurry as most boys are when they start on a new adventure. He was still in his pajamas as he started to climb.

Up and up he went until he reached the top, and there in the distance he saw a giant castle. He climbed off the tree and hungry as he was, decided to go to the castle and get some breakfast. Since he was used to getting everything he wanted, it never occurred to him that getting some food would be any different. Surely there was plenty of food in the castle.

Once he got to the castle he knocked on the huge wooden door, but no one answered. Danny put his shoulder to it and pushed with all his might. The door swung slowly open with a noisy creak, and Danny found himself standing in the biggest kitchen he had ever seen. The smell of fresh baking was everywhere, and his stomach growled as he looked at the giant loaves of bread lined up to cool on the counter in front of him. Danny stared at the back of the tallest woman he had ever seen, who was busy removing an enormous pie from the oven. Danny cleared his throat and the woman turned around with a surprised look on her face.

Danny pointed to the bread on the counter and said in a bossy voice, "Hey, big fat lady, how about you give me some of that bread."

"If you stay here, lad," said the woman, "You will most likely end up being my husband's breakfast. He is a giant and rather fond of mean boys on fresh bread for breakfast." Then looking down at the boy who barely reached the top of her counter she said, "Nasty little boys like you also make a very tasty stew. You are very rude and certainly not very nice. I think I will bake YOU for breakfast with a lot of spice." She took a huge wooden spoon and poked him in the ribs. "My husband will be home soon and he will be very hungry!"

For the first time in his life Danny felt fear and began to tremble as he stuttered, "b . . . b . . . but my m . . . m . . . mother will pay you a . . . lot of m . . . money if you get me home s . . . s . . . s . . . safe!"

"Money?" The woman laughed and pointed to the far side of the kitchen. "You see that hen over there? She lays golden eggs! I have all the money I need!"

As the woman started to approach him, Danny yelled out, "Wait!" Then he said as fast as he could, "I know what you need! I have the best MP3 player that money can buy. It can play endless songs! Surely in a place like this music would be a great treasure." Danny caught his breath and waited for her to reply.

27

"Music, you say?" She laughed again and said, "I have a golden harp that sings me any song that I wish whenever I like. Money and things will not save you now. If you had been nice, I might have made a stew with a little less spice."

Before he could turn around and run, the great castle walls began to shake. The sound of thundering footsteps grew louder and louder.

"It's my husband," smiled the giant woman. Quickly she grabbed Danny, pushed him inside the great big oven and closed the door just as her husband came in growling.

"I am so hungry that I could eat a dozen little boys! Tell me, wife, what's in the oven and smells so good? Are you making little boy stew?"

"Oh, I think you will like this one, he is extra mean and nasty. He should make a very tasty pot of stew.

Danny prayed as it grew warmer and warmer inside the stove. "I promise to be nice, Dear God, I promise to be nice, just get me out of here and I will never be mean again!"

Danny woke up covered in sweat. He jumped out of bed, ran to the window, and looked outside. There was nothing there. No giants and no magic tree, but he couldn't see the beans that his mother had thrown there just yesterday. He went downstairs and then outside to take a look around, but the beans were gone.

Danny's mother stood at the door and looked at him strangely. "Whatever are you doing outside in your pajamas?"

Danny ran into his mother's arms, gave her a big hug and said, "Nothing, Mother. Let's go inside and I will make you breakfast for a change." His mother looked at him in surprise.

28

"Well that is a very nice thing for you to do."
Danny just smiled at her and said, "From now on that's me, Mr. Nice Guy!" He closed the door behind them and thought to himself . . . Better safe than sorry. After all, no one wants to end up in a pot of stew.

© Siv Maria Ottem 2012

About the Author

Siv Maria Ottem was raised in the United States and studied Journalism at a local community college in Minnesota. Her strong Norwegian roots and family ties led her to Norway where she has been living now for over 20 years. Working mostly in the travel or health industry, her passion has always been writing. Living in Norway among Trolls has inspired her to write about them and the culture surrounding them. "Secrets of the Ash Tree," was first published as a short story in a Fantasy Anthology called Open Doors (Volume One) by Wayman Publishing. She is now hard at work writing her first book in a series called "Gods and Fairy Tales," which is scheduled for release early next year.

Siv now lives with her husband in southern Norway. Together they have two children, one live in mother, and two family pets. Siv also has two children from previous relationships that are currently living in the United States. For more information please visit her blog: http://sivmaria.blogspot.no/.

Shoe Business
Jane L. Patton

While frantically searching
for her sheep one day,
Little Bo-Peep noticed
children at play.

Their mother, poor thing,
was having some trouble.
"It's naptime," she yelled,
"kids, come here on the double."

"Excuse me," said Bo-Peep,
"I need your permission
To take all your children
with me on my mission."

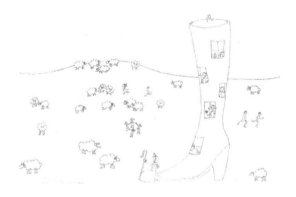

The Old Woman, tongue-tied,
leaned out her shoe door,
"A break from my 'sweet soles'?
Delighted, I'm sure!"

30

Off went the kids;
Bo-Peep took the whole crew.
Once back, sheep and children
lived in the old shoe.

Now, no more whipping
when it's time to sleep;
The kids are soon snoring . . .
they love to count sheep!

About the Author

Jane, a native Chicagoan, lives in San Diego, California. A graduate of Marycrest College, Davenport, Iowa, she has taught All-Level Music, Drama, and Kindergarten: in Iowa, Illinois, California, and Texas.

At one time a professional actress and vocalist with The Jim Patton Trio-"The Right Touch," Patton now concentrates on writing for children. She focuses her manuscripts on a variety of genres: plays for children (*A Dickens of a Christmas*); short stories (*Advent Angels*); poetry (*And the Crowd Goes Wild! A Global Gathering of Sports Poems*); and magazines (*A Sticky Riddle!*)

31

The Little Red Hen Moves to Beverly Hills
Deb Claxton

Once upon a time a Little Red Hen was speed walking around her wealthy gated community when she found some seeds on the ground. She took them back to her mansion where she found her friends, Skinny Stork, Really Rich Robin, and Narcissistic Nuthatch, sitting in her living room drinking wine.

"Look what I found. Who will help me plant the seeds?" asked the Little Red Hen.

"I can't I just got my nails done," said Skinny Stork.

"I don't want to get my designer jeans dirty," said Narcissistic Nuthatch.

"Why don't you just have your gardener plant them for you?" asked Really Rich Robin.

The Little Red Hen planted the seeds herself and they grew and grew until it was time to harvest the wheat.

"Who will help me take the wheat to the mill?" asked the Little Red Hen.

"I can't I've got a yoga class," said Narcissistic Nuthatch.

"Where are you going to take it? There's no mill in

Beverly Hills," said Skinny Stork.

"Why don't you just grind it up in a food processor?" asked Really Rich Robin.

The Little Red Hen ground up the wheat in her food processor and it was ready to bake into bread.

"Who will help me bake the bread?" asked the Little Red Hen.

"I can't, I have a meeting with my life coach," said Narcissistic Nuthatch.

"I'm going to spin class," said Skinny Stork.

"If you want bread why don't you just ask your cook to bake you some? My cook bakes the most delicious croissants," said Really Rich Robin.

The Little Red Hen decided to bake her own bread. Soon it was ready to come out of the oven. She sliced the warm bread and slathered it with butter and jam. Her friends found her in the kitchen.

"It smells so good in here," said Really Rich Robin.

"This homemade bread is really delicious but guess what? None of you can have any. You didn't help me plant the seeds, you didn't help me harvest the wheat, and you didn't help me bake the bread so I'm eating it all myself!" The Little Red Hen shouted.

"Take a chill pill. I don't eat carbs," said Narcissistic Nuthatch.

"Do you know how many calories are in that bread, butter, and jam?" asked Really Rich Robin.

"I'm on a colon cleanse," said Skinny Stork.

They left and the Little Red Hen ate up all the bread. She later regretted it after she got really sick, went to the doctor, and found out that she was allergic to gluten.

Jack Spratt
Variation by Fran Fischer

Jack Sprat could eat no fat.
His wife could eat no lean.
Mrs. Spratt became so fat
that when he stood beside her,
he couldn't be seen.

A Juror's Journal
Diane Weis Farone

Jury duty keeps popping up in my head and bugging me. Memories squirm in my mind like a bucket of worms trapped in a fisherman's bait pail. If I write stuff down maybe it'll flow out of my brain like the ink in my pen.

Jack didn't look like a bad boy. I guess his lawyer knew enough to have him all spiffed up in a suit and tie. Who did he think he could fool by tinkering with someone who grew up in overalls and bare feet? Why not make him more like Huck Finn, who after all was likable even when he strayed from the rules? That would have gone over better here in Grimmsville.

Jack had no words of regret, but then I guess he truly believed he did nothing wrong. His lawyer tried to make us believe it was self-defense in a hunter/prey/winner-take-all world. I had to ask myself how we could sit in judgment of him when maybe, but for the grace of God, we might find ourselves there.

We all had to agree, but we couldn't. The foreman's constant drumming of his fingers on the tabletop, between raking them through his thick hair, gave away his frustration and made me want to fix things. But how could I? People were pulling in different directions like opposing teams in a tug of war over a mud hole at the county fair.

Juror number six insisted, "Jack is responsible for the Giant's demise, ergo he must pay the consequences, which in this case requires capital punishment." Did he think he could overwhelm us with his highfalutin language? He was a professor on summer break, in love with his own words and far removed from the guts of the matter. If the rules were so clear and simple, we wouldn't need juries.

Juror number two had a different take, but just as simple-minded. "I'm not going to risk going to Hell for sentencing a possibly innocent man to any penalty but his own conscience." How did she make it through jury selection anyway?

You need to know the full story, as best I can tell it, to understand why this bothers me. You see, it's true Jack caused the Giant's death by cutting the beanstalk, making him crash to the ground and break his neck. But the Giant was chasing Jack. His lawyer asked us what we would do if a gigantic muscleman lumbered after us, breathing down our neck ready to snuff out our lives. Maybe it was self-defense. I only thought I wouldn't have traded a cow for beans in the first place, and I darn sure wouldn't climb some plant up to the sky. I hate high places with sheer drop-offs. Anyhow, I can't see how the Giant could be breathing down Jack's neck and still have far enough to fall to be killed when Jack chopped down the beanstalk.

Enough witnesses convinced me no one liked the Giant. He was a bully, using his superhuman strength to trample, like stampeding cattle, over anyone who stood in his way. He was a thief who grabbed whatever he wanted. You might even say he deserved to die; that the world was better off without him in it. That's what Jack's lawyer wanted us to think. But the jury didn't agree on whether the Giant's likability had anything to do with self-defense.

On the other side, the prosecutor told us Jack *enticed* the Giant to chase him to give him an excuse for murder. He wanted vengeance for a long-standing feud because the Giant took land and other stuff that rightfully belonged to Jack's family. According to the prosecution two wrongs don't make a right. We're supposed to let the law handle things, not take matters into our own hands like Jack did.

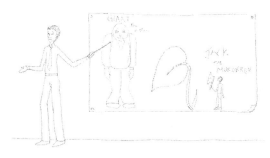

We pushed and pulled and bounced around like a rack hit by a cue ball down at the pool hall. And we sunk ourselves in different pockets, a hung jury. Then the state decided to cave in and do nothing more about it. So, they say Jack and his mother lived happily ever after with their ill-gotten (or recovered, depending on how you look at it) gains.

© Diane Weis Farone 2012

About the Author

Diane Farone, a lifelong fan of fairy tales and other truth-rendering fiction, has been happy to turn her writing efforts from academic publications in the publish or perish world of academia to writing for fun in her retirement. Ever the student she has been studying creative writing through the Writers Studio. Her stories have been published in *Rose Red Review (http://roseredreview.org/2012-autumn-karma-diane-farone/); Our Spirit, Our Reality; and Story Circle Network.*

The Princess and the Frog
Gayle C. Krause

Twelve pretty princesses stood near a pond,
waiting for princes to come from beyond,
to ferry them to the "Isle of Dance"
where they'd whirl and twirl in giddy romance.

But the youngest princess's prince didn't come.
Disappointed, she said, "This is so dumb."
Her smile turned into a small puckered frown
as she plopped on a log in her beautiful gown.

She imagined all the fun she would miss
when a frog on the log said, "It just takes *one* kiss."
She thought it disgusting, but then said "Why not?"
And the frog turned into a prince on the spot.

With no boat to row, on his back she did climb.
He swam to the isle. They got there on time.
His clothes were all wet. They drooped with a sag.
"I can't dance with you. You're as wet as a rag."

The Prince smiled and ripped off his clothes in a flash.
He adjusted his crown and his royal Prince sash.
The others gasped as they entered the dance.
The eldest prince snarled, "Now, what is the chance?

I thought that old king was the only odd one.
Look!
Your sister's with the mad emperor's son."

© Gayle C. Krause 2012

About the Author

Gayle C. Krause writes across the genres. Her debut YA novel, RATGIRL: SONG OF THE VIPER is forthcoming from Noble Young Adult (2013) and her picture book, ROCK STAR SANTA by Scholastic, Inc. (2008) is an original book club selection. Her YA historical romance short story, The Storyteller's Daughter is part of the TIMELESS Anthology by Pugalicious Press. (2012) And her poems have been published in MEANDERINGS, a Collection of Poetic Verse by Diversion Press (2009) and AND THE CROWD GOES WILD, an international children's poetry collection on sports Friesen Press. (2012)

http://www.gayleckrause.com/
http://thestorytelersscroll.blogspot.com/

Fairyland's Got Talent
Adam Graham

There was an old woman who lived in the shoe, she had so many children, she didn't know what to do. Her eldest son was a stout lad who took to singing in a magical way.

One day, the King's royal company was holding auditions in the town and the young man went to participate. After waiting in line for days, the emaciated young man got his chance to appear.

He walked to the stage and looked out at three judges seated at a table with a glass of grog in front of each of them.

The panel was made up of three of the King's Nobles, Sir Simon, Lady Brittany, and Lord Randall. An audience from the neighboring villages had assembled to see who would be added to the King's troupe of entertainers.

The shy lad hobbled forward in shabby rags.

"Hello," said Lady Brittany. "Welcome."

"Greetings," said Lord Randall.

The young man barely raised an arm. "Hello, your lordship, your ladyship, and Sir Simon."

Sir Simon shot a business-like glance at him. "So what's your name?"

"I don't have a name. Mother gave up names and just calls us by our number. I'm number one of thirty-eight."

"Wow," said Lord Randall.

"Thirty-eight kids. Where do you guys live?" asked Brittany.

"In a shoe," said the boy.

'Like a slipper?" asked Brittany.

The boy wrinkled his nose. "Of course not, don't be

silly, your ladyship. We live in a size eighteen boot."

Lord Randall gave an empathetic nod. "What does your mother do?"

"Well," said the boy. "She gives us broth without bread."

"Given the price of bread that's perfectly understandable," said Sir Simon.

The boy sniffled. "But then she whips all soundly and puts us to bed."

"Awww," said Brittany. "Poor thing. What are you going to do with the money if you win?"

"I want to buy mom a nicer place, maybe upgrade to a shoebox so there's room for the whole family."

Sir Simon tapped his fingers on the table. "So what are you going to do for us?"

The boy swallowed. "I gave to Ye Royal Band to play a song called, 'That Jazzy King.'"

"That sounds interesting," said Sir Simon. "Well, good luck."

The band began to play the music he'd written and everyone was amazed.

41

No one in the Kingdom had ever heard jazz, for it was an anachronism. The eyes of the three judges went wide. The crowd began to clap and rejoice greatly as the boy sang. He finished and all stood on their feet to applaud.

Sir Simon raised his hand. "That was phenomenal. This whole Jazz thing is just what we've been looking for. You walked in here and I thought perhaps you were a beggar or a pickpocket trying to get away from the sheriff by jumping into line. But you have something very special. And I think those who are here will be glad to say that they were here and they heard—" He paused. "Whoever you are, sing for the first time. You taught me not to judge people's talent by their physical appearance."

Lord Randall raised his hand. "Don't you have to learn that every city we go to?"

Sir Simon frowned. "Oh shut up, your Lordship. My son, I absolutely give you a *yes*."

Lady Brittany said, "You know when you came here, you looked pathetic, and I was just going to give you a pity vote to make the audience like me, but you don't need any pity."

The audience clapped.

Lady Brittany shouted, "It's a *yes* from me!"

Lord Randall said, "You know what, you're amazing. You have gone through so much and there you stand, my man, you are a star. And from now on, you're gonna get bread with your broth. And do you know why?"

The boy beamed. "Why, sir?"

"Because you may have been born in a shoe, but man, have you got soul."

Sir Simon scowled. "I can't believe you said that."

42

Lord Randall said, "From me, it is a *yes*."

"Three yeses, congratulations, you're joining our troupe " said Sir Simon.

And there was much rejoicing.

About the Author

Adam Graham is author of the Superhero Comedy Novel Tales of the Dim Knight and the Novella Sequels, Rise of the Robolawyers and Powerhouse Flies Again. He hosts the Great Detectives of Old Time Radio and the Old Time Radio Superman podcasts. You can visit him at http://www.greatdetectives.net and http://www.christiansuperheroes.com.

Simple Simon
Variation by Fran Fischer

Simple Simon met a pieman,
Going to the fair;
Says Simple Simon to the pieman,
Let me taste your ware.
Says the pieman to Simple Simon,
Show me first your penny;
Says Simple Simon to the pieman,
Indeed I have not any.
Says the pieman to Simple Simon,
Get lost, you creep!!

The Bitter Pea
EC Stilson

I've always hated being a magical pea. The royal guard stole me from my pod when I was still small and bitter. My fellow podlings were sacrificed for some stupid legend about peas and princesses. I saw Ben Pea-body get shoved between a million mattresses. We didn't call him Ben Pea-body after that, we called him Ben Smushed.

Then when my non-magical parents came to the castle and split up, they were obvious candidates for split-pea soup. Don't get me started on pea shooters and sweet pea lotions. The cruelty we've endured is virtually unending.

But humans don't realize how terrible it is being a pea, especially one that's magical.

Legend says that a princess will never smash a magical pea. All unworthy of royal life will smash us flat.

As a podling, I was kidnapped, then placed in a fancy bowl in the middle of Queen Nessa's mahogany table, just waiting for my turn to be pushed between the mattresses and murdered. Some other peas try making jokes about my plight, saying magical peas always pea the bed.

It isn't funny though. Every night Queen Nessa finds a new prospect to marry her son. Yesterday Pea J.—my cousin—was taken to test a would-be princess. Apparently she wasn't royalty because Pea J. turned into a stain and the woman got beheaded.

Tonight is my turn, I can just feel it. I'm at the top of the pile, and from what I've heard, at least my death will be swift.

As I thought about dying, the main serving girl started

45

setting the table. "Hello, dear peas," she crooned. She's the only person who's nice to us—that maid named Rapunzel.

She came here several years ago.

Even though she's nice, she tells some whoppers, about being locked in a tower by some witch. Then she said a prince came to save her, but he lost grip of her hair one time and fell about two-hundred feet. I thought he died, but Rapunzel went on telling us, the prince just poked out his eyes on some bushes, then wandered blindly through the desert until falling off a cliff.

She seems choked up about it, but I'm not too worried. It's better than death by mattress. AND it sounds made up if you ask me. What did the witch have against Rapunzel anyway, and why didn't the prince die the first time he fell a great distance? You wouldn't peg Rapunzel for an exaggerator, but she is.

Rapunzel's the only human who can hear our pea-brained thoughts and she loves us despite everything. In fact she even nods sadly every time one of us is chosen to test a princess. She's always there at meal times and that's when we get chosen. The rest of us peas sing Chopin's "Funeral March," in different harmonies. It's a powerful tribute, especially if the girl in question is obese and we know our fellow pea won't be strong enough to survive—unless she's a princess.

My thoughts lingered on death as dinnertime arrived and Queen Nessa babbled about money and clothing. I tried listening, but instead shook so hard I nearly rolled from the top of the pile of peas.

Was the legend even true about magical peas and princesses who wouldn't smash them? I'd never seen a pea or woman live through the ordeal. Wasn't there a better way for the kind prince to find a wife?

My thoughts trailed to how Queen Nessa is the complete opposite of her good-natured son. I caught some of her conversation with an adviser. "No prospects," she whispered. Then stood and shouted at him, "NO PROSPECTS. How do you expect my son to find a wife if we can't test a different woman by pea each night!"

I shivered hearing her thoughtless words. Forget the women; didn't she care about THE PEAS?

Queen Nessa stomped closer to the bowl, grabbed a pea next to me and smashed him between her two fingers. "UNACCEPTABLE! You find a girl for me to test, or it'll be *your* head." I gaped. Hadn't anyone noticed the smashed pea? She's just proved herself unfit to be royal! Only royalty won't smash peas. No one noticed except Rapunzel. She tried hiding her shock, but was unsuccessful as the adviser caught her reaction.

The queen followed his gaze and sneered. "Ah, yes. The serving girl, Rapunzel. Who always tells such whoppers! You're probably the least likely to be a princess, but the peas never lie." She grabbed Rapunzel by the arm. As the wicked queen dragged her from the room, Rapunzel's long hair trailed behind, skittering across the shiny marble floor.

The advisor plucked me from the bowl and followed them. The other peas were so taken aback they forgot to sing the "Funeral March" for the first time since I'd met them. I felt at a loss.

We moved closer to the bed chamber with the towering mattresses. I was terrified, but Rapunzel stood strong; her blonde hair spiraled around before resting on the floor dramatically.

Queen Nessa hissed, "Tonight you will be tested, serving girl. If this pea ends up being smashed in the night, you will be beheaded on the morrow! Too bad for you." Queen Nessa snatched me from the advisor and gave me to Rapunzel. "Put this pea in the mattress. Let me see you do it! And thus seal your own death!"

Rapunzel turned away and cradled me in her hand like a baby. Before putting me between the bottom two mattresses, she whispered, "Don't be afraid, little pea. You won't be smashed, or end up as soup or a stain on the sheets. I've told you many secrets, but I forgot to tell you one little thing."

What more could she possible say? I tilted forward, desperately, nearly bursting. She slowly lifted me toward her lips and kissed my cool green skin. "Stay strong, little pea, and let my magic save you, for *I* am Rapunzel. *My* parents were a queen and king. And *I* am a princess."

Nessa heard Rapunzel's fantastical words and cackled until she hardly breathed. "I vow with magic, that the day you prove you're a princess, is the day that I will die!" Queen Nessa spat.

Rapunzel nodded. "Then let it be," she said to the queen and placed me inside the tower of mattresses.

Rapunzel's words rang true despite how extraordinary they sounded. I wasn't worried anymore. After all, Rapunzel had given me all I needed to survive the night; she'd given me her love.

In Closing: The next day Rapunzel married the prince. She had the royal jeweler craft a ring where I could rest in place of a gem, safe from hungry mouths and would-be princesses. The princess called me her savior—her sweet pea.

Later, during that wedding day, though Rapunzel wanted beef, Queen Nessa insisted on pea soup. With the queen's final greedy bite, she choked and fell over dead.

The bowl of peas still resting on the table sighed collectively. Instead of singing Chopin's "Funeral March," we joyously sang "Ode to Joy" and *all* the people in the room actually heard it!

Death by split-pea had never seemed so sweet.

© EC Stilson 2012

About the Author

Elisa spends most of her time taking care of four rambunctious kids who are better than green eggs and ham. They're pretty darn fun, but despite that, after she had kids, her boobs shrunk, she lost hair, but gained a greater sense of humor!

When she's not scavenging through the vents, where her son—the Zombie Elf—likes hiding things, she's sewing, playing her violin, or writing.

Blog: ecwrites.com
EC Stilson on Facebook
@ECWrites on Twitter

A Little Skittle Spittle
Pat Hatt

Today you learn a skill,
That few truly know.
So just stand still,
And listen to my flow.

Give a troll a little,
Give a troll a lot.
As long as it's a skittle,
And nothing polka dot.

No, not peanut brittle.
No, not hot sauce.
If you want an acquittal,
Forget the reindeer moss.

It doesn't matter how.
It doesn't matter who.
No milk from a cow,
It looks too much like glue.

Lose the fancy bag,
Lose the clever grin.
He might start to gag,
When you bring the skittles in.

You need to color code,
You need to keep track,
Take an extra load,
Hide them behind your back.

Put them in his hand,
Put them in his shoe,
Forget nose land,
You'll just make him go achoo.

Do not stay to chat,
Do not run away,
You get a head pat,
For the right display.

He's not in the bed,
He's not in the loo,
Remember what I said,
Here's your final clue.

Turn left just a little,
Turn right just a lot,
Now take each skittle,
To his comfy closet cot.

You almost had it down.
You almost made it through.
Skittles can't be brown.
I thought that much you knew?

51

Then there was the this,
Then there was the that.
You even made him hiss.
I can't believe you called him fat.

I told you not to grin,
I told you not to talk.
We'll consider this a win,
Next time you better knock.

Now you know the who,
Now you know the why.
Welcome to the crew,
Let's give it another try.

© Pat Hatt 2012

About the Author

Pat Hatt can be found in the east coast of Canada. He hates writing these things but doesn't mind talking in the third person. He dabbles in a little of this and a little of that, not afraid to attempt something new.

He is owned by two cats, one of whom has his own blog, It's Rhyme Time. Yeah a rhyming cat, who knew? He would be considered a both person when it comes to cats and dogs.

He is also quite the movie and TV buff. As you can probably tell does not take himself seriously and has more stuff in his head than is needed. Thus the novels as just one more form of release. Thanks for the visit and enjoy!

Blog: http://rhymetime24.blogspot.com/
Twitter: http://twitter.com/rhymetime24

The Greaseman
Joshua Carstens

As he expected, there was a single knock on Pine's door. Pausing, he turned his head and listened for the faint sound of the envelope falling through the mail slot. He left the message where it rested and continued attaching his new left hand. It softly clicked into place, and Pine flexed the new fingers. If he had been physically capable of it, his face would have creased in a slight smile. After ensuring all of his joints were working in precision, Pine stood and stepped across the room to retrieve his orders.

It was always the same. Short, to the point, and signed with an embellished lowercase "g." He had received his instructions this way for over a decade, and even though the original *G* had departed from the world, the envelope still came twice every week from the real boy. Had Pine been able to feel emotion, thinking of *G* would have made him sad and angry. But Pine had long given up any pursuit of humanity.

He was a tool, plain and simple, and an effective one.

Instructions memorized, Pine held the paper to the flame of a candle. He waited, as he always did, and watched the paper disintegrate into nothing more than ash and blackened fingertips. Rubbing the burn marks off of his new hand with a towel, Pine found himself satisfied with the durability of the new appendage.

The job was easy, and Pine assembled his gear without further thought. Access points would be identified on the fly, which is how he preferred to run operations. If one made plans, something always went wrong. By going in virtually blind, Pine was able to adapt to changes faster than other greasemen.

54

It wasn't just gaining entry that made Pine exponentially better than the average thief. Having replaced each piece of his arms and legs with a sturdy yet flexible material, he could fit where others could not. The location for this job was one Pine had seen before, but never found a reason to go inside. Knowing what he did about the building, he tightened the mechanisms inside his leg parts. It was going to be necessary to bypass the ground floor, and the easiest way would be to jump.

While he had never been inside this particular building, Pine knew a soft touch would be necessary once inside. For that reason, he switched out his feet at the ankles for ones with a softer padding. It would ease the landing and make silent travel possible. Whenever possible, he avoided using the cushioned feet; they wore out too fast. Just in case, he stored the durable running feet in his bag. If the opportunity arose for switching to them, he would take it. Practice had brought the switch time down to three seconds per foot. Less if he abandoned the feet he was taking off.

With everything assembled, Pine sat on the padded chair facing the fire and watched the clock pass the time.

As the clock's hands moved, Pine caressed the box on the table next to him. It was the first piece he'd commissioned, and it completed the disguise. He opened the lid and stared at the eyeless face looking back at him. It had taken a lot of research and a good portion of his amassed fortune, but Pine had finally found *g*'s identity.

The plan was in motion, and with each replacement part, Pine came closer and closer to executing the final steps. Tonight would be the end of it all. His freedom would be assured, even if he was putting himself into a prison of his own making.

The job would go off as planned, without hesitation or an alarm being raised. Pine would make the drop as scheduled. He knew *g* would never do the pick-up on his own. But he also knew *g* wouldn't risk accepting the prize inside his own home. While *g* was getting the package, Pine would gain entry to his home.

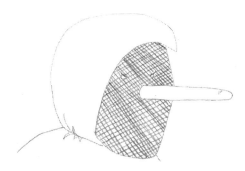

It had taken some time to get the shape just right, but Pine had pared down his wooden head slowly, one shaving at a time. Fitting the mask into place, he looked at himself in the mirror. The eyes were his, but the face was a perfect copy. Pine would make the switch, taking *g*'s place forever. Disposing of the real boy would be easy for someone like Pine. Piece by piece until he was gone. Replaced by the son *G* had crafted to perfection.

After tonight, he would be the one sending the orders.

Pine would become a real boy. He would be *the* real boy, even if it was a fake body. No one would know the difference.

Removing the mask, he stowed it in a padded space with his gear and glanced at the clock again.

Soon.

Despite all the heists Pine had run for him, g wasn't as smart as he pretended to be. Pine had no problem slipping into the expansive two-floor loft g used as his home and base of operations. Security was a joke, both inside and out. It was something Pine would have to improve upon. While he waited, he admired once again the quality and strength of his new appendages. They would serve him well for years to come.

The locks on the door clicked open one at a time.

The stubble-faced young man was too preoccupied with the bundle in his hands to notice the figure in the room with him. It was a wonder he had survived in this game.

"Hello, Gideon."

Startled, the real boy dropped the bundle. It hit the ground with a crunch, its value gone in an instant. Gideon didn't notice.

"How did you find me, Pinocchio?"

"I go by Pine now. You should know that better than anyone."

"Fine." Gideon's face turned into a snarl. His voice was a rough growl, like a caged animal. "What do you think you're doing here?"

"I would think it would be fairly obvious," Pine said.

Reaching into his bag, he pulled the Gideon mask out of its padded sleeve and clicked it into place. The way it attached, Pine was able to manipulate it in ways his wooden face never could. He mimicked Gideon's narrowed eyes and snarl. The real boy pulled a knife and lunged at his doppelganger.

Pine had tightened the joints and springs in his arms while waiting in the loft. The fight was over before

57

Gideon knew what hit him.

Looking down on the crippled man, Pine spoke again. "Real son or adopted, you're not your father, Gideon. And you never will be. Geppetto loved me more than you, and that's why you killed him. You took his place. It's time for me to take yours."

As he wrapped his hands around Gideon's throat, Pine swore he could really feel the last of the man's heartbeats.

© Joshua Carstens 2012

About the Author

Joshua Carstens is a Nerd, and proud of it. Yes, that is Nerd with a capital "N." Joshua holds an MA in Professional Writing where he focused on Creative Writing, and a secondary emphasis in Applied Writing with particular attention to editing and design. He will edit anything you put in front of him, whether fiction or non-fiction and any genre.

Blog: http://vivelenerd.blogspot.com/
Twitter: http://twitter.com/Vive_le_Nerd

Three Goldilocks and the Bear
Roland D. Yeomans

Once upon a time the world was not as it is now. It was a time of what two-leggeds would call magic and myth. But of course there is no magic, only things not understood. There is no myth, only deeds not remembered truly.

Do not blame two-leggeds. After all, they are but human.

In that time, animals spoke. They speak still. The ears of two-leggeds are just too full of convictions which are not so, to still be able to understand what they hear.

In that age, the world had voice . . . as well as shape and substance.

Now, the forests are so few and the rivers so tainted that she seldom walks among us. But from the full moon, her face of shadows still gazes down upon us. Her thoughts still shimmer in the night sky in the colors of the Northern Lights.

In that long ago time there was once a bear who walked among legends until he himself became one. If you close your eyes and let your mind break free of its moorings, you will slowly see him in the dark of your imagination. There. Can you not see him? You are in fortune.

This is the moment his life became myth.

Sit safe and snug by the fire and let me tell you the tale of it:

Standing erect, the grizzly bear looked up into the endless night sky. His name was Hibbs. There is a tale of tragedy, power, and truth to his name. But that is a tale for another campfire.

Though Greeks called the world Gaia, the Lakota

59

Estanatlehi, and the Norse Miðgarðr, Hibbs called her . . . "GrandMother," he whispered staring up at the face of shadows in the full moon.

Across the great waters in the forests of the bear's land of birth, it was the warming season when the geese return. Here in the Norse Black Forest, the cold wind plucked at his flannel shirt, the fringe to his leather pants, and his face fur. Hibbs did not mind. He enjoyed winter's breath. However, he did not enjoy being in strange territory. In lands unknown, enemies could lurk unrecognized in plain sight.

Hibbs whispered again, "GrandMother, why have you sent me here?"

The grizzly listened to the silent shadows. No answer. He sighed. Hibbs knew that GrandMother thought him slow of thought. That fact hurt him. What hurt worse was that she was often right.

The breath of the night brought sobbing to his quivering ears.

Much might be strange in the Black Forest, but he knew well the cries of despair, for often he had heard such cries from his own lips as a misunderstood cub.

Hibbs smiled. He was a healer. He would heal this anguish.

Grizzlies could move silent as secret sin, and in such a manner did Hibbs move. A few feet later and he spied a woman sobbing on her knees. With the aid of the full moon, he saw her long hair was the gold of a winter's dawn. He cleared his massive throat so as not to startle her only to be startled himself.

As she raised her head to him, he saw her gaunt face had so many wrinkles on it, there was literally no room for any more.

To allay any possible fear, he said softly, "Goldilocks,

60

what ails . . ."

"Urðr," she snapped. "My name is Urðr."

"Of course it is," Hibbs smiled. "Are you lost like me?"

"I am hungry," said Urðr.

Hibbs gestured to the bushes around them. "There are berries here."

Urðr smiled strangely. "I only eat flesh."

Hibbs made a face. "To eat flesh one must kill, and I am a healer so I eat berries and things covered in scales, Goldilocks."

"Urðr!" snapped the old woman.

Hibbs shrugged. "So you keep saying. I see no bow or spear.

How do you catch prey?"

The old woman lowered her head like a wolf. "I use snares."

"I see none," said the bear.

"It is right in front of you," laughed Urðr.

Hibbs snorted, "I will be careful where I step."

"I am sure you will. Take me to the home I share with my sisters. You will have to carry me since I am too weak to walk."

Hibbs glowered, "I heard no request merely an order."

Urðr murmured, "Since when does a healer have to be asked?"

Hibbs nodded. Goldilocks had a point. He swept her up in his mighty arms. He noticed then that her eyes were blue, not the blue of a robin's egg, mind you, but the fiery blue of a lightning bolt . . . and just as deadly.

As he walked, Hibbs noticed how remote her face appeared though it was so close to his. He also glumly saw how sharp her teeth were.

And they were much too close to his throat . . . and

growing closer.

"Do you fish?" he asked her.

Urðr jerked in surprise. "No."

"I do. Have you ever seen trout fly through the air over wild streams? You nod yes. Well, I catch them in mid-air. I am very, very . . ."

Hibbs smiled with his own very, very sharp teeth. They were much longer than the old woman's and larger, too. Urðr pulled back her head. And she no longer smiled.

Following Urðr's directions, Hibbs walked into a clearing where there was an enormous, rune-covered well in front of a rustic cottage.

Urðr sighed, "Urðarbrunnr."

Hibbs was impressed with the gigantic well, but it was the towering Ash tree that took his breath. He stretched his massive head back and still could not see the end of its branches in the dark night.

Hibbs frowned when he saw four mighty stags eating the shimmering buds and shoots from the trunk of the huge Ash tree.

"You said you were hungry, Goldilocks."

Urðr frowned, "Dáin, Dvalin, Duneyr and Durathrór are the charges of my sisters, Verðandi and Skuld, and me."

Hibbs' head was beginning to hurt from all the strange sounding names. "I will bring you to your sisters and leave this place."

Urðr shook her head. "What kind of hosts would that make us? We shall have you for dinner."

Hibbs stared at her lightning eyes, both remote and deadly. The Lakota loved bear grease. The grizzly bear had been lusted after and hunted before. How many unwary travelers had been these sisters' dinner?

Suddenly, he knew why GrandMother had brought him here. 'Do you?' mocked her icy voice inside his head.

Hibbs sighed. One day he would guess GrandMother's intention correctly and die from the shock of it. Until then, he would tweak the crooked nose of this crone.

The bear lumbered quickly to the towering Ash tree, dumping the old woman atop the three gnarled roots of the thing. "Here, Goldilocks, chew on some of those sprouts. I'm thirsty."

"No!" screamed Urðr.

Hibbs paid her no mind. He quickly lumbered to the rune-covered well. With a swift dip of his huge paw, he scooped out a chill mouthful of rainbow water. He sipped it all lustily. His mouth exploded as if struck by the lightning of Urðr's eyes. Hibbs staggered. Whole constellations of stars, fiery waterfalls of colors, and strange images flooded his mind.

Inside his mind, GrandMother's laughter bubbled like an icy spring. "Slow of thought no longer, beloved GrandSon. Now, you know why I brought you here."

Hibbs' head felt as light as a cloud, seeming to threaten to float off his wide shoulders like one. The wooden door to the cottage burst open, slamming shut like an angry thunder boom.

A blonde maiden rushed him, scissors upraised in her tiny fist.

A small girl with a flimsy veil concealing her face raced out after the young woman. The little girl cried out.

"Verðandi, no! It is not his present we must punish but his future!"

Verðandi twisted more fluidly than mere flesh and bone should be able to do. "Then, Skuld, end his future for his blasphemy!"

63

Hibbs chuckled, "Two more Goldilocks! Shame on you for your anger. You were thinking to make a meal of me. All I did was drink of your well of wisdom. We are even I think."

Skuld held up a vibrating thread of golden brown. She brought her gleaming scissors up to it. Through the gauze of her glimmering veil, Hibbs saw razored teeth gleam in the young girl's cold smile.

"Dolt of a bear, our arrival to this dung-heap of a world heralded the end of the golden age of the gods, whom we surpass in age. We three rule the destiny of gods and men."

Hibbs shivered, and Skuld laughed, "Yes, fear us."

The bear sighed, "I fear the One whom you have insulted."

Skuld snorted, "We do not fear the spirit of Midgard."

Hibbs shook his massive head, his brown eyes deepening. "Not GrandMother. You may end the lives of men and gods but you are powerless against the Great Mystery."

Skuld laughed like icicles dancing. "I have never seen the thread of the one of whom you speak. But yours I see before me. And so . . ."

Skuld snipped with her scissors. The long blades promptly bent.

64

Skuld dropped the silver shears now red-hot and smoking.

Verðandi hushed, "This cannot be!"

Hibbs walked sadly away. "So say all two-leggeds when the world proves larger than the grasp of their minds."

He locked eyes with Skuld. "Your arms are too tiny to box with the Great Mystery."

The young skull girl glowered, "Who?"

Hibbs snorted, "Exactly. He comes by His name honestly."

Urðr snarled, "Curse you, bear!"

Hibbs smiled, "Goldilocks, next time eat berries and not something you do not hold claim to."

As he walked away into the depths of the Black Forest, Hibbs swore to himself that he would never again trust another female. He felt his furry head caressed by icy, invisible fingers. GrandMother laughed within his mind: 'On one issue at least, men and women agree. They both distrust women.'

About the Author

I've been writing most of my life. Most of my old writings burned up when my home burned to the ground. But now, I have an e-book, THE BEAR WITH TWO SHADOWS, on sale at Amazon: http://www.amazon.com/THE-BEAR-WITH-SHADOWS-ebook/dp/B004MDLWD0/ref=pd_sim_kstore_13.

Hibbs also appears to fend off the Twilight of the Gods in post-Katrina New Orleans along with the Lakota shaman, Wolf Howl, in END OF DAYS.

Georgie Porgie
Variation by Fran Fischer

Georgie Porgie, Puddin' and Pie,
Kissed the girls and made them cry,
When facing a sex discrimination suit,
He refused to testify and remained mute.

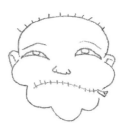

Where are they now?
Jan Marshall

After attending an event where volunteer clowns cheered up the evening, I had the following dream, as background circus music played and moving vans appeared.

Though many showbiz celebrities choose to live in our over-55 communities, the dream revealed our newest neighbors were from the cartoon, comic strip and fairy tale world.

I met Cinderella, recently divorced from her prince with the foot fetish. They split when she refused to wear glass shoes. Turns out he was CEO of Pyrex® and could get them wholesale, so he had a vested interest in her tootsies and those of a few of her hot friends.

She now dates Dr. Scholl's®. He explained that glass slippers, unless custom-fitted with orthopedic inserts, cause bunions, not Brussels sprouts as she first thought. The Prince is now rooming with Betty Crocker® and the Pillsbury Dough Boy®. Please, don't ask!

Another truck brought Peter, Peter, that Pumpkin eater. Don't get me wrong; pumpkin itself is nutritious, but as a home, even in a dream, I guffaw. He put his wife in a pumpkin shell which happened to be in a co-op, so he could not get a reverse mortgage. While keeping her? I mean, really! I am a women's libber and I truly object to this "keeping her" business whether he keeps her "well" or not. It is simply wrong in this day and age, except perhaps at Thanksgiving.

While in sleepy land, I received an email from Goldilocks writing that she wanted to move to our community but didn't have the down payment to qualify.

She now lives in Hollywood over a Chinese restaurant where she grows dill and asked me to meet her for a drink.

When we talked about her past, she revealed, "He was such an animal," referring to her relationship with the papa bear. While she was being reviled because of her indecisiveness, she later sadly, was diagnosed with A.D. D.

Goldie said Papa asked her to call him "Big Daddy" at intimate moments, though that is another story for another time, actually never—duh—since she told me the sordid and frankly exciting details that I was sworn to keep confidential as we were getting loopy at the old Brown Derby. To be truthful, I do not remember much except for a deep yearning to walk in the woods or head for the nearest zoo with a bit of honey dabbed behind my ears.

After Brenda Star, Ace Reporter, was fired from the newspaper cartoon pages, she moved to a senior community with her mystery man, Basil. It turns out Basil wasn't such a mystery man after all. His real name is Irving and she was mighty disappointed to learn the distinguished black patch he wore was for pink eye.

Today, a handsome man moved in next door. He

was wearing blue tights. The only man I ever loved in tights was Stewart Granger in the film Scaramouch. I'm sure he loved me, too, though I have not heard from him recently. I wish I could tell him, "The sword wounds have healed nicely."

MY OPINION on Male Tights: NO, except if you want to learn the religion of a guy in a hurry. As for shorts: NO, No and No. What is it about older men with bad knees, arthritic joints and gorilla hair that prompt them to believe Bermuda shorts are a turn-on? Perhaps to me yes, though to other sexy old broads, not so much.

Meeting Red Riding Hood in a consignment store where she was selling her cape and her copy of *He's Just Not That Into You*, she confided that in the infamous court case she was questioned by a cruel, macho prosecutor.

"Why were you walking in the forest alone? Did you run out of alleys? You do know what the color red indicates, you ignorant slut, you." OMG!!!! I hate that.

Speaking of Red, a belated card from Santa insisted that Rudolph the Red-Nosed Reindeer is not an alcoholic, as some have claimed, but simply has a bad case of rosacea! (Gosh, it seems like the fake world has lots of ailments.)

I asked the new neighbor, in those cute tights, his name, and he said he was Superman (that's what they all say) and he sighed that his "Big S" had been retired. When he told me he was faster than a speeding bullet (been there, done that), I suggested he see a Urologist. Then I slammed the door in his face. "I Don't Get No Satisfaction" is NOT my favorite song, with apologies to fellow Medicare member Mick Jagger.

A banging noise at the door happily but confusingly awakened me. Yes, it was only a dream, but I could not fathom why I was wearing blue tights? Maybe I overdosed on chocolate and went into a coma and simply forgot the why of it.

Oh well . . . I see it's the cute guy in the brown shirt and great gam's delivering a book from Amazon, *Gulliver Regrets Traveling with a Senior Group of Formerly Famous Folks*. He writes that if he hears the phrase 'remember when . . .' one more time, he is going to climb up a beanstalk and throw water balloons.

Privately though he regrets even more, disrobing in front of that wicked witch who threw little kids into overns, who ruined his love life by giving him the nickname, Tom Thumb.

About the Author

Jan is founder of the International Humor and Healing Institute established in 1986. She worked with board members Norman Cousins and Steve Allen as well as prominent physicians in promoting hope and humor in healing. As a long term cancer survivor, "Jan's Army" acknowledges and sends "Badges of Courage" to other heroes.

Jan is currently the humor columnist for Senior Correspondents and writes satirical essays for several online magazines and newspapers.

Connect with her directly on
www.facebook.com/janmarshallauthor
www.twitter.com/janmarshmellow
www.linkedin.com/in/jankellermanmarshall
www.Pinterest.com/justjanmarshall

The Littlest Princess
Kate Buhler

Once upon a time, in a land far, far away and long ago forgotten, there lived a King and a Queen. They were very happy for they ruled a prosperous kingdom, had many friends, and lived in a time of peace. The only thing that could make them happier is if they had children. But, alas, the Queen had a hostile uterus and the King had a dangerously low sperm count so they thought they would never have the joy of raising a family . . . especially a boy to be heir to the throne. They could take or leave a daughter.

But, one day, as the Queen sat alone in the garden, a flower opened and spoke to her. It said, "You shall have the perfect child that you have always wished for but you shall also have six worthless daughters who will bring nothing but a headache."

Then the flower withered up and died.

In due time, the flower's prophecy was fulfilled and the Queen gave birth to seven beautiful daughters. Each day the girls grew more and more beautiful. But none were more beautiful than the Littlest Princess. Even though the Littlest Princess was the most beautiful princess and the favorite child of the King and Queen, she idolized her older sisters and worked to be just like them. This was not very wise of the Littlest Princess, however, because they were the six terrible daughters the flower had warned of.

The eldest princess was the greediest person on the planet. Whenever she went shopping, she bought everything in the store just so she would have it and no one else could. The eldest princess's greed extended to food also. At every meal, the eldest princess would eat until she was sick and soon her weight passed that of a baby elephant. One day, as the princess was eating a whole chicken, the wishbone was lodged in her throat and she choked and died. And so the Littlest Princess learned the virtue of Moderation.

The second princess was always in a hurry and never had time to do anything properly. She constantly drove her horse through the village at such a fast pace that she would run over children playing and old people crossing the street. One day, all the princesses decided to go swimming in the moat. However, the second princess had just eaten. The other princesses warned her to wait an hour before swimming but she was too impatient. The minute she hopped into the water, she got a cramp and sunk to the bottom where she was eaten by an alligator. And so, the Littlest Princess learned the virtue of Patience.

The third princess was the meanest person on earth. All she thought of was herself and she constantly bullied others. Her favorite thing to do was ride through the village, mocking ginger children for their red hair, freckles, and soullessness.

One day, as she rode through the village torturing gingers, a giant ginger came out and stepped on her and she died. And so, the Littlest Princess learned the virtue of Kindness.

The fourth princess was the most promiscuous girl in the world. Instead of having three meals a day, she liked to have three men a day. The fourth princess typically wore nothing more than fishnets and a tank top.

One day, as the princess walked outside, the sun began to shine so brightly that the princess's skin simply melted off for lack of covering. And so, the Littlest Princess learned the virtue of Modesty.

The fifth princess was the stupidest girl in the world. The Princess would constantly get lost in the castle and forget how to find her way back. Sometimes she would go missing for days before they would find her in a corner; shriveling away because she was too stupid to feed herself. One day, she ordered a coffee from McDonalds' but didn't read the warning label about Hot Liquids. She poured the hot coffee all over herself and died instantly from third degree burns. And so, the Littlest Princess learned the virtue of Intelligence.

The sixth princess was incredibly smart but also very cunning. She often made deals with people then backed out or stabbed them in the back. One day, she backed out on a deal with a crack whore who snapped and killed the sixth princess with her rusty switch-blade. And so, the Littlest Princess learned the virtue of trustworthiness.

And now, the King and Queen had the perfect child they had always wished for and the three of them lived happily for many years until the King and Queen died of old age. Then, the Littlest Princess became the wisest queen and people came from across the land to see their queen's goodness and beauty. And when the wisest queen finally died, her daughter became Queen (although the daughter was a manic-depressive, meth addict who put the country into massive amounts of debt and started numerous wars which eventually lead to the downfall of the country).

And they all lived happily ever after.

© Kate Buhler 2012

About the Author

Kate Buhler is a recent graduate of Fordham University. She is currently living in Buffalo, SD taking time off before committing to a future of 9 to 5s. Kate writes a weekly blog humbly titled "KB Thinks For You: The Only Things You'll Need To Know From the Only Person Who Knows Them All" as well as a blog called "A Week in the Life of Ivan Denisovich" which details the life of her chronically dissatisfied cat, Ivan.

Blog links:
http://kb-thinks-for-you.blogspot.com/
http://ivandenisovich.blogspot.com/

The State vs. Winkie
Barry Parham

Here's something that's been bothering me: "A kid'll eat ivy, too. Wouldn't you?"

That's just irresponsible parenting, pure and simple. You don't encourage children to eat landscaping.

You just don't.

But nursery rhymes are rife with such aberrant advice and odd behavior. As a kid, I never worried much about monsters under my bed. But I do remember reading nursery rhymes and thinking, "These people are twisted."

So yesterday, I committed to some intensive long-term research, while waiting for my bagel to heat up.

To you that may not qualify as long-term research, but I usually set the toaster to "dark," thank you very much.

And my research paid off! Nursery rhymes are extremely twisted. Most were based on actual European historical events, and many have had lasting effects on American culture.

Witness:

Tom, the piper's son, stole a pig. Not his fault. Tom was a victim of his father's bad decisions. Then, as now, piping rarely pulls in a family-sustaining income.

In "Sing a Song of Sixpence," a blackbird pecked off the nose of the laundry maid, prompting someone to invent drop-off dry cleaning.

A troubled truant named Jack Horner spent his childhood sitting in a corner, shoving his thumb into desserts. Mr. and Mrs. Horner finally tired of this public school curriculum, and home schooling was born.

They called him "Simple" Simon. Yes, he was. Expecting freebies from Pies Art Us; trying to catch a whale in a bucket; plum-hunting in a thistle bush; fetching water with a sieve. Yes, he was.

Wee Willie Winkie ran around an obviously un-gated community in his pajamas, rapping on windows and yelling unseemly questions in keyholes. "Are the children in bed?" The maniac was deftly detained by Britain's original neighborhood watch group, the Vikings. Mr. Winkie's legal team was led by celebrity attorney Gloria Allred's ancestor, Erik the Allred.

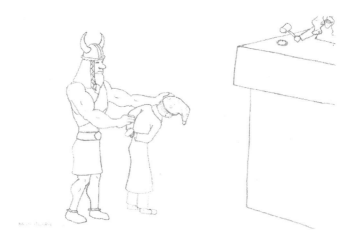

"Georgie Porgie" is alleged to be George Villiers, first Duke of Buckingham, who allegedly mated with a king. And a queen. And the queen was married. It was that season's top-rated episode of "Ye Olde Jerrie Springer Houre."

A crooked man lived in a crooked house with a crooked cat after pocketing some crooked money he found on a crooked road. This man went on to establish Chicago politics.

Humpty Dumpty fell off a wall. This was in the days

before large imaginary wall-scaling eggs had access to Medic Alert bracelets. Fortunately, he was found by his snooty neighbor, Mrs. Hollandaise, who dutifully dialed IX-I-I. But all the king's men couldn't help Mr. Dumpty, since his medical treatment was not covered during that fiscal period. Welcome to Universal Health Care.

"Mary, Mary, quite contrary" was "Bloody Mary" Tudor, who invented vodka. She was the daughter of the nefarious Henry VIII, a dodgy Midwestern ex-cop who went through wives like the rest of us go through paper towels.

The tolerance-challenged militant who penned "Goosey Goosey Gander" found a man who wouldn't pray, so naturally he threw the man down a flight of stairs. Gloria Allred filed an amicus curiae brief, Fox News reflexively issued a goose-meat recall alert, and Sean Hannity called for a boycott on foreign-made stairs.

Three little kittens lost their mittens. Then whined about it. Then found the mittens. Then, like little kitty idiots, they ate pie with their mittens on, so the mittens got dirty, triggering a whole new round of whining. So they washed their mittens and hung them out to dry, which was pretty amazing, considering cats don't have opposable thumbs. And then a rat showed up. It was just one of those days.

The Jack Sprat story is supposedly an encoded allegory about Richard the Lionheart, good King John, and Robin Hood, proving once and for all that they had hallucinogenic drugs in the Middle Ages.

I met a man with seven wives. Boy, was he miserable.

"One, two, buckle my shoe." According to my research, these words "have no traceable connection with any events in history." Much like the stuff I write,

77

and America's current fiscal policy.

And then there's "Three Men in a Tub." Imagine the message that's sending to our young people.

But let's wrap up on a lighter note. "Ring Around the Rosy" describes one of the tell-tale symptoms of the Bubonic Plague. Didn't know that, did you? At the time, medical experts (barbers with leeches) thought the disease was spread by bad smells, so everybody carried pouches filled with flowers: a "Pocketful of Posies." Now ponder the line, "Ashes. Ashes. We all fall down."

Sleep tight, kiddies! And don't let the bedbugs bite!

© Barry Parham 2012

About the Author

Barry Parham is the award-winning author of humor columns, essays and short stories. He is a recovering software freelancer and a music fanatic.

Parham is the author of the 2009 sleeper, "Why I Hate Straws," his debut collection of humor and satire including the award-winning stories, 'Going Green, Seeing Red' & 'Driving Miss Conception.'

In October 2010, Parham published "Sorry, We Can't Use Funny," another award-winning collection of general-topic satire and humor, and the more targeted "Blush: Politics and other unnatural acts." He followed up in 2011 with "The Middle-Age of Aquarius," a growing-old-but-not-so-gracefully vehicle for the award-winners 'Comfortably Dumb,' 'Snowblind' and 'The Zodiac Buzz-Killer.'

"Full Frontal Stupidity" (2012) is Parham's 5th collection of humor, satire and observations, and features more award-winning stories, including 'Skirts vs.

Skins' and 'Scenes From a Maul.' Most recently, his work appeared in the 2011 national humor anthology, "My Funny Valentine," and his essays are slated to appear in two more collections in late 2012.

http://ivandenisovich.blogspot.com/
http://www.amazon.com/author/barryparham

Mary Had a Little Lamb
Variation by Fran Fischer

Mary had a little lamb,
its fleece was white as snow,
And everywhere that Mary went,
the lamb was sure to go.
It followed her to school one day,
which was against the rule.
The cafeteria lady was surprised
to see a lamb at school.
She offered to take care of it
and Mary said, "All right."
At lunch she got the "special"
and took a great big bite.
"Yummy," she thought
and she had another slice.
She knew that all the other kids
had thought her lamb was nice.
The thought of a ham sandwich tomorrow
simply made her drool
And she wondered if she could get her pig
to follow her to school.

Red's Coming of Age
Shane Stilson

A warm light evolved behind Red's eyelids. She buried her face into the pillow, unable to escape the ocular transmitter embedded around the focal point of her inner eye. This was no ordinary light passing through the thin covering of eyelid. The lunar solar cycle lasted thirty days and they lay deep in the dark of the moon. This light came from inside her head, projected from the back of the eye onto the lens of the pupil. The transmitter had been installed the day before, her coming of age day, the day they said she had stopped growing and could be fitted with the standard bio-peripherals.

Red floated into wakeful consciousness and a mellifluous voice greeted her. Red jumped and looked around, but no one was there. "Good morning Redonica Tsukinodé. This is the first day of the rest of your life."

Red searched the ruffled covers, most of which lay in a tangled lump on the floor. She'd been told what would happen. It was little comfort. She felt naked, like a stranger watched her in her crimson bedclothes. "Who are you?" she asked.

"I am your personal bio-peripheral assistant. There is no need to vocalize. Feel as though you are speaking without actually using the muscles and I'll understand."

"What time is it?" Red tested silently, her hand running through strawberry blond hair streaked with bands of blood rose red.

A display of green characters formed on the lens of her eye and she focused on the words. A calendar indicated it was the fifth of October, 2056, 6:01 in the earth morning. "Six a.m., earth time?" she groaned. "School doesn't start for another two hours."

81

"Your bio-peripheral contract clearly states that you agree to abide by the earth based galactic timeline found to be optimal for maximizing education and punctuality."

A knock came at the door to her room. "Hey, Red, is the wench talking in your head yet?" Red's dad sauntered in, kicking his way through disassembled electronics scattered across the floor.

"Yeah, Pa, and she's kind of bossy."

It wasn't often Shale Tsukinodé heard fear in his daughter's voice and he didn't like it. Shale nodded to a glass of green fluid held discreetly in his right hand and put a finger to his lips with the other. "I'm here to talk to you about that." His whispered words barely reached her ears.

Red's face widened, in awe at the green fluid her dad seemed to be offering her. "Transmugenic accelerator," she whispered in kind. Her father pressed the finger deeper into the skin of his lips and handed the glass over. She drank down the thick draught, fighting not to throw it back up. The emerald elixir sloshed strangely in her mouth, as though it moved on its own.

Shale slapped her on the back, his tone suddenly relaxed and affable. "I wrote the reconstruction routine myself, darlin'." Red coughed, still fighting not to throw it back up.

"Great, thanks," she said sarcastically through a wheezing breath. "That's nasty stuff. You do it every day, don't you?"

"The daily dose is just a booster to ensure no loss of data stored in the fluid, but well worth it. It's the great equalizer." His tone turned uncharacteristically serious. "Make sure you get all of it down."

Red sat bolt-upright in bed. She grabbed her father's shoulder and gasped. She felt she was a glass of carbonated water being poured over cubes of sparkling ice. Popping bubbles formed in her stomach and rose in her limbs. It reached her brain and her vision cleared as though she had been looking through a dirty space freighter window for the past sixteen years.

"Whoa . . ."

"That's my girl," her dad smiled. "Welcome to your new life," he leaned closer, "your real new life."

"Is this legal?"

"I don't know. Is it to only allow the elite and their children access to the Juice? Is it right that even those who mine the accelerator that the Juice comes from on Europa don't share in the fruits of their labor?" His words gained in volume. "No, darlin', the bureaucratic, elitists can go to hell. You deserve more than they're offering." His eyes faded as he spoke, lost in memory. "If they weren't so greedy and self-righteous, your mom wouldn't have died."

Red looked down, there wasn't a day over the last four years that she hadn't thought of her mom.

Shale sighed and sat next to his daughter on the bed. "Honey, there's something I've been keeping from you. I. . . Well . . .," he struggled; it wasn't supposed to go down this way.

"What?" Red looked her dad in the eye. A flickering of green light flashed across his pupil. She had seen it many times, but the reason held new meaning. It indicated he interfaced to some sort of data being shown to him there.

"I don't mine transmugenic accelerator on Europa."

A void opened in Red. "But where do you go every day then?"

"Honey, it's not fair, the inequality." Shale looked side to side, checking for prying eyes. "Red . . . I'm a Juice

Runner."

Red stared at her father, someone she had thought she knew better than herself, now a stranger. Juice Runners were the most hunted and hated of outlaws by the imperial regime. They had taken on legendary status among the masses, hijacking shipments of refined Juice and then selling it back to the common folk at a fraction of its real world earth price. "Does Grandma know?" she asked.

A devious smile crept across the elder Tsukinodé's face. "Grandma? Grandma's the mastermind behind the operation."

If Red had been shocked before, she was dumbfounded now. Exams at the lunar equinox, the Dark Side of the Moon Dance, graduation; they somehow felt trite and inconsequential now.

"Red?" her dad prompted her gently.

Red stared at the sheets covering her legs.

"Redonica, there's something else."

Her head snapped up to her father's tender eyes. "What else could you possibly say?"

"The heat is on. They're on to me hotter than a moon rock on the bright side of the lunar equator."

Red's brow wrinkled; irritated anyone might dare hurt her father. "What do you need me to do?"

"There's over a thousand deca-liters of Juice in the back of the Hood Drive Freighter. They're going to pick me up as soon as I leave the house, but they don't suspect you. I need you to pretend to go to school but then peel off and deliver the shipment to Grandma's house on the far side of the asteroid belt."

Red's jaw fell. "What about school?"

"School?" her dad laughed. "You've graduated."

"No, I haven't. I've got another six months."

84

He laughed again. "No, you've graduated."

Red opened her mouth to ask if he'd been at the local neuro-stimulation bar last night, then closed it without uttering a word. For years, her father had been taking her into the asteroid belt, he in his supped up space commuter, she in the spry space freighter refitted with a Hood Worm Drive. During these excursions, she had learned to hug the envelope of moon-sized rocks, using the inertia of the larger asteroids to shield her own ship's gravity signature; to dart in and out of the collections of smaller satellites, timing her movements with the seemingly random patterns of the field's rocky resident's. These were high risk games of hide and seek that her friends scoffed at when they found out how she spent holidays and weekends with her father. The previous Earth Day, the week before, had been the first time she evaded her father and beat him to the other side of the belt, just short of Jupiter and the fabled mines of Europa.

"Red, your reaction times and intuition out matches even those hyped up on super-saturated accelerator. With the Juice, you'll be unstoppable," her father stated proudly.

The doorbell rang through the narrow halls of their small moon town home. A green light flashed across Mr. Tsukinodé's pupils. His eyes took on a remote cast as he focused on the image projected across his inner lenses. "They're not waiting for me to leave, Red." He chuckled. "They're trying to override the door's security locks." A muffled yelp reached Red's ears from the direction of the front door. "A little electroshock will do you good, nimrod." He grinned and his eyes refocused on his daughter. "I didn't park the Hood in our garage. It's stashed in the community garage one block to the west. You'll have to put on a space suit to get there. They'll be covering the underground passages."

Tears welled in Red's eyes. "What about you, Dad?"

A familiar roguish smile covered his face and the doorbell rang again. "Don't worry about me. I know this is sudden, and even now you're free to choose a different way of life." His words sped by. "But, you have to choose now, in this second, what the rest of your life will look like. I'll love you either way."

Red threw her arms around her father's broad shoulders. "Daddy, I'll meet you at Grandma's house." She felt a pent up breath ease out of his body. "I love you."

"Okay, the guys at the door are getting anxious, but one last thing." His words brushed her neck like a final goodbye. "The Juice you drank. It's supposed to be clean. It supposed to be . . . unused." He leaned his forehead against her shoulder for strength. "I made a choice, for the both of us." He shook his head as though to cast off lingering doubt or fear. "It was your mom's. I took it from her when she died. It's got all her memories, her dreams. This isn't how I wanted to do things. I just found out they were coming." He hugged her tighter than he ever had before. "Get the suit on. Get to the Hood as fast as you can. Deliver the Juice, and say 'hi' to your mom for me." He let go and stalked from the room before she could see him cry.

His last statement confused her, but all the drills he had forced her to go through kicked in and shoved her questions aside. She went to the closet and took out an emergency space suit. She pulled it on, activated the air lock on the door to her room and opened the small window on the opposite wall. Everything not tied down whooshed out the hole to the nonexistent moon atmosphere. She followed the floating bed sheets into the dark morning and bounced through the domes of adjacent houses. She landed in the entry to the parking garage a few seconds later.

The airlock wheezed as the specially formulated breathing mixture rushed under the opening door. Red took off the helmet on the run, already going through the Hood's start up sequence in her mind. A different voice, yet still familiar, spoke to her. "The Hood's in the second row on the left." A green outline flashed around her beloved vehicle. "Hurry up, Cherry-Head, they know you're not in the house."

"Mom?" Red skidded to a halt.

"Yes, honey, but hurry. They're coming. They bugged your transmitter with a new type of device yesterday and it took longer than your dad thought for me to deactivate it. They heard much of your conversation with him."

Red ran through the garage, the bulky suit rubbing between her legs. She popped the hatch and jumped in. Red froze; the usually empty passenger seat had something in it. The lights flashed on in the cockpit and she recognized her dad's remote access droid, The Huntsman, sitting in the seat. The roughly humanoid-shaped machine should have provided an early clue to her dad's illicit activities. Any civilian caught with this type of military grade hardware in their possession would have earned themselves a one way ticket to the penal colonies on the expanding edge of the galactic frontier.

"What's up, Diddy?" The tone in Red's voice belied the fondness she felt for the droid.

The black eyes in the sleek head flared like fluorescing liquid mercury. It cocked its head to the side, as though cracking its neck after a long sleep. "Little G! Are you ready to rock the Casaba? Your dad bring you

87

in on the down low?" the Huntsman asked.

"You know he did, Axe-man. He said I grad-ji-ated." Red flashed a fake hand signal and winked.

"No doubt. You shredded his ass in the roid field last weekend. The Hood was on the other side and at granny's house before he even realized you'd spoofed the spacial sensors and he was chasing space dust. Nice!"

Red flipped switches and checked dials, going through the vehicles start up sequence. "Thanks, Diddy, but we've got a grand of D-liters in the back and the fuzz is looking to repossess it." Red hit a red button and the hatch closed.

"Oh, yeah? Your dad's already put you on a job?"

"You know he did and it's time to stop flapping your resistors and get on it." Red winked. "How about some appropriate music, maestro?"

"Yeehaw. Axe's got the moves to groove." The Huntsman weaved its head back and forth as a heavily distorted orchestra of classic music burst from speakers in its chest.

Red moved her hands in time to Axe's grooving, while maneuvering the Hood out of the parking space. She leaned forward dramatically and the freighter ramped up to space speeds, down the exit lane. A sign cautioning to slow down to merging speeds ripped from its fasteners as the airlock opened and the back-draft of their exit ushered them into the lunar night.

A group of imperial police cruisers hovered around her house and the usual parking garage she used. It only took them a few seconds to realize who blew into space one block over. Red and blue lights flashed across their sleek bodies as the cruisers turned in pursuit.

"Oh, ho," Axe sang in the Hood Freighter. "The fuzz is hot tonight. What's the plan? The spacial sensors indicate a deep space warship lies in synchronous orbit on the other side of the moon."

"What type?" Red asked.

The Huntsman cocked its head to the side, "From the gravitational pull, it looks like the new Wolf Class."

"Cherry Head," her mother's voice rang between Red's ears. "Now is not the time to delay. Execute."

Red nodded to herself. "Then it's straight to the roids. A wolf's too big to get through there. Time to bring the nasty, Diddy. And, turn up the noise. No one can catch the Hood."

Red hit the Hood's overdrive and they ricocheted around the gravitational edge of the moon and out into space. They passed the massive wolf ship on the other side, the Huntsman giving a little wave with his fingers in good-bye.

The commander on the bridge of the Wolf Class Penetrator growled in irritation. "That's a Hood Drive. Why didn't we know they had a Hood Drive?"

His number two smirked in admiration. "No one puts a Hood Drive in a dumpy freighter like that," she laughed.

The commander gave his number two a withering glare. "Send the dogs on her tail. She's undoubtedly heading to the asteroid belt."

The lieutenant pushed a button and a squadron of drones rocketed off the starboard bow and after their prey. "This one's good, sir. I can feel it. I'm not sure they'll find her."

"Doesn't matter. I know where she's going. All they need to do is to slow the target down. Set a course for Grandma's house."

"But sir, that vehicle, no matter how big and ugly it is, it's too fast for us."

"That's why I've got something special planned. Plot the fastest course and get the engineers to warm up the new cloaking device." The commander lounged in his chair, a devilish grin on his face.

The dog drones caught up with Red as she piloted her craft into the outlying asteroids of the field. Red's hands gripped the controls lightly. "Axe, get ready to deploy the decoys on my mark."

The Huntsman rested a metallic finger on a blinking blue button. "When did you build these?"

"I made a bunch more after the one worked so well on Dad last weekend."

Red threaded the closing eye of two house-sized rocks on a collision course and a drone exploded behind her, unable to pass through. Normally, she would have had to check the gauges projected on the transparent material of the cockpit as she piloted the Hood. Instead, the Hood's computer had automatically synchronized its data with Red's newly installed bio-peripherals and the readings appeared as green dials in the corners of her vision, projected on the inside of the lens of her eye.

Ten drones flew through the plume of their disintegrating comrade, still on her tail. A larger asteroid came into view and the Hood dove toward the pockmarked surface. The vehicle's computer outlined obstacles in her vision and displayed the probability of successfully negotiating anticipated trajectories.

"Ready, Axe," Red whispered. She rounded a deep ravine, the Hood blocked from the drones' view. "Now!"

The control systems on the drone ships froze as a dozen identical gravity signatures flew in as many different directions. Red shot out of the melee of mixed signals, two drones still on her tail.

"Two of the dogs are still on you," Red's mom whispered in her ear.

"I see them," Red responded.

They spent the next few hours dodging through the maze of rocks until Red finally lost her remaining pursuers in a maze of tunnels running through a porous asteroid giant. An hour after that, they sat on the far edge of the field, the interstellar causeway a few parsecs away, Grandma's space station floating just beyond the fringe of asteroids. Red nodded to the Huntsman and the droid crawled out the back dock. In a few moments, he floated next to the Hood and gave Red a nod.

"Got any reading on Grandma's house? Anything look out of the ordinary?" Red asked inside her mind.

"Gravitational signature seems correct," her mom responded.

In the heat of leaving, Red had not had time to consider the magnitude of who spoke to her. "Mom, is it really you?" Tears welled in her eyes.

A sigh of sadness settled in Red's mind. "As much as I can be, Cherry Head, but know this, I love you." Red tried to absorb what now lived inside her, but failed to come to an adequate understanding.

The Hood's intercom crackled to life. "Red. Red, is that you hiding on the edge of the field there?" A husky voice filled the interior.

"Grandma? You sound a little funny, and your image is not coming up on my screens. Is something wrong?" Red nudged the Hood closer to the space station, inspecting the exterior.

"Oh, the confounded transmitter is on the fritz again," Grandma groused.

"Well, it's no wonder, your antenna must've taken a

direct hit from an asteroid." Red nodded toward the top of the floating house. "It's hanging on by a thread." Red flew closer and the inspection made her do a double take. Something didn't seem quite right. "My, Grandma, the station's observation windows seem bigger than I remember."

Grandma chuckled sweetly. "The better to see you with, my dear. It does get lonely out here in the depths of the cosmos and the view is all I have to comfort me."

"And, the size of those new subspace collecting dishes? You must be able to get broadcasts of the earth based vids with those lobes."

"All the better to hear you with, my dear," Grandma chimed. "Sometimes I just set it to a random frequency and listen to the rhythm of the universe."

"Careful," Red's mom whispered and an outline of a gun turret on the space station flashed in Red's vision. Red had piloted the craft quite close by this time and recognized a defense contractor's piece of hardware when she saw it.

"When did you get the plutonic rail guns? I don't remember those. You could fend off a small army."

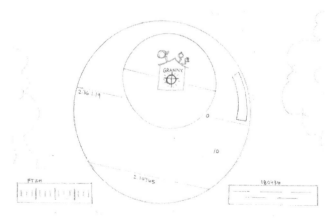

Red moved to turn the Hood around, but too late. The space station began to open across the middle and the image to waiver in space. The bulk of a massive imperial warship, coming out of cloaking mode, soon replaced the facade. Red jerked to engage the Hood Drive, but too late. A flash from the guns blew across the ship, the weapon set to overload the computer and knock out anyone with embedded peripherals. A gruff laugh stung Red's ears before she fell unconscious. "All the better to eat you with, my dear."

Red floated in darkness. She felt as though people lifted her, wrapping metal hands about her head, probing her mind. Then someone pushed a button in her brain and she opened her eyes. She lay on an elegant bed, the top cover, a midnight blue, with iridescent stitching in the shape of exploding supernova. Chairs and a table sat across the room, the legs bolted to the floor in battle cruiser fashion. Round portholes laced the far wall, the universe beckoning outside.

"Juice Running is a serious offence, Redonica Tsukinodé," a mustached man said from behind the desk. His booted feet rested casually on the corner of the table top. "The penalty is either death or a life of servitude in a deep space penal colony."

Red blinked and spoke into her mind. Something echoed back, too faint to hear, but insistent, as though it strove to be heard.

"There's no sense in trying to contact your bio-peripheral assistant. We've disabled the modifications your father made to your programming."

A mumbling bubbled into Red's mind. It fought with a new barrier placed there, but still failed to make itself understood.

The man stood. His straight-backed posture frightened Red. "But, I've been thinking, Redonica. He rounded the desk. "Perhaps there is a third option for you."

The voice in her mind modulated, coming in and out of focus.

"Do what I say, what I want, and it will go easier."

The voice nearly screamed in her mind, then fell deathly silent. Redonica feared it had gone; that it had lost whatever battle it fought. Why she hoped, she did not know. Her mind still ached from being knocked out, and what help could it be anyway? The man reached out his hand to touch her face as he came to her.

"Cherry Head," Stella Tsukinodé spoke to her daughter, from within her daughter's mind, "did you know your mother had a PhD in bio-organism encoding, or that she was a third degree master of bushi- jutsu?"

"I do now," Red said out-loud and her eyes flared green as information downloaded out of her mother's memories and into her brain. The man's hand stalled an inch from her face. The hesitation proved his undoing. Red took him by the wrist, whipped his arm around and had the commander pinned to the floor, face down, before he could do anything about it.

"Huntsman!" Red activated the communicator peripheral embedded within her. "Locate Grandma and cut us out of this beast!"

"Finally, what took you so long?" Axe responded, followed by a massive boom that rocked the ship. Raucous music sounded from outside of the hull. A hissing around the portholes indicated the ship already lost pressure.

Red kicked the commander in the stomach and then the head. He writhed on the floor and slipped into

94

unconsciousness. Red scanned the room and found the closet looked for. Another blast preceded a shower of sparks indicating a neutron welder sliced though the hull of the captain's room. She found the emergency space suit she had hoped for, in the closet, and locked herself in. She put the suit on and cracked the door in time to see the body of the commander sucked into space by the pressure in the ship blowing out the compromised hull.

Jets on the Huntman's back propelled him into view and Red pushed herself out to meet him. "Nice plan, you nearly got yourself killed," the droid quipped.

Red laughed. "Where's Grandma?"

"Already in the Hood and waiting for us. She escaped almost as soon as they brought her aboard the Wolf. That's one tough Grandma, taught your mom everything she knew."

Red smiled, she recognized the truth of the statement from the memories she now shared through her mom. "Let's get out of here," Red said.

Together, they located the Hood and left the disabled cruiser to lick its wounds. The Hood's cockpit window came to life with an image of the Wolf ship's number two in command.

"You can't hide from me, Little Red Riding Hood. I'll find you no matter where you go." The distraught woman's face scowled with a disfiguring infection of hatred. "You're father's been given a death sentence of hard labor to be served in the deep mines of Europa. By the fabric of space and time, I swear you'll join him!"

Red flashed a roguish smile and disabled the com-link.

Grandma groaned in mock fear as she adjusted her peg leg in the passenger seat. "Now there's a woman who's got a serious twist in her girdle."

Red chuckled, but hadn't really heard what Grandma said. There was no way she would let her dad languish in the mines for the rest of his days, not when she knew exactly how to bust him out.

About the Author

A vast world of exclusive character biographies and sketches may be found at www.middledamned.com.

In his 'free' time, Shane Stilson configures the brains of robots to aid soldiers in their day-to-day and combat activities. This experience, combined with a long history of training in Japanese martial arts, informs a uniquely descriptive writing style.

Blog: http://middledamned.blogspot.com/
Author Site: http://www.middledamned.com/

Treasure in the Tower
Gayle C. Krause

The miller's sons had ground the grains
that made the village bread,
but his eldest two took farm and home
when they found out he was dead.

The youngest son inherited
his father's old, black cat.
He didn't recognize him
in boots and feathered hat.

The wise cat told the naïve boy
to find a royal bride.
For a wise and wealthy life,
he'd need a princess at his side.

The puss in boots accompanied
the boy across the land
looking for a princess
who'd accept the boy's poor hand.

They sought out foreign kingdoms.
Every castle. Every town.
But soon the boy's bright smile
had turned into a frown.

A princess wouldn't marry
a measly miller's son.
"Don't worry," said the clever cat.
"Our search has just begun.

97

I'll help you find the princess
that will make your poor life, rich.
They say she's lived her whole life
as the captive of a witch."

They traveled to the north
through an ancient, gnarled wood,
when they came upon a clearing,
where a single tower stood.

Hanging from the turret
was a long, blonde, silken braid.
"Climb it to the top," said Puss.
"There you'll find your royal maid."

The miller's young son listened
to the wise old cat's advice
and he climbed the golden braid,
though he found it filled with lice.

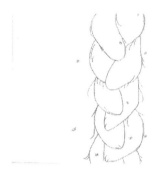

At the very top, indeed,
a princess waited there.
The boy was quite surprised.
She was anything but fair.

Her skin was green. Her teeth were black.
On her nose, a hairy wart
"Come. Kiss me, now," she said
as she let out a snidely snort.

The miller's son looked at the cat.
The cat said, "What the heck?"
With just one kiss, gold filled the room,
but the boy turned into Shrek.

Prince of Fools
Robert G. Ferrell

In a time that none can recall, in a land that probably never was, a prince was born. He was a baby, who cried and drooled and went poo-poo like all the other babies, but by virtue of accidentally being born the son of a king and queen, his social status was immediately far above that of all the other crying, drooling, poo-pooing babies in the kingdom, despite the fact that he had done nothing whatsoever to deserve this beyond completing a few thousand cell divisions, sitting around in a warm bath, and being fed constantly for nine months. Like all the other babies.

As the prince evolved from mewling, helpless infancy to whining, fractious childhood, he came to understand that his was a position of absolute privilege in a world full of people scrambling day to day for mere subsistence. In other words, it was good to be a prince.

One fine afternoon the prince was dragging his sleepy and therefore reluctant knot of sycophants (he called them 'courtiers') down to the village to watch him best all the other children in whatever game they happened to be playing (princes always win, or else), when out of the western sky there came a screaming roaring crackling sound that made the kingdom gnash its collective teeth and cover its collective ears in pain.

The prince was annoyed that an apparent act of God had interrupted his peasant abuse, and he dispatched one of his father's knights to tell God to play somewhere else. The knight obeyed without question, for that was what knights did best, but an hour later, his horse returned alone, dazed and smelling like an aborted barbecue.

The prince rolled his royal eyes and made several choice comments concerning the competency of the knightly class at anything but wenching and tournaments before sending out another knight, this time with a companion and more weaponry. Nothing was ever heard again from either of these hapless emissaries or their mounts, and the prince was sorely wroth.

He was so wroth, in truth, that after the king had fallen asleep that evening he tiptoed into the royal study and absconded with the royal seal and the royal sealing wax. With these he proceeded to declare war on whatever it was that had despoiled his princely pleasure (costing his father three expensive knights and their equipment in the process, which were going to come out of the prince's royal allowance), mobilizing even the royal reserves in the ensuing campaign.

One by one the squadrons marched out of the walled city, until every last soldier in the king's armies was deployed. The prince sat alone on the battlements, anticipating his royal revenge.

By the evening of the following day, it was pretty clear that things weren't going too well. The only messenger who had made it back to the castle died of exhaustion and post-traumatic awe syndrome on the drawbridge; his final utterance sounded like "dragon" and was followed by a rude sort of noise made with the tongue and lips. The prince was even entertaining thoughts of giving up and blaming the whole incalculably costly fiasco on his sister when what little daylight that remained was harshly and utterly extinguished by an impossibly enormous blot that appeared between the prince and the waning sun.

The prince realized that he was looking at more than a blot, and he raised his eyes reluctantly along a

101

mountain of scales until they met the burning orange orbs of the dragon, who was roughly the size of the king's summer palace balanced on the king's winter palace, with a smattering of keeps and manors thrown in for good measure.

"Ah, little princeling," boomed the behemoth, "it was you who sent me all those appetizing morsels: for this I thank you from the bottom of my stomach. You are a generous and thoughtful host." The prince was so scared he was about to wet himself, but he warmed nonetheless to the sound of the dragon's praise and puffed out his pitifully miniscule chest ridiculously. The dragon smiled even more broadly and continued, "Alas, however, it appears that you are now the only thing left for me to eat." The prince was frightened almost out of his wits, but his royal cunning had not quite deserted him and he replied as boldly as he could manage.

"Nonsense! Why eat me, one little boy, when an

entire village of peasants awaits you, lean and sweet to the tooth?" As he spoke, the prince spread out his palm toward a cluster of miserable huts cowering at the edge of the forest beyond the Royal Keep.

The dragon considered this. "I see your point," he replied, whereupon he flew away and consumed the whole village in one massive bite, but not before gobbling down the surprised prince and half of his father's castle.

MORAL: It is good to be a prince, but far better to be a dragon, especially one the size of the king's summer palace balanced on the king's winter palace, with a smattering of keeps and manors thrown in for good measure.

© Robert G. Ferrell 2012

About the Author

Robert G. Ferrell is a lifelong computer geek and amateur radio operator (KF5SAR) living just outside San Antonio, Texas who also exhibits avid interest in writing, history, quantum physics, music, art, and ornithology. He was a finalist for the 2011 Robert Benchley Society Humor Writing Award and has been a humor columnist for ;Login: Magazine since 2006. He has several dozen publications to his credit, the scope and range of which can only be described as eclectic. Or possibly, dyslexic.

Links:
http://www.scribd.com/rferrell_1
https://twitter.com/RobertGFerrell
http://robertgferrell.blogspot.com/
http://8baud.blogspot.com/

The Vampire's New Clothes
Neal Levin

Dracula decided
he was sick of wearing black.
He wanted something colorful
to put upon his back.

So what would look magnificent?
He paused and tried to think.
A not-so-gentle hot magenta?
Maybe shocking pink.

Perhaps fluorescent yellow
or a mellow yellow-green
Or baby blue or navy
or a something-in-between.
A color more like orange? Purple?
Maybe bloody red.
It could be white or maybe bright
with polka dots instead.

Perhaps he'd go for something
sort of earthy, maybe clay.
Forget it, that's too boring.
It's like brown or tan or gray.

He'd much prefer a color
that was powerful and bold.
Like maybe something neon,
something silver, something gold.

He had so many options.
Would he ever make the call?
It turned out, in the end,
it didn't matter much at all.

He couldn't quite decide
which looked the best upon inspection.
No matter what he wore
he couldn't see his own reflection.

About the Author

Neal Levin enjoys writing humorous children's poetry, especially poems that involve word play, surprise endings, and funny ways of looking at the world. His poems have appeared in several anthologies published by Meadowbrook Press, including *Rolling In the Aisles* and *If I Ran the School*. He has also written poetry for a variety of national magazines, such as *MAD Kids* and *Pockets,* and is a three-time winner of the *Saturday Evening Post* Limerick Laughs contest. He lives in Michigan.

Personal Website: http://www.neallevin.com/
Poetry Foundation:
http://www.poetryfoundation.org/bio/neal-levin

Hanzel and Gretyl: A Boomer Fairy Tale
Timothy Hurley

Once upon a time there lived a kindly gray-haired, grandfather Hanzel and his sweet-as-strawberry-pie, spinster sister Gretyl. That witch-in-the-forest thing when they were kids was tough, but what happened to them in their retirement—well, it's just so hard to believe. Here's how the story went.

Hanzel and Gretyl lived in a yellow ranch style house with a professionally landscaped front yard. But they didn't live in the actual house. That's where Hanzel's ungrateful son, his son's nasty second wife, and their bratty grandson lived—with a 150-inch plasma screen television, Evil Step-daughter-in-law's boxes of yarn, and Bratty Grandson's superhero comic book collection. The spare bedroom, ideal size for an elderly, platonic couple, was Evil Step-daughter-in-law's macramé studio.

The humid basement was where Hanzel and Gretyl lived with their two-burner hot plate and 17-inch TV and minimum channel cable service. Hanzel spent his days carving wooden toys and humming Pink Floyd tunes. Meanwhile Gretyl made scrumptious molasses cookies two at a time on the hotplate.

On Friday evenings while the upstairs family watched the big screen stream a Netflix movie and scarfed delivery pepperoni pizza, Hanzel and Gretyl huffed and puffed up the rickety basement steps. They knocked, wiped their feet, and shuffled, bent over in the manner of old folks, into the off-white living room. They proffered a wooden toy and cookies with an inquiring smile and arthritic, trembling hands.

106

And every Friday night Bratty Grandson scowled at the plate of cookies and said, "Auntie Gretyl, you know I like sugar cookies."

Ungrateful Son would mumble, "Thanks, Pops," and then shove a folded slice of pizza into his mouth. Hanzel would sniff and mention how much he liked the smell of pepperoni. Friday after Friday Evil Step-daughter-in-law would silently point at the basement door, and Hanzel and Gretyl would return to their apartment, put on sweaters and gloves, and reset the rattraps.

One particular Friday night Gretyl heard voices. "Listen," she said. "Up above. They're talking about us."

Hanzel cocked his ear to the ceiling and turned up his hearing aid until it squealed. "They're plotting," he said pointing to the bedroom above.

They could hear Evil Step-daughter-in-law's squeaky voice. "Your father and aunt are costing us money. We should rent out the basement and invest the money in corporate bonds."

"You're right, of course," they heard Ungrateful Son reply. "And that doesn't even count what we should do with their entitlements. But how will I get rid of them?"

107

"Take them to the mall and leave them where they can't find their way home."

Ungrateful Son said that was a brilliant idea. He would do it Saturday right after Grandson's soccer game.

Gretyl wrung her hands, "Whatever will we do, Hanzel? They're going to throw us out on the street. Can they take our Medicare? I don't know how to use vouchers."

Hanzel touched his temple. "I have a plan."

The next day, after Bratty Grandson's team lost the soccer game, Ungrateful Son said, "We'll drop you at the mall, Grandpa Hanzel. You can go to the hardware store and buy a new carving knife." He looked at Evil Step-daughter-in-law and winked.

"Good idea," said Step-daughter-in-law winking back. "You can buy sugar, Auntie Gretyl."

"I could use a new sweater," Gretyl said. "Mine has holes. I think the rats are chewing it."

Hanzel asked, "The old mall close to home? Or the new, unfamiliar one far away?" He shoved his hand into his pocket, felt around, and mouthed to Gretyl, "Trust me, I have a plan."

"Try the new one," Ungrateful Son replied. And suddenly he whipped the steering wheel, made two left turns, a right turn, and then another, even more disorienting left turn. They all lurched left and right and then pitched forward as the car came to a stop at the Great Maw Mall.

Hanzel stared at the looming building and the rotating neon sign. He worked hard at looking confused. "However will we find our way home?"

"Oh, it's a short walk," Evil Step-daughter-in-law said through gritted teeth. And with that Hanzel and Gretyl were standing on the concrete while the car zoomed off, leaving the smell of gasoline to drift onto the sidewalk.

Hanzel smiled at Gretyl and shoved his hand back in his pocket. "Trust me."

Much later that evening as Ungrateful Son and Evil Step-daughter-in-law were chuckling and examining a bond prospectus there was a knock at the front door. Ungrateful Son opened it, and there stood Hanzel and Gretyl, a little grimy, sweaty, and smelly, but invigorated by their long walk from the mall.

"How on earth did you fi . . . ? I mean . . . oh, you're home already," Ungrateful Son said.

Hanzel held up his iPhone 5. The screen displayed a map of their neighborhood, and a little blue dot blinked at the family's address. "Good thing I preordered online."

"Good thing I wore my Nikes," Gretyl said smiling and pointing at her reflective-orange walking shoes.

That night Ungrateful Son turned off the circuit breaker to the basement. He chortled, "Let's see him charge that phone now, heh, heh, heh."

Sure enough, when Ungrateful Son dropped them at the mall the next day, Hanzel's battery icon read thirty percent.

"Why do we have to come to the mall again?" Hanzel affected a worried look.

"Just because." And again the car sped off.

Even though he remembered to turn off all his apps and shut down the wifi, Hanzel's battery succumbed before iMap delivered them back to 1234 Tree-Lined Street. They wandered up One Street, and down Another Street, and turned right on Not-Taken Road. The houses looked alike. The trees looked alike. The children on bicycles looked alike.

"One Street looks just like Another Street," Hanzel

said.

"Dear me, how will we get home?"

"Don't worry your sweet little head. I'll think of something."

A carload of teenagers drove by in a red Prius, loud music hip-hopping from the open windows. "Get a horse," they guffawed and waved with one finger.

Gretyl smiled and waved back. "What a catchy tune," she said.

By and by Hanzel and Gretyl came upon a split-level house painted purple with black trim. The onyx-colored picket gate was open, and there was a trail of low carb snacks on the walkway leading to the front door.

Hanzel sampled a fresh piece of broccoli raab. "Healthy," he said.

Gretyl took a bite from a whole-wheat oat cookie. "Scrumptious."

They reached the door, which was the color of a very ripe banana, and prepared to knock. But before they could, the hinges screaked and the door opened. A woman stood in front of them wearing a longhaired wig the color of cornflakes, a pink and blue flowered muumuu, and Birkenstocks that revealed her black toenails. An unfiltered cigarette bounced up and down in her lips when she spoke.

"Those things'll kill you," said Hanzel.

"Come in, dearies. I'm Wicked Wendy. Lunch is ready."

"My, my, Wendy," said Gretyl. "You could use a shave."

"And a shower," Hanzel said sniffing. The couple stepped through the doorway and the three walked down the dark hallway.

And before they knew how it happened Hanzel and

110

Gretyl were in the basement in a brick-lined pit on a dank, dirt floor. Gretyl wiped her hands on her navy-blue-with-tiny-white-polka-dots dress. "We always end up in a basement," she wailed. "Does this mean there's no lunch?"

From the floor above they heard a sound. Thigga thigga thigg. Electric sewing machine, Hanzel thought. They also heard Wicked Wendy's cigarette-baritone humming. "Mozart," Gretyl said. Looking up she closed her eyes, clicked her heels together three times and murmured, "There's no place like home. There's no place like home."

"What are you doing, Gretyl?"

Gretyl opened her eyes and touched the damp brick. "Guess it only works with ruby-colored tennies."

Hanzel was on his knees, his fingertips feeling the dangerously under-lit bricks. "Eureka!"

"Did you find something, Hanzie?"

"I found the electrical outlet. Don't ask me what it's doing in a sinister basement torture-pit, but right now it's mighty convenient to the plot." Hanzel snapped open his man-bag and extracted a long white cord. "Lucky for me I remembered to bring my charger." He located the slot on his phone and shoved in the plastic thingie. Instantly a bluish light lit the pit, and a rat scurried round the perimeter.

"Oh, Hanzel, look, Wicked Wendy has rats too. I wonder if she knows."

"No time for that, Gret. I've got to get us out of here before this story goes over the word limit. He pushed on a button, and an irritating female voice said, "What can I help you with?"

"Locate police."

"I'm sorry," the irksome voice said. "iMaps cannot

locate that service."

"Damn," Hanzel said.

"Don't swear, Hanzie. There might be children reading."

The thigga thigga thigging above got louder and then stopped. The humming also stopped. They heard footsteps. Hanzel tapped 9-1-1 on the screen.

"911, hold please." Hanzel held and heard Mick Jagger sing all of "Paint it Black." Then Nine-one-one Lady came on the line. Hanzel whispered that she should send the FBI quickly because Wicked Wendy was preparing to make a sundress out of them.

"What kind of dress, Sir?"

"That doesn't matter right now. Just send Jodie Foster." Hanzel explained about the pit and the chianti and the liver and the thigga-thigga-thigg.

Nine-one-one Lady said she hadn't seen the movie. "You want the Federal Bureau of Investigation?"

"Yes, please. Now."

And before anyone could say Jack Webb, a gaggle of officers in black SWAT uniforms bumped their way up the sidewalk with an ax, chopped down Wicked Wendy's front door, and hauled her off in plastic handcuffs. Special Agent Columba took names down in her notebook and offered Hanzel and Gretyl a ride home in her Peugot.

"No thanks," Gretyl said. "We need the exercise. But thanks for the rescue."

On their walk home, Hanzel and Gretyl noticed a man in a blue pinstripe suit sitting on a park bench reading a leather-bound copy of *Tartuffe*. He looked up and introduced himself.

"I'm a sympathetic banker," he said. Hanzel thought it odd but fortuitous to meet a sympathetic banker on a weekend and he quickly summarized their story. The gentleman took Hanzel and Gretyl into the bank, booted up his computer, and clickity-clacked on the keyboard.

"There," he announced. "I foreclosed Ungrateful Son's mortgage." Next he did a short sale, and faster than anyone could say 'credit default swap' or understand what that meant, the house belonged to Hanzel and Gretyl. The sympathetic banker shook their hands and drove them in his silver SUV to their new home.

"Thank you," Gretyl said. "You're so kind and just. What's your name?"

"Just John," the banker said.

"What's your last name?" asked Hanzel.

"John," said the banker.

"John? Nothing more?"

"No, Nothing More's the comptroller. I'm the bank manager."

"Does the bank manager have a last name?"

"John."

"What's his first name?"

"No, his first name's Just."

"Just what?"

"No, Just John."

By then they were at the house, and Hanzel yelled into his phone, "Siri, find movers near me."

The movers arrived and moved Hanzel and Gretyl's hot plate and sweaters upstairs, and lugged Evil Step-daughter's yarn, and Bratty Grandson's comic books, and Ungrateful Son's stuff into the basement. Except for the television.

"I think the Utes game is on," Hanzel said settling into the easy chair and putting his feet on the ottoman. Gretyl came smiling from the kitchen with a plate of sugar

113

cookies.

"This'll tide you over until the pizza arrives," she said.

As the months went by down in the basement, Ungrateful Son read several David Foster Wallace novels, Evil Step-daughter-in-law moved from macramé to existential acrylic painting, and Bratty Grandson took up carving and decided he didn't want to be bratty any longer.

He said, "Call me Just Grandson."

And they all lived happily ever after.

© Timothy Hurley 2012

About the Author

Timothy Hurley is a writer, retired physician, and family man with four children and six grandchildren. Coast-hopping between New York City and San Francisco Bay Area, he writes literary, speculative and humor fiction. His heroes, M. Twain, E.A. Poe, and E. Hemingway, among others, are not returning his emails. His works-in-progress include collections of New York and Mars short stories, The Grumpy Old Men's Club, and a memoir of his medical career. When not writing, he reads, and often walks the neighborhoods of New York searching for the perfect pizza. Timothy and his wife, the architectural historian and author, live in Brooklyn. They will celebrate their forty-fourth anniversary the day the Mayans bring the world to an end, but they're not afraid. Timothy blogs occasionally at *The Lunatic Assylum (http://thelunaticassylum.com/)*, his name for Earth, and tweets at *@timothyhurley3*. Email Timothy at *thelunaticassylum@gmail.com*.

Belle and the Beast
Melynda Fleury

In the Southern corner of France a wild group of large men had begun a reign of tyranny. They went from village to village taking what they wanted. The leader of this band of brigands was named Beast.

Beast was fierce and without mercy. Women and children did not escape his cruel torture. He stood over six feet tall, and his beard grew wildly down his pristine shirt. His boots were always clean and shiny.

Today was no exception. This village had lots of gold and grain. His men had gathered more furs than they could sell in a year. Beast looked up the hillside to see what appeared to be a vacant castle. Surely, if there was a lord there he would have made his appearance known by now.

Beast trotted up the hill calling for his men to follow. As he entered the halls the riches within caught his breath. Someone had to be there to defend everything. Yet, only an old woman stepped from the shadows, broom in hand, waiting for him to approach. He was in a great mood and decided to oblige her silent command.

"To whom does this castle belong, old woman? Fetch him now that I might kill him and claim it as my own."

"You may have it, Beast. It belongs to me. My daughter will be returning soon and we are the only ones who live here."

"Two women owning a castle? Ridiculous! If what you say is true then I claim it for myself," Beast bellowed with laughter. "Is she fair, your daughter? If so, maybe I'll make her my wife and allow her to clean the place and serve me."

Again laughter rang through the halls as his men

115

imagined Beast married to anyone.

"She is fair. She won't marry you though, Beast. She will give you a fight like none you have ever seen." The old woman smiled.

"Enough! If she is fair I shall marry her. If she is disobedient I shall beat submission into her."

"That you won't, dear, although you are more than welcome to try." Still smiling the old woman began to walk away.

"I did not say you could leave, woman. What is your daughter's name?"

The old woman continued to walk away.

"Come back here, hag, or I shall beat you into submission." Beast began to feel fury building inside of him at the old woman's lack of respect.

Suddenly, she turned to face him.

"Her name is Belle. For your insolence I curse you to become what you are named. A beast. Not a brave, beast but cowardly, to roam these halls forevermore or until you win my daughter's love. Your men shall also be cursed. I know not what affect you shall suffer."

With that curse the woman vanished. All was quiet. Had she really just cursed Beast and his men to a life of imprisonment? Surely, no one had that power. Yet, fear overcame Beast as he watched his strong hands become covered in hair. His nails grew long and pointed. The bones in his body contorted and rearranged themselves in a painful way.

The terror that he had inflicted on so many others now weighed him down. His clothing ripped as his body shifted.

Looking at the fear on his men's face convinced him to run to a mirror. Before him stood a creature of unparalleled horror, a man yet not a man. He had become, a beast.

Running from the room he pulled the castle door open and tried to cross the threshold, yet his body refused his commands.

A voice singing prettily stopped his effort. A child stepped from the woods, small basket on her lean arm. She was tiny. He was terrified. "Hello? Who are you?" A little voice drifted softly into the room where Beast huddled.

"You had better come out now. No one is supposed to be here but me. You are in biiig trouble." The stern command forced his body into action. Slowly he emerged and looked down.

"Boy you must have made her mad! She made you extra ugly. Well, no matter. You better go now before she gets back."

The child reached for Beast and he pulled back. "Go away. She won't let me leave until I make her daughter Belle love me. Then I will imprison her."

"You wouldn't even get close enough to her. She would just turn you into a frog. What are you anyway? What's your name?"

"My name is Beast." He said quietly and tried to shrink back from the child reaching for him. "Where is this Belle?" One of the men had come forward sporting a long black and white coat, reminiscent of a skunk.

"I'm Belle." The child smiled so sweetly that the other men began to come out and grin.

"Beast, we could just hold her captive 'til the woman returns for her. Make her change us back." The other men's faces had changed. One had a pig snout, while another's face had spots like a hyena. His biggest man had grown large ears and his nose had distended like an elephant's trunk. The other two men stood back slightly, but the tallest man now looked like a giraffe.

As Beast looked up at his men the child moved away, out of reach. He cowered at the thought of touching her. He might give her whatever he had caught. Wait! Since when did a child matter?

The last man, who had evaded Beast's sight, made a grab for the child as she snuck away. The man's rat-like face came only inches from the child as she reached up and gave him a slap.

"You don't touch me. I don't like to be touched. I'm the boss around here and you will all do whatever I say. You . . ." She pointed at the rat. "I want you to go fetch some dinner. You . . ." Her little hand pointed towards elephant man. "You may sweep the floor and mop it. It's getting dirty."

On and on the chore list grew until she turned to Beast. "Since I can tell you are a coward and weak, you will be my maid."

At this the other six men laughed. Beast a maid? Turning sharply the child lifted her hands and the men began to move, without their consent, to do her biding. It was as if they were marionettes and she the puppet master.

The men quickly learned to obey their little tyrant queen. She was a harsh mistress, for a child, and expected whatever task she assigned to be done promptly and without question. As long as the men complied they were rewarded with treats and special meals. Games often took place in the evening time. If she was displeased however, she punished them just as a parent would a child. They were sent to bed without dessert and game time.

Months of working for the child had turned these stoic creatures into her abject servants. They loved her. Often

118

they would make her something special in the kitchen or bring her flowers from the window boxes. Beast, after getting his ears soundly boxed for brushing her hair too hard, still cowered every time she came near.

"Beast, why are you so afraid of everything?"

"I didn't used to be, Belle. Your mother made me this way before she left. Where is your mother?"

"We've gone over this Beast. She won't return until the curse is over." With that she gave him a pat on the head and walked away.

"I must make this child love me." Beast thought about the ways the other men had gained her love and respect. He couldn't think of a single way of endearing himself to her.

One day however, Belle asked him to go on a walk with her.

"I can't leave the castle, Belle. I've tried. The curse is too strong."

"You're with me, silly. Of course you can leave as long as I say so."

119

Smiling, Beast went with the child, and they walked hand in hand, 'til they came to a cliff.

"Belle, don't get so close to the edge. You might fall." Panic set in as she teetered by the side. The drop would kill her.

"That could break this curse." Beast thought but as she began to tumble he reached forward and grabbed her, pulling her close to his heart.

"Don't ever do that again!" He bellowed.

"If you were to fall, you'd die!" He put her down gently and looked into her tear-filled eyes.

"Oh, Belle! I didn't mean to frighten you. You can't do things like this though. No one wants to see you hurt or killed. Just promise me you won't go that close again. Don't cry. I'm sorry."

Feeling like the monster he resembled, the big man/beast put his head between his hands wearily. "I'm not crying because you scared me, Beast." Belle's small hands lay calmly on his head in comfort. "I'm crying because you finally learned to care about someone other than yourself, which means you will be going soon. I shall miss you."

Beast raised his head and shook it from side to side. Was it true? Had he really started to care about this child?

The answer was yes. He loved her dearly and didn't want any harm to come to her.

Suddenly, his body shifted. The hair that covered his body fell in billows around them and his nails retracted.

"You did it, Beast. You broke the spell." Belle smiled kindly up at him then threw her little arms around his waist.

"I guess you and the boys are going to leave now aren't you?" She sighed as she began walking back to

120

the castle.

"I won't leave until your mom gets back, Belle. You shouldn't be left alone. It can be dangerous and you are always getting into mischief." Beast smiled at the child.

"You looked better the other way." She grinned and ran back to the castle.

"And mother has been here the whole time. You don't think she would have left me with a bunch of strangers do you?"

Her laughter flowed back up to him and he smiled.

As he entered, the old woman stood before him. Her face changed and her back straightened. Before him stood a beautiful woman, holding Belle's little hand.

"It looks like you have won my daughter's heart, Beast."

"Woman, I ought to throttle you!" Beast grinned.

"Or beat me into submission? The woman grinned back.

"Are you going to stay and marry my mom?" Belle reached up and grabbed his hand.

"I might if she promises not to use magic on me again."

"Wait. I might not want to marry you. You won my daughter's heart that doesn't mean you won mine."

"Yes, it does or you wouldn't have changed me back. We are here to stay, woman. Get yourself ready for a wedding."

"I'll think about it."

"Yea. I'm gonna have a dad. We will be Beauty, Beast and Belle." Belle skipped off and told the men they had lots of work to do. After all everything should be perfect for a wedding.

About the Author

Melynda Fleury was born so long ago she prefers not to remember the year. The mother of three active children, that keep her busy and amused, her books reflect her life. Although she is now blind as a bat she tries to focus on the funny side of life. Her first and second books, Just Nonsense and More Nonsense, have hit number 1 on the charts in family humor and women's humor. Her newest book True Nonsense has been said to be funnier than the first two. If you are looking for a fun, light-hearted read, these are the books for you.

Come join her *crazy world*!

Blog: http://www.melyndarockinthecrazy.blogspot.com/
Twitter: @Lynsworld

Pillaging
Kai Strand

Sneaking up to the cardboard enclosure, Amber whispered, "Hello."

She gently shook the box. "Anybody here?" She'd watched the tall guy leave, but needed to make sure no one else was around.

If she had counted it out right, it was Wednesday and the guy usually rode his bike over to the Home Depot. Amber had been watching the tall guy for a while. Peeking around the corner of the box she said one more tentative, "Hello?"

The stench hit her head on. A combination of sweat soaked manmade fibers and wet dog. "Hmmm," she mused out loud, "he doesn't smell as bad as most."

Amber scurried over to a pile of clothing and dug into it as if it were a chocolate cream pie. She pulled out a black sweater.

"Too itchy." Amber dropped it back onto the pile and yanked out a denim button-up shirt.

"Too lightweight." She tossed it aside.

Next she tugged out a blue, zip-up sweatshirt. She pulled it over her goose bump covered arms and dragged the hood over her greasy, blonde hair.

"Just right; warm, soft and with a nice, deep hood for the rain."

A pile of shoes beckoned to her. At fourteen years old, her feet had recently grown. She looked down at her own tennis shoes; toes flapping like a duck's bill and laces only long enough for half the eyelets.

"It's worth a try." Shrugging, Amber slipped off her shoes and plopped onto the ground.

First she tried on another pair of tennis shoes. They

fit well enough, but she noticed the sole tearing away on the right shoe.

"Too drafty."

Then she tried on a pair of water shoes. They were way too big and she could feel the cold concrete of the underpass through the flimsy bottoms.

"Too wimpy." Amber kicked them off.

The only other shoes were a pair of army boots. Doubtful they'd be comfortable enough to live in, she slipped them on and laced them up.

"Wow, these are perfect!" She flapped her feet in the air in front of her, enjoying the secure fit around her ankles.

Amber's stomach growled. Spying a small box in the opposite corner, she crawled over to it. Lifting the flaps, she was pleased to discover the tall guy's food stash. She pulled out a foam take-out container and opened it. Inside were the remains of an omelet. Her stomach knotted and roiled in protest to the cold eggs.

"Too bad." Amber closed the top and put the container aside.

Next she found a bag of bread. Opening it she peeked in and the woodsy scent of mold assaulted her nose. The bread was covered in green fur, far too much to consider removing it and eating what was left.

"Too gross." Amber sighed and wrapped the bread up again and then rubbed her nose trying to dislodge the smell of mold that clung inside.

She noticed a fast food wrapper and lifted it out of the box. She opened the wad as if it were a present. Inside she found the remains of a burrito.

"I love Mexican food!"

"Hey!"

Amber whipped around, the burrito poised in front of her salivating mouth. The tall guy filled the entrance of the cardboard enclosure.

"You're stealing my stuff!" His bloodshot eyes glared.

Amber shoved the burrito in her pocket, flung the cardboard wall nearest her over her head and sprinted up a hill to the freeway. She ran southbound on the northbound side of the freeway until it felt like her lungs would burst. The tall guy hadn't followed her so she climbed down the slope into the neighborhood below.

Amber had broken the cardinal rule. Thou shalt not steal from thy homeless neighbor. She would have to hang out on the south end of town for a week or so until the tall guy forgot her and what she'd done.

She pulled out the burrito and ate it while she wandered down the alley behind an apartment complex. The tortilla was soggy but the delectable blend of spices thrilled her tongue with each bite. Finished, she wadded up the wrapper and tossed it into a dumpster. Amber paused and considered the dumpster.

Heaving a big sigh she accepted that she would have to start fresh building a new shelter.

"Ah, the glamorous life of a homeless fourteen-year-old. If Mom could see me now." Amber hefted herself onto the side of the dumpster and started the gnarly process of finding discards to turn into a temporary home.

"The boots were worth it."

© Kai Strand 2012

About the Author

Kai Strand writes fiction for kids and teens. Her debut novel, *The Weaver*, was a finalist in the 2012 EPIC eBook Awards. She is a (very lucky) wife and the mother of four amazing kids. The most common sound in her household is laughter. The second most common is, "Do your dishes!" She and her family hike, geocache, and canoe in beautiful Central Oregon, where they call home.

To find out more about Kai's books, download companion documents, find links to her published short stories and discover all the places to find Kai both virtually and in person, visit her website: www.kaistrand.com. She loves to hear from readers, so feel free to send her an email or visit her facebook page, Kai Strand, Author.

Lake Josephine
M Sullivan

Beneath the shoreline, winter scrub
the ice ends . . . blub . . . blub . . . blub.
It swallows pucks and hockey sticks,
with quaking gasps and painful cricks.
Josephine, alone, too near,
skates along without a fear.

Disappears.
For spring we wait,
to find her under where we skate.

About the Author

M Sullivan is an award-winning writer, a storyteller, and a pediatric nurse. He has performed songs and stories throughout the country in libraries, schools, bookstores, and museums. His work has been published in numerous magazines, including Highlights, Crow Toes Quarterly, and Bridal Guide Magazine, of all places. His

127

work has recently appeared in "An Eyeball in My Garden," "And the Crowd Goes Wild," and "In the Garden of the Crow." He lives in Richmond, VA, with his wife and three children. For more information, please check out his website at www.msullivantales.com.

Rose Amongst the Briars
Leetah East

The rain poured heavily, leaving everything sodden and slippery. Duke Devon gripped the saddle's pommel as he attempted to pull himself out of the mud. The pressure on the horse's side made it step away from its would-be rider. Devon tottered off balance, barely catching himself.

"Thrice cursed beast!" Devon hollered. He yanked on the reins, forcing the uncooperative horse closer so he would have the required leverage to get out of the mud. As he did so, a bright flash filled the sky all around them, and an explosion that made his ears ring followed directly afterward. The lightning strike spooked his horse and it went running as fast as the mud allowed, paying no heed to the useless tugs at the reins.

When Devon's ears stopped ringing and his sight refocused to the dark of the rainy eve, he pulled hard on the reins, finally acquiring the appropriate response, and they stopped. Devon looked back at where they had come. Less than a hundred yards from where he had been stuck there was an enormous wall of briar thorns. It was this which had been struck by the lightning and was now visible in the glow of the fire that lit the section of gnarly thorns.

"So then, where have you taken me, Nawlah?" Duke Devon inquired of his horse as he turned his attention back to his immediate surroundings. He could see the outline of a small hut on the horizon. "At least the gods guided your flight in the right direction." Giving a nudge with the heel of his boot, he urged his horse in the direction of the hovel.

The old man who lived in the hovel agreed to let

Devon in out of the storm and stabled his horse in the barn. Devon was soaked as a drowned rat and looked like a man that just crawled from his grave with all the mud covering him. The old man must have thought that description fitting as well, because as they sat around the hearth, allowing the Duke to dry himself, he began to tell the tale of the Forsaken Kingdom.

"There once was a king and queen who ruled their kingdom with wisdom and justice. They were loved by their people and envied by all surrounding kingdoms. When they had a daughter it was their wish to have her rule as they had, so that the prosperity might continue. But they feared that because she was a girl that others might think it easy to overthrow her. They called upon the Fae to give her gifts that would help protect her from this inevitability. For the celebration of her birth the Fae came to bestow their gifts. Twelve Fae arrived at the celebration and each gave her a gift.

"The gifts were of the highest value to one who would rule, but before the twelfth Fae could bestow a gift, the spirit of death came and kissed the little babe on the cheek, telling the king and queen that their daughter would not live to see the eve of her fifteenth birthday, for she would be wounded with the spindle of a spinning wheel and die.

"The king and queen mourned the fate of their daughter, and through her, the fate of their kingdom. They commanded the twelfth Fae to remove this curse that death had placed upon their little girl. The Fae told her that she could not change death's promise, but that she could give her a gift that would allow her to live, after death, though she would sleep until the man who would rule beside her released her from the sleep. The royal couple was so distraught that they begged the Fae to

130

give this gift of life. They only wished that their daughter might still live and protect their kingdom. And so the Fae gave this gift and returned to their habitation.

"The king ordered all spinning wheels be burned the next day to prevent death's promise from being fulfilled. And so, on the morn of their daughter's fifteenth birthday they believed death had been defeated. But the princess was found in her room at midday, pierced through the heart with the spindle of a spinning wheel. They pulled it from her breast and the wound closed immediately; there was not so much as a trace of blood. However, the princess's heart did not beat and her chest did not rise and fall with breath. And so, they placed her on her bed and bid none to enter save for prospective princes.

"But that evening the entire kingdom fell to the flesh rot disease and not one soul survived. A neighboring king called it an act of the gods for communing with the wild Fae. He sent men to bury the bodies in a mass grave that encircled the forsaken land. And so they did, but the men who were sent also died of the flesh rot. So, the only ones who have ventured there since have been kings and princes in search of this damsel that they might have her for a wife and lift the curse from the kingdom. But none have been able to even penetrate the wall of briars that grew tall and thick over the mass grave surrounding the kingdom."

"Is that the wall of briars I saw this evening?" Duke Devon asked.

"The same," replied the old man. "And you will go there in the morning when the weather has cleared and you will wake the land from its slumber."

Devon laughed. "And why would I do that? If I remember correctly, you said that every king and prince that has gone there has been thwarted by the briars alone. I have had enough snags in my life; I don't need to purposefully walk into a hedge of them."

"As you say," said the old man. And he stood up, retiring for the evening, leaving Devon in his thoughts.

Why would I knowingly go into a cursed briar patch that covers cursed graves to find a cursed princess and awaken her cursed land? That just sounds like hell to me! Of course, the old man is probably senile and a bit crazy. He lives out in the middle of nowhere and probably gets a kick out of telling these stories to random travelers to see if they will believe him and kill themselves. Ridiculous. I'm not going to fall for those shenanigans.

In such thoughts he dozed off to sleep, tossing and turning as images of a beautiful maiden came to him, teasing him with a kiss and then turning into a hedge of thorns that would tear his lips and leave him bleeding for want of the maiden. By the time he awoke, he had determined to find this maiden if there was even a chance she existed. And if she didn't he would kill himself in the effort and no longer have anything in life to worry about.

Devon thanked the old man for his hospitality and mounted Nawlah, his steed and headed back in the direction he had come the following night. In the daylight and good weather, he found that the wall of briars was much closer than it had seemed the night before. The rains had put out the small fire and left the section of briars charred and crumbling.

Dismounting his horse at the charred section and keeping the image of the beautiful maiden in his mind (and faithfully ignoring the thoughts of his lips tearing from the rose thorns), he gingerly took a step toward the wall. He paused, unsure what he had been expecting, but when nothing magically tried attacking him, he felt more confident and moved closer. He placed a gloved hand on the briars and they crumbled to ash. Brushing across the entire burnt area he created a space large enough to step through.

He maneuvered carefully, clearing the charred hedges step by step before proceeding, until he could see the shape of something large through the hedge. Another fifteen minutes and he had passed through the briar hedge and found himself facing a grand castle about a mile off.

The castle too, was covered in thorns. As he approached he was nervously excited to note that these thorns were actually roses, just like the ones from his dream. He placed his hand gingerly over his mouth as a sort of instinctual protection, then began assessing how he would enter the castle, for this, he was sure, was where the princess must lay waiting for the kiss that would awaken her.

He began walking around the perimeter to find a way to gain access to the inside from the ground and much to his delight, found the main gates wide open, held in place by the numerous rose vines and briars. He walked around the castle, noting the grandeur that had been left to decay for nearly one hundred years, if the tales were true.

Eventually, after roaming through a large part of the castle and not finding the maiden for whom he searched, he came to a locked room. Try as he might he could not force his way through the doors, the rose vines were too many and too thick with age and growth. Weary, he sat on the stone marble floor and looked longingly at the door, knowing that what he had been searching for must be there, just beyond reach. He looked at the hundreds of roses that sprouted from the thorns all around the door, far more than had been on any other part of the briars.

As Devon looked at the roses the image of the kiss from his dream entered his thoughts.

He gingerly took a rose in his rough hand and kissed it. The moment he did, sharp pains pierced through him, like thousands of little thorns thrusting into his flesh. The vines moved from the doors and it opened. Devon writhed on the floor in agony, aware of the opening of the doors but unable to do anything but scream in agony.

Briar Rose, for that is what her parents had named her at birth, stood from her bed for the first time in ninety-seven years. It had been unpleasant, hearing all and knowing all but being unable to directly respond to the world in which her body resided. She mourned for the flesh rot that took her kingdom. The gift of life the thirteenth Fae had given her had bestowed some invaluable abilities. After ninety-seven years she now had the power to reclaim her kingdom and in those ninety-seven years she had also been able to defend it from invaders by growing the briars over the bodies of her citizens.

Princess Rose stepped from her room and looked down with pity at the man who had freed her from the immobility of the magical sleep. His form was strong; this was not a prince from a court, but a man who had dealt with the world and its trials. The tortured look in his cold, dead eyes called to her soul and she knelt, held his head in her hands and kissed him on the lips. He stirred, then stood with her and bowed in gratitude and awe.

"My Prince. I have been awaiting your arrival for nearly a century. What took you so long?" Briar Rose smiled at him.

"M'lady, I apologize for my tardiness. Until last eve I was unaware of your condition. I swear by my title I would have come sooner had I known you were waiting for me," Devon said.

"You are here now, and that is all that matters. It is time I introduce you to our people," said Briar Rose.

"But there is no one here M'lady. All of your subjects died the same eve you passed," said Devon, feeling sad he had to pass such news to Lady Rose.

"True, but like me, they too will live in death. I may appear living, but my heart does not beat and my skin remains cold in death. Only the gift of the last Fae provides life to me now and to you also. For when you kissed my roses, they killed you, but when I kissed you, I gave you life again. And this life is eternal. No one can kill what is already dead," said Briar Rose.

"Now 'tis time to awaken my people. Their rest has

been long and now they must arise to reclaim their lands." Briar Rose walked out to the hedge of thorns and caressed them lightly with her cold fingers. The ground shuddered. Only small tremors, at first, that made it difficult to stand, but then the ground shook so violently that the neighboring kingdoms felt the rumbling of the earth. The briar hedge fell away in great shreds as the flesh-rotted corpses of her people rose from the ground beneath them. The mass of unearthed peoples gathered around Briar Rose, their queen. She spoke to them, to answer their questions of why this thing had happened to them.

"My parents wanted their people to be free of the threats of the outer kingdoms and so it is! There is no greater blessing than this undead life. None will dare challenge us. None can live where we are. Those who are foolish and think to overtake us will be overtaken by us. They will become as we are. Death can claim us no longer for the gift of the last Fae was the gift of life, and so even in death we live!"

A great roar of morale rose up from the voices of the undead horde. Every man woman and child, whose ears it touched, quaked in fear.

About the Author

Leetah East is a wife and home-educating mother to four children. She devotes what spare time she has to her passion.

Her writing has been published in various anthologies.

Please visit her website:
http://candyboutique.wix.com/candiss.

The Old Woman Who Lived in a Shoe
Variation by Fran Fischer

There was an old woman
who lived in a shoe.
She had so many children
she didn't know what to do.
She knew she had too many,
but they were all so cute.
They needed a bigger place to live in
so she bought a knee-high boot.

The Evil Queen
Afobos

Deep underground they toil and dig, looking for the treasures of the great dwarven king. The mines of Abergnor snake beneath the earth. For a thousand years and more, countless dwarves have dug for the precious stones, wealth and gold, all for their city that stretches cathedral-like under the wondrous mountain that is their home.

The mountain king, the great dwarf Borthenor, has ruled these lands for three centuries in peace and love and with a hand that's strong. The dwarves dig deep and the mountain's blood runs rich. It glistens to the lantern's glow, its brilliant hue golden, as the veins on the wall reflect the light from the workers' picks. The dwarves dig, and sing a song as old as time itself, when the Gods themselves built this world.

Proud men they are, and love what they do, working with their strong and gnarled hands, muscles bulging and time well-spent. They are a simple folk and fear no beast as they defend their homes from goblin and troll alike, and now from the human queen whose taste for power has brought the tall humans knocking at their doors.

The faerie folk speak of her with hushed tones and call her power dark and evil, and talk of demons that she conjures forth to do her bidding in the four corners of the world. The seven brothers listen to the tale of the evil queen by the emissary of the elven king, as everyone in the great big hall drinks their beer with eyes wide and hands fondling great long beards.

The tall and lithe elves, even though opposites of the dwarves, are still respected as brothers, and the king of the elves has visited Borthenor on many a celebration to honor his clan.

The elf continues his tale and proceeds to describe the evil deeds the queen had done to the elves, and fairy folk of the great oaken dale. The poisoned wells and the taxes imposed. The threats on the king himself. And the humans walking in fairy realms with no fear, and trampling living things, without even a prayer to the Goddess as they do what they may. The dwarves mutter and make signs to ward off the devil of a queen, and finally the elf steps down from the table, and the king nods to him as he sits, and someone brings him some more mulled wine to warm his parched lips.

The feast in the honor of the elven lord is finally done. The brothers escort the tall and thin elf towards the dying light of the day above to see him safely to his home.

Times were once that no one feared the walk through the forest realm. Even the trolls stayed clear of the magic the elves had woven like so many spider webs gleaming turquoise green and brightening the night's air. The queen's spells have turned the magic to something else, something dark, and what was once peaceful forest trails are now twisted dark paths that wait for the pure of heart.

There was talk of uniting all the people of the seven realms. Yes, even inviting the troll and goblin kings to join in strength to fight the evil that the black queen spread throughout the realms, through black demons that float on fear's dark slimy wings, come out of places mired with rot and steeped in darkness and despair.

The brothers found the hidden trail that remained safe, still warded by their own potent powers, guarded by the mage Dindril's powerful earth magic. Once out of dwarven lands, they turned back laughing as they pass the wineskin to make light of the darkness that lingers in the air.

Suddenly brother Heingerd stops and turns in the fork to the left, out of the protection of the warded path. The others call to him but he runs to a shape in the tall grass and bends down to see the form of a fair maiden with milky white skin and beauty so fair that it breaks his heart.

"A human so far from home, how did she get here?" Alignor asks as he bends to see if she still yet lives. He is doubtful since her skin is as white as snow in contrast to her long and silky raven hair. "She looks as if she sleeps," Doc, the brother that knew of the arts spoke, marking the beatings of her pulse to the beatings of his own. He claimed that she lives and is but unconscious and to bring her with them to their home, away from the evil in the air.

It took two of the brothers to carry her home while the others, with hands on swords, made ready for attack by beast or man or any foe. Haven's Gate at last was reached and they found the long winding path that led inside the mountain to their well-lit keep. Lain on their biggest bed and covered with soft warm furs, they lit the lamps and watched her sleep as two of the brothers ran to tell the king of her and to see what he would have.

The brothers watched her as she slept and finally she stirred. Her eyes opened and she caught it all in, and stood up in the bed frightened not knowing where she was. Doc came closer and spoke softly to her, telling her they found her on the forest floor, and just brought her out of the dangerous night and welcomed her in their homes. Her face relaxed and a beautiful smile formed on her lips. The brothers were stunned at her beauty, as if the sun was lying on their bed. Doc's heart skipped a beat.

They begged her to spend the night and she agreed, saying that her home was not hers anymore for her stepmother tried to have her put to death and dead she would be if not for the kindness of her would-be executioner who risked his own life to let her live.

The dwarves were stunned with this news, and at that moment Borthenor walked in, followed by the two brothers who brought with them the old king. She shared her story once more, and they were aghast to learn of her treatment at the hands of the evil queen. Borthenor invited her to stay in the Dwarven kingdom for as long as she deemed necessary.

Her face brightened, and she thanked the mighty king, who, under the spell of her beauty as well, melted inside and longed for the princess to just touch his hand. A red color overtook his old face and he grinned.

He didn't think he still had those childish needs inside his old self, and wondered what his wife would think of his wanting a young maiden, younger than a sapling and he, an old gnarled oak with great grandchildren of his own.

The king left, and she was brought food and drink. Famished she told her tale of escape from the castle and the wicked queen. The queen envied her beauty it had seemed, and was known to brag to herself of how she was the most beautiful in the realm in her great ornate mirror as the princess caught her at it more than once.

The brothers chuckled at that news, and slapped each other with mirth, their hearts growing warm towards this child that appeared in their midst. She told them how the servants swore they heard the mirror speak in a gravelly demon's voice, telling the queen that she was the most beautiful in the realm except for the princess who was more beautiful still.

Her servant confessed that the evil queen was livid at the news, and she struck the first servant that walked into the room and called out to her entrusted man as the servant left the room.

A day later, as Snow White walked in the courtyard, an arrow flew toward her breast. She ran into the forest without food or rest. That was two days ago, before she finally woke up in a strange bed.

The brothers took it all in and shaking their heads, they vowed to guard the princess fair. Her smile alone was enough for them to swear fealty and give their lives to her care.

Two weeks later she had become accustomed to living in the great cavernous hall and living with the brothers for whom she sang and played the lyre, telling them wondrous stories from the human courts.

One day, she cleaned near the cave, singing to herself as she washed their clothes by the dale. Her voice was beyond belief and her beauty reflected in the water's edge as the old beggar came by on her mule, pretending to be a harmless seller of wares. She told the princess that she reminded her of her granddaughter that had died while still young, and with a fake tear in her eye offered her a gleaming red apple, because her singing had touched her heart.

The princess took the offered fruit, and thanking her, took a bite. The old hag watched with glee, making sure the poison worked its evil as it took root. The princess fell on the soft green grass, and the old hag's form wavered as if in a dream, transforming first to the evil queen's cold beauty and then into a black smoke that withered the grass it touched as it disappeared.

Snow White lay there as the forest animals came to mourn. It wasn't long before she was discovered by the brothers and pronounced dead by Doc. They all cried having lost something more precious than gold.

As they carried her back to their domain, a rider approached and asked who she was. They placed her on the ground and looked at the stranger, their eyes full of sorrow and despair. "She is a princess and now she is dead. We know her as Snow White because she was most fair."

The man looked at the beauty lying on the grass as if asleep and he could see her chest lay still and she was at her final peace. His heart told him that she was the woman in his dreams, that had haunted him these past two years and here she was, out of his reach.

He asked the dwarves a favor, one first and last kiss. They looked at him as if he was mad but reluctantly they agreed. He bent down on his knee and kissed her rosy lips, and as he straightened to get up, a gasp was heard. The brothers saw the heaving of her chest and her breath visible in the crisp morning's mist.

A miracle of love was witnessed as tears streamed from their eyes to fall, moistening their long beards. Snow White opened her eyes to see the prince, whose face went ashen at the beauty come to life from his dreams.

She reached out to him and he to her. This time they kissed for real as the brothers watched and witnessed the meeting of a princess and a prince. That marked what was destined to be the coming of a new age for all the realms and many centuries of peace.

The realms would unite to drive the evil queen's reign to the darkest depths of hell, where it will be her fate throughout eternity, to exist in misery as the hag she portrayed, ugly and alone, with mirrors as her only companions.

About the Author

Afobos was born in Greece. His family immigrated to the states in the late 60's ,and he's lived there since. He's always loved writing mostly for his own pleasure. He's had poetry anthologies published as well as sci-fi novels and also a book called: Zen and the Art of Massage. Afobos is a very diverse and talented writer. Please look for him on Amazon.

A Good Day for Magic Fish
Larry Lefkowitz

Usually it takes me a while to catch the first fish. But that day as I sat in the skiff on the lake, they simply weren't biting. Changing flies, changing fishing spots—nada. I was dozing off from the lack of action and the sun, when the fish jumped into the boat. I pounced on him before he could jump out of the boat. "Wait long enough and they come to you," I shouted triumphantly, the old fisherman's wisdom.

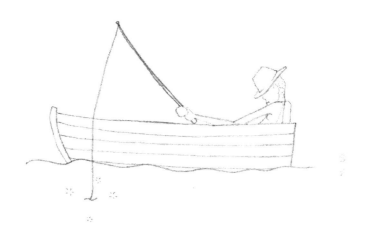

He turned out to be a disappointingly small fish, though a pretty one—a type I had never seen before. With gold scales that put those of your aquarium goldfish in the shade. I picked him up to toss him back. He was too small for frying.

"Don't do that," the fish pleaded. "Not before using your three wishes"

A talking fish. Trouble. If you tell people a talking fish jumped into your boat, even bait-sellers will give you the

145

wary eye.

"Get off my back," I growled, in a bad mood since I hadn't caught any fish that Molly could fry up. Molly traditionally threatened me, before I went fishing, to brain me with the skillet if I failed to bring back fish to fry. She never did but her biting comments if I didn't, made me smart, anyhow.

"That doesn't count as a wish since your 'I'm not on your back' is a metaphor. Precise phrasing is all-important."

I remembered something about a fish and three wishes which my mother, between swigs of whatever alcohol was handy, told me as a child.

"I have three wishes before you get the hell out of my boat? Is that it?"

"Essentially, yes. Although your somewhat truncated version is from the pre-modern era of legends. The traditional 'magic fish' was somewhat cruel. We contemporary piscatorial wish-granters are a different breed. We see psychiatrists. We suffer guilt. If I jumped out of the boat without granting you three wishes, I would suffer angst and have to sit through too many sessions of remedial therapy. In short, you are the beneficiary of three wishes."

On the ropes from his spiel, and worried about Molly's reaction to my not catching a fish, I mumbled, "I wish I caught a good eating fish today."

Suddenly the biggest lake trout I had ever seen was lying in the bottom of the boat.

"Sorry," said the golden fish. Not to me, to the trout. "I'm only a conduit. The legend, you know."

With the last of his strength, the trout nodded, sadly it seemed to me.

This wish business actually worked. Too bad I

wasted a wish on the trout, though he was mouth-wateringly meaty. Must have weighed fifty pounds, at least. My 30 pound test would have snapped with this hombre. Too bad I wasted a wish on him, though. Still I had two big ones to use.

"How long have I got?" I asked the golden fish.

"To use your wishes?"

"Yeah. Not 'til I turn belly up."

The fish frowned, maybe disturbed by my dead fish . . . metaphor. "There is no statute of limitations."

It was my turn to be disturbed. "Give it to me in English."

"That is, no time limit. But you could give some thought to me. I cannot complete the carrying out my task until you use your last two wishes."

"You jumped into my boat, I didn't jump into yours."

"I am not authorized to go into the reasons for the form and purpose of our meeting. Let us say that the fact that you always toss back undersized fish and remove the hook gently out of the fishes mouths have not gone unnoticed."

With all the gab, I didn't notice the wind spring up and the water turn rough. Before I knew it, a storm bore down on the boat. And of the three of us in the boat I was most at risk. I was a poor swimmer, even before the beer made me more like a sinker in the water than Tarzan. My companions didn't have a problem. I looked up at the rain coming down in sheets, filling the boat. "I wish I was back at the dock," I murmured.

I was. I slapped my forehead with the palm of my hand. Wish number two—gone. When you fish alone you talk to yourself. I had long since given up on trying to get Molly to come fishing with me. "Together with you in a trailer is more than enough," she would say. Or "Your

147

dinghy is not my idea of a Love Boat." For some time Molly had been urging me to take her on a cruise, but what good was sitting on a big boat if you couldn't fish from it. When I told her that, she refused to talk to me for a week. Go and try to figure out women.

I lugged home the trout tightly gripped under my arm. In the other hand I carried the golden fish in a bait jar of water. I feared he might try to jump out, head for a sewer or something, but the golden fish, who could read thoughts as well as grant wishes, raised slightly a cautionary dorsal fin. "I'm under contractual obligation to you."

"Until the third wish is granted."

"Precisely."

Soaked to the sin, I headed for the trailer park and the trailer which I shared with Molly, who I met two years before working behind the counter in 'Fish Tackle for Your Mackerel'. Molly claimed she had nothing to do with the name, but it smacked of the style of one whom, in her words, "tried her hand" at poetry and liked to read books.

When I kidded her that she was named for a tropical fish, she would say she identified with a Molly Bloom from a book. "Why her?" I asked.

"She made do with the men in her life," she replied. Molly was a cynic. Not someone that you came to with a tale about three wishes.

How did Molly end up with me? Her ex was a hunter. "I prefer to fry fish than cook deer," she would tell anyone who asked how we met. Yet Molly was enough for me, cynicism and all. There's nothing lonelier than living in a trailer park without a woman.

On the way, I fantasized on which wish I would use. I considered wishing for another woman, younger and prettier and gentler than Molly. But then I told myself, you're used to Molly. Those Barby doll women are nothing but trouble. No, I would not use the wish to wish for something for me alone. I would wish for something for Molly and me, if that was permitted.

"Permitted if you phrase the wish jointly; that is, collectively; that is—"

"I wish you would stop with the legalese," I cut him short. Human lawyers were more than enough; I didn't like to have a fish lay down the law for me.

"Easily done!" he said joyfully. "And that is your third—and need I add, last—wish."

"You did that on purpose!" I thundered.

"Well within the parameters of the legend," he said before he disappeared in a golden flash.

I resolved not to tell Molly or anyone else about all this. I'll just give her the trout. We'll dine off it for a month, at least. Some would say a wasted wish, but they won't have tasted it. And Molly will stop threatening to leave—at least for a month.

About the Author
Larry Lefkowitz

As I was born, a certain heavenly brightness . . . no, I'll leave that off and settle for:

The stories, poetry, and humor of Larry Lefkowitz have been widely published in the U.S., Israel, and Britain.

Lefkowitz is looking for a publisher of his Humorous Fantasy and Science Fiction Stories.

Goldilocks and the Ugly Sister
Elaine Mann

There was no doubting Goldie's beauty. Her blonde curls tumbled lushly onto her shoulders, her bright eyes were like big, blue marbles, her skin was clear and her cheeks a healthy pink. By contrast, her sister Cissie was actually rather ugly. It was said that when the twins fell into the gene pool whilst Goldie had the softest of landings, Cissie hit every rock on the way down and a few more on climbing out. Cissie had poker-straight, mousey-brown hair, one eye looked east and the other west and her coarse skin was covered in fine, dark hair giving her the appearance of a small, furry animal.

Unkind people used to call the twins 'beauty and the beast' and when their mother said that Cissie was a little monkey, she wasn't always referring, in an endearing fashion, to her behavior.

When the girls began school, of course Goldie was popular. She not only became one of the 'in' crowd, she created it. Cissie was never included in Goldie's little gang of wenches, but she did become the butt of their jokes and cruel pranks on more than one occasion.

Steadfastly, the little girl tried and tried to be accepted, but whilst others might have allowed her to tag along, Goldie always made sure she was left behind.

But, instead of being thankful for her beauty and her easy life and going easy on her less fortunate sister, Goldie resented Cissie's ugliness as if it were a personal assault.

Their parents didn't help the situation although they did try. Their mother, in particular, always insisted the girls stick together when they went out to play. Goldie hated being lumbered with Cissie and to be fair, Cissie didn't much enjoy this forced companionship either.

Goldie made her do things that she knew were wrong, like stealing apples from Mrs. Black's tree. Of course, when they were inevitably caught, Goldie apologized profusely for her sister's awful behavior and was rewarded with a bag of apples while Cissie took the blame. It was Goldie who broke Mr. Green's windscreen with a stone, stole money from their mother's purse to buy sweets and put a pink sock in the white wash. The list went on and on and with each misdemeanor Cissie took the blame and fell more and more out of favor.

The surprising thing was that nobody ever saw through Goldie. Her behavior was awful, her nature cruel, she delighted in hurting people and she was sly and altogether nasty. Beauty, it seemed, really was only skin deep. All the while Cissie was patient and kind, honest and true, but she was never given any credit or praise. To use the old cliché, they were like chalk and cheese.

Goldie was proudly shown off at every gathering. She had the leading role in the school nativity play, naturally, no one expected anything less, and while she played

Mary, Cissie was a sheep. Goldie was chosen to be her cousin's bridesmaid, Cissie was not. No one wanted the ugly child to spoil the wedding photos.

Goldie sang a solo in the church choir, Cissie was asked to mime and stand behind Billy, the tallest boy in the group. When teams were chosen for school sports, Cissie was always the last to be picked whereas Goldie, of course, was a team leader. One wondered how long this situation could continue. How much rejection could a little girl stand?

Holidays were miserable for Cissie. The themed activities favored by the rest of the family left her cold.

She couldn't paint, her photography skills were zilch, she was scared of heights and her skiing was a joke.

Goldie excelled at everything.

This year the family chose an outdoor centre in Canada for the torture. Horse riding, gold panning, trekking, everyone was very excited, everyone except Cissie. The hours during the flight were hell for Cissie.

The motion of the airplane made her feel sick and, while the rest of the family watched movies and stuffed themselves with food, Cissie spent her journey barfing into a bag.

Their cabin on the edge of the wood was luxurious and it even had a hot tub, which unfortunately made Cissie's skin erupt in hives. Goldie cruelly nicknamed her pizza face. The camp site Hoedown was a show down, Goldie danced all evening, Cissie sat alone clawing at her itchy skin.

One afternoon, near the end of the holiday, while their parents were drinking bourbon and lolling in the hot tub, Goldie decided to go for a walk.

"Take your sister with you," their mother called.

"And don't go into the woods," their father added.

Goldie huffed and puffed and stormed off with Cissie running at her heels.

"Don't walk beside me, pizza face," Goldie warned. "I hate you and I don't want you with me. Stay back where I can't see you."

Cissie obediently did as she was told. The girls walked on in silence. Then suddenly Goldie made a sharp left turn and disappeared into the trees.

"Goldie, Goldie, come back. We're not allowed to walk off the track," Cissie called, but Goldie ignored her and kept going deeper and deeper into the woods.

After a while it became very dark and Goldie began to think that perhaps this wasn't such a good idea after all. She turned around and around looking for the path home, but soon realized she was hopelessly lost. She tried calling for Cissie, but there was no reply. Cissie, too, was lost and she began to cry. This was the last straw. Goldie had abandoned her in a dangerous wood, in a foreign country. Surely this time Goldie would get into trouble.

The girls had no idea as they meandered on, searching for a way home, that they were actually only a few feet apart. They both heard the low growls of the bears at roughly the same time. They'd been warned by the Park Ranger about the dangers of straying into the woods and now they could hear that very danger getting closer and closer.

Both girls began to scream. Daddy bear, Mummy bear and Baby bear looked up and sniffed the air.

"I smell dinner," Daddy bear said.

"I hear dinner," Mummy bear said.

"My mouth is watering," Baby bear said and they all nodded contentedly.

Goldie and Cissie emerged into a clearing and could

see each other at opposite ends. The bears stood between them, blocking their way.

"Eat her," Goldie yelled throwing sticks at the bears. Cissie cried, "Leave my sister alone. Come here, chase me. Don't hurt Goldie."

The bears looked bewildered.

"What is that little, furry bear saying?" Daddy bear asked, nodding his big head in Cissie's direction.

"She's speaking with a foreign accent," Mummy bear replied.

"Maybe she wants to share our meal," Baby bear added.

Goldie started running and screaming, "Take Cissie. Keep away from me. I'm too beautiful to eat. Take her, she'll make a much better dinner."

While Goldie disappeared into the woods, Cissie remembered everything the Ranger had taught her and gradually backed away from the bears. Once she was hidden from view she, turned and ran and ran until she emerged from the trees into safety.

Goldie was never seen again and neither were the bears.

And the moral of this story is, sometimes it's better to be an ugly, hairy creature with common sense than a beautiful but sly airhead.

© Elaine Mann 2012

About the Author

Elaine Mann lives in Scotland. She has written several children's books and stories. The first book in her series 'Natalya's Magical Jigsaws is called 'The Penguin Olympics' and is available now at Amazon.

Rumpelbumpelstiltskin
Janie Goltz

My father's blabbering mouth
has brought trouble again, you see.
But this time, Lord in Heaven,
the trouble's all on me.

Father bragged to every man in town
that I could do no wrong.
Mine the loveliest face around,
his voice cried loud and long.

Worst of all, he made a claim
that brought my name to fame.
And not a one seemed to see
that I was not to blame.

"Spin straw to gold!"
they laughed at me.
"We'll see how
this can be."

But the King decided then and there
I'd make his fortune abound.
Now the dogs are in the dairy
and the cattle are in the pound.

The King shut me in a room alone,
commanded me to work.
I stared at stacks of smelly straw
and longed to flee to die kirche.

155

But I was trapped.
I had to stay.
As night set in,
I began to pray:

"Lord, deliver me
from spinning straw to gold.
Or I'll be in this room
until I grow very, very old."

And at that moment
my savior appeared.
He was not the One
in my Bible so dear.

He was short and stumply
kind of rumply
curly haired
like a small bear.

He sneak-snaked out
from behind some straw,
Took one look at me
and started to caw:

"I'll help you out—make all well.
Spin straw into gold. Get you out of this cell.
Just one thing you must promise, you see.
Your firstborn child you'll hand over to me."

I had no children,
planned on none.
I made the promise
and my freedom won.

156

The King saw the gold
and made me his wife.
Promised he'd love me
for the rest of my life.

But after
about a year or so
Something within me
started to grow.

It wasn't a chipmunk.
It wasn't a tree.
It was a baby,
a baby for the King and for me.

When the little prince arrived,
I tried and tried
To take care of his needs.
It seemed he constantly wanted to feed.

Up all night,
visiting charities all day,
I didn't have a
single moment to play.

And then the little man
turned up.
He wanted my baby
and wouldn't settle for a pup.

I could see that love for my baby
burned in the little man's eyes
So I let him take my child,
knowing he was in for a surprise.

He thought I was shaken
to my very core,
When really I knew
it was an open door.

"Guess my name
within three days.
And your prince I'll return.
That's the only way."

As he skittered out
the babe began to fuss.
He stopped by the nursery for nappies
and then he cussed.

"Hush, little child.
Gol darn ya, my dear.
You musn't shed
a single tear.

You now have a dad
with a claim to fame
And Rumpelbumpelstiltskin
is my name."

Silly, little man.
He had no clue.
I heard every word
and didn't miss a few.

158

The nursery monitor
gave me his funny name
So I could begin
to play my game.

I let him take charge of my babe.
I hadn't a care.
I took a nap, got a mani-pedi,
and walked about in my underwear.

Oh, Rumpelbumpelstiltskin,
you just wait and see.
You'll be back
and begging to me.

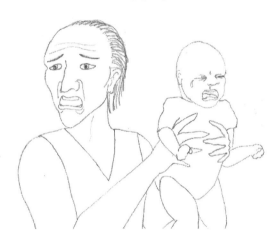

In two days' time
an exhausted R.B. arrived.
"Guess my name," he mumbled,
"And I'll give you the prize."

"Is it George or Charlie or Bernard?"
I teased.
"Perhaps you are Bertram
or is your name Pekinese?"

But then R.B.
simply burst into tears.
"I love this baby,
but I don't know how to calm his fears."

"Oh, Rumpelbumpelstiltskin," I cried,
"Now don't you see
The fishes in the water
and the birds in the trees?

A baby needs attention,
one, two, three.
I'll teach you all you need to know
and make you part of our family."

So Rumpelbumpel
learned to care for our babe.
He changed nappies, made funny faces,
made his name the simpler Gabe.

We shared
childcare work.
Gabe seemed
always to lurk,

Ready to help,
ready to please,
Never a better fellow has hailed
from the seven seas.

160

Now we live together
in our beautiful home,
And I have time
to write my poem.

We're the King, the prince,
mommy me,
And the very best nanny
that ever could be,

I'm pleased to say
I call him my friend
And Gabe,
you never away shall I send.

About the Author

Janie Goltz is just a girl who fell from a star, and Kansas she says is the name of the star. Now she's on her way to The Emerald City. As she travels, she writes stories and a blog and she edits books. Janie owns Janie Junebug Writing & Editing. You can find her blog at dumpedfirstwife.blogspot.com. She is, indeed, a dumped first wife, who now lives with the wolves who raised her. Janie plays slobber ball and eats mice with the wolves, and she has been described as having a strong sense of the ridiculous. She is the self-described Queen of Grammar.

Cinder, Ellie: An Exclusive as told to Bob Grimm
Susan Kane

Bob Grimm was given an address from his distant cousins (the Grimm Brothers) and told to meet with Ethel Gutmater. She had some info on Ellie Cinder, who had recently made headlines, 'Poor Girl/Rich Prince: What Really Happened'?

Bob found himself at a two-story walk-up behind the Cinder home. The first floor was a barn with a mangy donkey, farm equipment, and a pile of rotten pumpkins. Knocking fiercely on the door, Bob waited for an answer, half hoping Ethel was gone. He really could do with a strong cuppa.

But, no. An old woman stuck her head out the window above and hollered, "If you're selling home renovations, I don't need any!"

Bob looked up, squinting at the old worn woman. "I'm . . . that is . . . the Grimm brothers are my cousins, and they said you wrote to them about . . ."

"Come on up, kid. I've been waiting for you. Sure took your time . . ."

The door buzzed open and Bob headed up the narrow stone stairs. Waiting at the top was a frumpy old woman. "I'm sorry to be . . ."

"No problem. Just get in here. There are mice all over the place—I've had a heck of time with them. Bold little scamps."

They settled into the hovel-like home, and the old hag introduced herself. "Ethel . . . Ethel Gutmater." Bob gazed at Ethel and thought, *this is possibly the ugliest woman I have ever seen.*

162

Ethel chuckled. "Yeah, I know what I look like, kid." She handed him a cup of tea, strongly sugared and black as tar. Just the way he liked it.

"Well, then, Bob. Just let me do the talking and you write down what I tell yuh. No questions. Don't need any. Got it?"

Bob took a slurp of the tea, nodded, and started writing.

"Well, let me tell yuh. The Cinder family has lived in that fancy house for ages. Miz Cinder is okay, but not an easy person. I can hear her yellin' at those girls day and night."

"Her two daughters, Ginny and Annie, are just about the dimmest and homeliest girls I've ever seen. Ginnie? Face like a horse. Annie? Shaped like a pumpkin. And then there's Ellie."

Ethel paused, gathering her thoughts. "Ellie showed up on their doorstep one rainy night last year. Miz Cinder's ex dropped her off, saying he had to run, that Harold King's men were chasing 'im. Owed Ol' Harold some money, I guess. Sure enough, a few minutes after he took off, along came thugs with flashlights."

Bob paused and wondered silently, *how the heck does she know about this?*

Ethel laughed heartily. "Hey, I got ears and a good pair of binoculars! You think I go out much? So I watch the Cinders and that family over there, the Whites."

"Well, Ellie was all right, the prettiest piece of fluff I've ever seen. Nice to the animals, even those crazy mice. Miz Cinder wasn't a bit happy about Ellie, but she saw a good deal. Free maid, free servant, whatever. She put Ellie to work in the house, and that girl could work. Cleaned everything, made the place look better'n than it ever has."

163

Ethel stood up and hobbled over to the window. Bob followed her, notebook in hand.

"See over there, the back garden. Well, that's where it all came together."

As Ethel wove the tale, Bob tried to not think anything, but just write about how the story came to be.

"Now then, the mayor, ol' big Harold King, decided it was time for his son, Hal to get outta the house. Marry, have kids, stuff like that. So he threw a big party, real fancy. Invited every single young girl around. Harold didn't want any old hag like me showing up." She chuckled.

"Just about that time, I got this mail-order delivery from T.J. Maxx. *I* didn't order anything; it was addressed to some girl in Hoboken. But I opened it up, and pulled out the cheapest-looking ball gown I have ever seen. All satin and lace, puffy sleeves, a light blue, and it came with clear plastic slippers. Thought it was a Halloween costume.

"Well, the night of the big party, Miz Cinder and her girls gussied up and took a taxi. That was when I heard Ellie in that back garden, and she was crying up a storm."

Ethel hobbled back to her chair, plopping down with a sigh. Bob followed, and picked up his cup. It had been empty when he went to the window, but now a new cup, hot and steaming, sat in its place.

She continued after Bob breathed in the tea. "So, here she was down there. I thought 'Oh heck, what can I do?' So I picked up that cheap dress, shook it out, and wiped off those shoes. Went down to Ellie, and asked her what she wanted to do."

Ethel paused. "Had to feel sorry for the girl. She was all snotty and blotchy-faced, miserable as a wet dog. So

164

I showed her the dress and told her to wash up, 'cause she was going to the party.

"Well, Ellie jumped up, raced into the house. Heard water splashing. She came back, all fresh-faced and clean. Ellie had even combed her hair up nice, tied a blue ribbon around it, and had lipstick on. Think that was from Ginnie; it was her color of pink.

"Ellie stripped off the rags and slipped into the ball gown. It fit her, a surprise to us both. Even the shoes fit her little feet. But, then there was the problem of getting to the party."

Bob tried to squelch his thinking, but couldn't. *Take a taxi, of course!*

"Taxi? You're kiddin', right? Taxis are expensive, and neither of us had the coin. Well, that was when I noticed that son of the White family. He was always a bit of a peeping tom. I called him over and told him to hitch the donkey up to the cart, and to dump the pumpkins in the barn."

Ethel picked up the knobby cane by her chair. "He pulled the donkey and cart around to the back garden. The donkey was none too happy about this at all. Ellie sat on a barrel in the cart and the mice darted around her feet. That White kid sat holding the reins, beaming and thrilled. But, that donkey was not moving, so I swatted him on the rear with this cane, and he took off. I waved the cane at them, and told her to get home by, say, midnight.

"Well, you know pretty much about the party. How Ginnie and Annie made fools of themselves by line-dancing and doing something called 'gangnam'. How Miz Cinders hit on ol' Harold and they disappeared for a while. How Hal saw Ellie and danced with her. Yadda, yadda, so on and so forth. How Ellie and Hal ended up

165

outside on the terrace, and he put some moves on her. How she ran down the stairs at midnight, lost a shoe. Et cetera, et cetera."

Bob wrote furiously, trying to keep up with Ethel.

Ethel chuckled. "That donkey was chomping at the bit to get home, so he bolted. When they all got here and in the barn, that donkey came to dead stop, hurling both Ellie and that kid out and into the compost, which was mostly manure. He ran home crying, and Ellie raced into the garden. She ripped off the s*&t covered gown, and tossed it over into the White yard. Ellie hosed herself off and hobbled inside wearing her one shoe."

"Miz Cinder and the two girls were back at the house minutes later, so Ellie hid the shoe under the kitchen sink with some sponges and rags, ran upstairs and was just in bed when the Cinder women staggered through the door."

Bob tried not to, but the words formed in his head. 'How did you . . . ?"

"Binoculars, kid, binoculars! You are sure one dim Grimm, I tell yuh." Ethel cleared her throat. "Well then, the next day everyone was buzzing, and I mean buzzing. There were hangovers and vomit everywhere. Ol' Harold was miserable. He knew that Hal had at last found true love, so he kicked that sleazy boy out the door, and threw the plastic shoe at him. Told him not to come home, unless he found that girl in the cheap blue dress.

"Hal revved up his Harley and took off. Went to every house, down one street, up the other. No single, of the right age, female could fit into the shoe. Hal was getting desperate, his head hurt, and he wanted to throw up. At last, the Harley stopped in front of the Cinder house.

"Hal staggered to the door, shoe in hand. He heard groans inside and Miz Cinders opened the door. She was a mess, so were the girls. She let him in and he said what he had been saying at all the houses: The girl that can wear this shoe will be my wife . . .

"Miz Cinder and the girls gazed at him through bloodshot eyes. Before they could say or do anything, Hal vomited on them, spewed big time. Man. He covered them all with it. They raced to the back garden, and up-chucked as well.

"Ellie heard the noises and walked into the room just as the Cinder women headed out to the garden. Hal was on his knees, wretchedness written all over him. He mumbled the words about the shoe. Ellie shook her head and thought how awful this was for him. She led him back to the kitchen and cleaned him off. Vomit didn't bother her; she had cleaned up after the Cinder women drinking binges many times.

"After she had settled him down with a strong cup of coffee, he repeated the thing about the shoe. Oh, here's a cup of coffee for you, four sugars, black, just the way you like it."

Bob found the cup at hand, and downed it. He didn't ask or think a thing.

Ethel sighed in dismay. "Well, Ellie pulled out the shoe from under the sink. Hal fit the other shoe on her tiny feet. They hopped on the Harley and sped off to the mayor's big house. The mayor was an ordained minister of the Methodist Church, and pulled together an impromptu wedding. Ellie and Hal leaped onto the Harley and headed off on their honeymoon. Happy ever after and all that crap."

Bob was confused. *Why are you so unhappy About . . . ?*

"Hey, kid. They can do whatever they want. But what bothers me the most is that Miz Cinder and Harold King got married shortly after. She moved in with him, and left the daughters to get by on their own in that house over there. They are the worst neighbors. They toss garbage over the fence into the White garden and at my front door. Let me tell you, I never seen so many vodka and gin bottles in my life, which is a long long time."

Bob said, "And that does what?"

"You have no idea about real estate do you, kid? Property values have plummeted as it is. Now with those two trashing up the neighborhood, throwing wild drinking and dancing parties, the Whites and me can't sell our homes. And we would, if we could."

Bob excused himself, thanking Ethel for all the information. As he stood up to leave, Ethel asked, "Hey, you wanta hear the low-down on Snow White? Now there's a story for yuh. You come back sometime, and I'll give you another exclusive."

Bob left Ethel at the door, and ran for his life out of the town. Ethel knew too much, and he didn't want his life laid open like a story book.

© Susan Kane 2012

168

About the Author

Writing an autobiography is a dicey thing.

On one hand, it could sound like I am the epitome of teaching (for twenty years), or an adventurer who worked tirelessly by my husband's side in our hotel in Ireland (for three + years).

There is also the part where our three children were born and raised, guided through some bumpy roads, and netted us three grandchildren (I love that part).

I could make myself appear to be a well-educated writer who is part of an elite group that focuses on writing in the classroom (I bet you were thinking "elite group of assassins), or I could go all humble and refer to my farm country roots with a barn full of stories. (*Now, there's a book to read when it gets published!*)

No matter what is chosen to go down on paper, none of it sounds real to me.

Basically, the bits of my life experiences have been carefully chopped into pieces, tossed into a blender, and ended up to where I am now. Which is here: Open Doors Anthology. I hope you enjoy my contribution, "Cinder, Ellie: An Exclusive"

To read some of Susan Kane's,
please visit her blog
(http://thecontemplativecat.blogspot.com/)
or Author Site
(http://susankanewriter.blogspot.com/).

The Petite Gourmands
Bonnie Ogle

Hank and Gretchen were not what you call adorable. Far from it. The siblings gave their father heartburn and turned their mother's knees to jelly every time they demanded a snack. Which was often.

At the dinner table, the young gluttons grabbed for whatever they wanted. Their mother had recently stopped serving vegetables, which became missiles when launched by stubby fingers, leaving vivid stains on the ceiling.

The beleaguered parents had also caved on security and ceased admonishing their mischievous offspring about leaving the safety of the yard. "No sense of adventure," Hank told Gretchen, as he climbed over the locked gate.

"Just ignore her," Gretchen answered, following after him, knowing without a backward glance, that their beleaguered parent was wringing her hands.

Unbeknownst to her, the small urchins, who helped themselves to confections stored in cookie jars or left on sideboards in a third of the domiciles in the village, had now become the area's most successful thieves.

"Where to this time?" Hank asked Gretchen, the brains of the operation.

"I think we're ready for the big time. We've messed around enough with the likes of this," she answered, and pulled a wadded up piece of tofu from her pocket.

"You kept that stuff?" Hank held his nose. "What for?"

"Mrs. Whittaker's hounds. This is sure to slow them down." Hank nodded, appreciatively.

Mrs. Whittaker's kitchen had been in their sights for months. The lady Whittaker was renowned for her

170

afternoon tea parties and seasonal banquets, all lavish epicurean affairs featuring recipes coveted by every local chef, not for commercial gain, but for their own gastronomic pleasure.

Mrs. Whittaker's house was situated in the woods, at the edge of town, secluded, and protected by two hefty canines that neither intimidated nor deterred the voracious brats. Gretchen, the strategist, had correctly determined they could drop bits of the tofu behind them to keep the dogs off their heels. After weeks of assiduously reconnoitering, they were ready. "I'm faster, so I'll go first, and when I get to the house, I'll toss the bait while you climb up the spout," Gretchen ran along the previously determined trajectory, and scrambled up the spout, reaching for the nearby window, and as Hank began his decent, covered him with her remaining tofu.

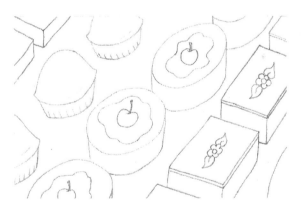

Standing side by side in the upstairs bedroom, the children huffed and puffed. "Seemed too easy," said Hank.

"Smell that!" Gretchen sniffed.

"Mmmm," was Hank's only reply as he rushed for the stairs.

The path was clear, no one in sight. Entering the kitchen, they stood staring across the room toward the oven. Skirting the central counter, laden with goodies, they crossed the room.

"Dare we?" Gretchen asked.

"We dare." Hank opened the door and they peered at Mrs. Whittaker's dinner. Unaware of the two-legged shadows falling across the room, they inhaled the heavenly aroma, and became one with the evening's repast.

The guests arrived by seven, sipping champagne and speculating on the evening's entre. Expectations ran high, as the last guest took his seat. The widow Whittaker stood at the head of the table, and welcomed her guests. "It is with great delight, I present to you, for the very first time, my most lavish creation." She continued, "As diligently as you strive to glimpse the recipe in my personal cookbook, I assure you I have not committed it to the written page. I confess that I may never again be able to reproduce it."

About the Author

Bonnie Ogle is a retired first grade teacher, now teaching at a natural history museum. She is a children's writer, whose most recent publications include the children's picture book, Arthur the Arthropod and Beaver Woman for Boys Quest Magazine. Bonnie is an inveterate ballroom dancer. Visit Arthur the Arthropod.com for more about centipedes!

Headless Horseman
Neal Levin

The headless horseman didn't care
for fortune or for fame.
He didn't care for prominence
or worthiness of name.

He didn't care for diamonds
or for silver or for gold.
He didn't even care about
his dinner getting cold.

He didn't need a haircut
and he didn't need to diet.
He didn't need insurance plans
or even peace and quiet.

He didn't need diplomas
and he didn't need degrees.
He didn't need a tissue
since he couldn't even sneeze.

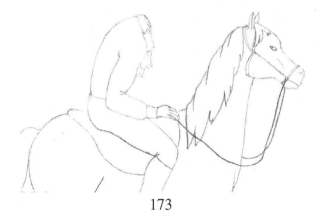

He didn't want a brain surgeon.
He didn't want a shrink.
He didn't want some know-it-all
to tell him what to think.

He didn't want a family
or children or a wife.
The only thing he wanted
was to get a head in life.

© Neal Levin 2012

Mirror, Mirror
Eve Gaal

Once upon a time, there lived a beautiful, hardworking young woman called Snow. Orphaned as a child, she lived with her nasty aunt Zelda. She was born during one of those incredible storms that seized the sky, freezing everything into standing ice sculptures; an immobilized world, where no one went anywhere unless it was absolutely necessary. Though outside the walls of the hospital, silence reigned and snow sparkled in the hushed silence of packed powder. Inside the nurses ran abuzz about the baby with pale skin and dark hair. Thus, they named her Snow. Growing up, the kids at school teased her about the name, which eventually came to mean she was as pure and virginal as a snowflake. Heart-shaped lips and large dark blue eyes evoked stormy seas above a graceful swan-like neck and bony shoulders.

Snow had one horribly vain and stupid problem and that was that she constantly liked checking herself out in the hallway mirror. Every time she applied her red lip-gloss or mascara, she'd hear a voice tell her she was the fairest in the whole county. She lived in Orange County, California which happened to be the beach blonde capital of the entire universe, but this colorblind mirror kept telling her she was a gorgeous fox. Though she was nice looking, perhaps good enough to audition as a television extra in Hollywood, she'd never be the cover girl at Cosmo.

She'd bat her eyes and hurry to her amusement park job to greet all the little children with sticky fingers and security guards who didn't look into her eyes but usually looked much lower. *Must have something to do with*

175

security, she figured. One of the guards however, was rather nice and attractive. He touched his hat when she walked by and bent into a slight bow as if she were a queen. Most days Mike blushed every time she walked by, but today he stared like all the others. One especially dopey guy stared at her purse. Perhaps he was hungry and wanted the apple sticking out the top of her tote bag.

She was glad to be at work where she could get away from her crazy aunt who thought herself much prettier. The aunt looked into the same hallway mirror and heard the mirror tell her that she used to be attractive, but now there was someone taking her place. The aunt hated that mirror. Utterly pissed off, Zelda zoomed out to the garage, climbed into her Camaro and zipped down Pacific Coast Highway to find Snow. That blasted mirror probably meant that Snow was the fairest and she couldn't take it. She was indubitably sleeker, blonder and maybe not as curvy, but certainly more intriguing than her wholesome looking niece.

Feeling insecure, she first stopped at Neiman Marcus and bought some expensive face creams and a new bright colored lipstick. When it boosted her morale, she wandered over to Bloomingdale's and picked out the latest pumps and a silk top. *Snow hardly makes more than minimum wage and can never afford beautiful things,* she thought. *What makes her think she's so cute? Wait until she takes a bite of that apple!*

That's right, Snow was now having lunch and she took a bite of her apple. Her vindictive aunt had injected the apple with a natural sleeping remedy. She figured, if Snow fell asleep on the job, she would be fired immediately. Out of work, she'd start to neglect her beauty. Pretty soon, Snow wouldn't have any friends and she'd become a lazy, fat, ugly, couch-potato and no one would ever consider going anywhere with her. Of course, she'd stay alone and unloved, becoming an old maid. *That would show the little minx!*

Snow did fall asleep in the break room and Mike the security guard tried to move her to the first aid department but he didn't want the park guests to notice. So he went to the wardrobe department and asked for seven green elf hats. He outfitted the entire security force with green hats and they held onto her and marched Snow over to the first aid clinic where she continued to sleep.

Many of the guards had gone to rehab before they were hired and placed into their current positions. Dopey had been on meth, Sneezy on coke and Sleepy took too many pills. Doc was also a part-time EMT and Grumpy worked the swing shift. Happy and Mike worked the day shift and Bashful worked at night. All of them lived in the same apartment community so they could keep an eye out for each other. They had developed deep friendships throughout the years during and after their rehabilitation and wanted to remain close friends forever. Mike lived around the corner in a big house but he still remained very friendly with the guys from work.

The night that Snow fell asleep, the guards kept stopping by the medical office to see if she was alive. They didn't call an ambulance because it was too much fun to monitor her breathing. Besides, she looked pretty healthy and they figured she'd be okay. On the way out the door each guard planted a kiss on her cheek and said, "Wake up and be mine."

During this fiasco, her aunt arrived at the park and asked for Snow, but they told her that she was out to lunch. Zelda paced back and forth on the red carpeting and stared out the window. The smell of kettle corn wafted into the building and soon, she wandered over to buy herself a large box of the delicious smelling snack. Night was falling and Zelda went home because she was tired of waiting and her new shoes from Bloomingdale's were hurting her feet. Once at home, she looked in the hallway mirror. Her bunions bulged from the front of her new pumps. Kettle corn hung from her hair and sticky syrupy residue had smeared her perfectly outlined lips. Under her now stained silk top, her leggings showed a prominent lump near her stomach and miracle of miracles, she actually saw that perhaps today she wasn't the fairest in all the land. Picking up a vase, she hurled it at the offending mirror and marched to collapse onto her bed. Shards of mirror flew everywhere.

It was close to closing time at the park, and the head of security allowed Mike and a nurse to stay with Snow. Finally, the nurse went home and Snow was alone with

Mike. Slowly, her eyes blinked and she awoke to see seven hats stacked on the table next to the gurney. *Oh my goodness, she thought. What have I done?* She looked over at the security guy and noticed him shyly looking down at his shoes. "Hey," she said, "how long have I been lying here?"

"Several hours," he replied, coming over and taking her hand. "Are you feeling all right?"

"Yes." She wondered why he held her hand. He was a nice looking man, but she never thought of any of her co-workers as possible boyfriends. Besides, she was a virgin. "I'm fine," she said, letting go of his hand. "What happened?" She asked rubbing her face.

"You fainted for some reason. Our staff rescued you and brought you here. They all kissed you on the cheek," he paused, realizing it sounded weird. "Sorry."

She immediately sat up. "What? That's gross. Why would they do that?"

"They like you?"

"Well too bad. Uck," she said, vehemently wiping her cheeks.

"I think they thought it would be like the Snow White story where you wake up from their kiss and ride off into the sunset."

"Right." She was horrified and started to climb off the bed but felt woozy.

"Can I give you a ride home?" He smiled, reaching over to support her. She looked like she was going to fall.

"I can. . ."

"No, it doesn't look like you can," he interjected. "I'll take you home." He grabbed his keys and they went out to his SUV. On the way out, she almost fell twice and he pulled her up and hugged her. She thanked him and

179

hugged him back. On the way home, he asked her out.

When they walked through the door, they tenderly walked across broken remnants of the mirror. Mike helped her clean it up and they threw the mirror out. Her aunt came out of her room and started screaming about all the noise they were making while they worked to clean up the mirror. Sensing the tension in the room, Mike decided to leave. "See you Friday," he called before driving away.

"Friday?" Zelda asked. "What's going to happen on Friday?"

"Nothing," Snow replied. "We're just going to go on a date. Is that okay with you?"

"You can't go out with him. He's just a security guard at an amusement park. Are you looking for trouble?"

"He's sweet and sensitive. I've seen him for months at work and I can tell he's not like the others."

"You're asking for trouble Snow! I can feel it. Don't do it. Do you want to end up being a nothing?"

Snow ran to her room and closed the door. If anyone was a nothing, it was her aunt who had a lot of possessions but very little feelings.

Snow heard a scream coming from the other room.

"What happened now?" she asked.

"Nothing. Stubbed my toe. Get lost."

Snow tried watching television, but again she heard a very loud crash coming from the kitchen. When she went to investigate, it looked like her aunt had dropped the pickle jar.

Afraid of getting yelled at, Snow timidly asked, "Can I help you?"

"No. Vamoose. I can do it."

Snow went to sleep and on Friday, she went on the date with Mike Prince. Not only was he kind and gentle but he enjoyed treating Snow like a lady. They went to a nice dinner and a movie, and when he brought her home Snow asked him into the house. Inside, her aunt limped by and whispered something very derogatory. Snow gazed at her aunt who used to be quite attractive and wondered what happened. Bandages covered at least three of her fingers and a strange fistula throbbed on the end of her nose.

"Mike, I have to go," Snow whispered.

"Yeah, no problem," he said, with a small nod and a smile.

"What are you smiling at?" Zelda asked with a weird look on her face.

"Nothing ma'am, I'm leaving."

The next day at work Mike ran into Snow near the break room.

"I've got a problem with a buddy of mine and I won't be at work. Can I see you later in the week?" he asked.

"Of course, can I help with your problem?"

Mike's face looked serious. "It's Dopey. I'm going to take him for a detox at the rehab clinic. He's been clean for two years. I really don't know what happened," he said shaking his head and wringing his hands.

"I've got a strange problem too. Ever since my aunt broke that mirror, she's had nothing but bad luck every single day. Today she burned her breakfast and locked the keys in the Camaro. I really would rather help you and Dopey than go home to one of her tirades," Snow suggested.

"Sure, sure, of course," Mike answered. "I'll pick you up after your shift and we'll drive him to rehab. I appreciate your company."

Snow went with Mike to Dopey's apartment where they found him lying on his couch. He looked extremely despondent. A half-eaten pizza littered the coffee table along with empty soda bottles. When Dopey noticed Snow standing behind Mike, he sat up and patted down his flyaway hair.

"Buddy, what's up? You haven't been to work, you haven't called and we were worried," Mike stated, looking around at the dark messy room. "Mind if we open some shades?"

Obviously groggy, Dopey nodded and pointed to the window. "Yeah, no problem."

Snow ran over to the window and did her best to let light into the room. Turning around she whispered, "Hi Dopey. Are you okay?"

"I'm okay," Dopey said. "It's that aunt of yours Snow. She made me do it."

Mike and Snow looked at each other wondering what he was talking about.

"What?" Mike asked. "What did she make you do buddy?" Mike was patient and caring and didn't want to come across too harsh. They had been friends for a very long time. He took hold of Snow's hand and they crouched down next to the couch.

"She wanted to make sure I switch apples in your purse. She told me you're going to get fired and that when you pass out I could even have my way with you because she was sick of you being a virgin. Of course I didn't." His face turned red. "Well except for that one small kiss." Mike stood up and wandered over to the window.

Inhaling and taking a deep breath, Mike asked, "So you're not on any meth or speed?"

"No," Dopey answered. "I'm just ashamed because I always had a crush on Snow. I also feel like I'm guilty of a bunch of crimes that could have hurt the cutest

182

girl I've ever known."

"Relax," Snow said, patting his arm. "I'm fine."

"Am I going to jail?"

"That's up to Snow. If she thinks you need to learn your lesson the hard way, and she presses charges well then there's not much to talk about—is there?"

"Oh, Mike, it's Zelda. She's horrible. Dopey, I won't press charges and I forgive you but don't listen to anything she says in the future. Promise me?"

"I promise," Dopey said sitting straight up and looking at Mike.

Tears were falling from Snow's gorgeous eyes and landing on Mike's arm.

"I'm sorry," she said, trying to wipe them away, but they kept on flowing. "I don't have any family and ever since I've been dating Mike, she's become meaner and meaner."

"Snow, look at me." Mike took hold of her chin and slowly raised her face to look him in the eye. I've worked with you over two years and though we've only dated a couple of weeks, I know you're the one for me. I love you, Snow. Will you marry me?"

Snow nodded that she would. "Could we wait six months just to be sure?"

"Of course," Mike replied. Then they looked over at Dopey who had tears flowing from his eyes too.

"Give me a break Dopey," Mike said. "She can only marry one of us," and at this they all burst into laughter.

The months passed slowly but Snow and Mike planned a wedding in Las Vegas inside Caesar's Palace. Zelda had so many problems that Snow stopped trying to keep track.

On their special day, all of Mike's friends wore the elf-like hats for a joke. Dopey was the best man. Snow's dress was magnificent and as they walked by walls and walls of mirrors on their way from the wedding chapel, they stopped to admire each other and Mike said, "You are the fairest in all the land." When he lifted her veil to give her a kiss, the mirrors began singing and applauding. Meanwhile, back at home her aunt was facing seven more years of very bad luck while Snow and Mike were going to live happily ever after.

© Eve Gaal 2012

About the Author

Eve Gaal, M.A. Human Behavior

More of her writing can be found in various anthologies such as **God Makes Lemonade and Fiction Noir-13 Stories. Rusty Nail Magazine** has her poem in the September issue about a *Writer's Blog as Viewed by an Optimist*. Her non-fiction story about pie will be in the December issue of **Epiphany Magazine** and a humorous story appears in the current **Wit and Humor Magazine on iTunes.** *"Kidnapped Writer and "Front Page Kiss"* are short stories available on Amazon. Check out her blog at http://thedesertrocks.blogspot.com

A Mother's Tale
Rayne Debski

I had to throw them out of the house. The market crash put my stocks in the trough, and my paycheck from Maggie's Farm was barely enough to keep the landlord from the door. My three sons spent hours hanging at the corner trying to pick up girls who would take them to the drive-in for burgers and fries. When I asked the boys to get jobs to help pay expenses, Robert, the oldest, strummed his guitar and sang, "No, no, no, not me, babe." Andrew, the middle boy who resembled his father too much to ever amount to anything, sat on his sorry little pork butt drawing soup cans. "Not by the hair of my chin," he said. And Jack, the one who, with his high grades in Life Skills had shown the most promise, paged through my Julia Child cookbooks and said perhaps he would scavenge for turnips and apples to make a casserole.

I wasn't the only parent whose adult children lived at home. Up and down the road, sons and daughters who had been laid off from their jobs knocked on their parents' doors and moved into their old bedrooms. But my boys—they had never pursued jobs from which to get canned. The next time they went to the corner to hang, I packed their belongings and changed the locks.

With the three of them gone, the house had more breathing room. I'd lived most of my adult life there, always conceding space to my sons for their toys and hobbies. Now in the first days of my solitude, I stretched out on the living room sofa without having to dislodge Robert's piles of sheet music. On the kitchen counter I replaced Andrew's tubes of oil paint with a simple vase of daisies. I did miss Jack's meals, but not the stacks of

185

pots and pans he would leave for me to clean. When a breeze blew across the plains, I opened all the windows and let it sweep through the house inhaling it like a drug. I was in Fat City.

What was I thinking! I knew the boys would have to scramble to find shelter, especially with the recent tornadoes. I assumed they would use their heads. Through the grapevine I learned Sam Wolf had given Robert and Andrew no money down, interest free loans to buy trailers at his Happy Hides Mobile Home Park. He attempted to make the same arrangement with my third son, but Jack was starting Hearth Cooked, a catering business, and needed a fireplace. Sam offered him the brick caretaker's cottage. I had known Sam since high school. He was unscrupulous even then, chasing little girls in the woods and stealing food from McGregor's garden. In later years, when he collected our rent, he eyed the boys closely, pinched their pink bellies, and called them his Little Pigs, even after they were grown. Some said he used his deep rumbling howl to summon the tornadoes that destroyed the homes of those who owed him money. He licked his chops and collected on their homeowners insurance. I told myself the boys were smart enough to keep him at bay.

Months passed. I hadn't heard from my sons. Consumed with worry, I drove to Happy Hides, hid my car behind a tree, and gazed at the dilapidated structures they called home. Andrew hadn't bothered to install tie-downs or lightning rods to keep his abode safe. Unfinished canvasses were strewn across the weedy front yard like discarded toys. Next door at Robert's, cracked windows were mended with duct tape. An overturned plastic milk crate served as the front step. I squeezed my eyes shut hoping that when I opened them, things would be different. I had spent years preaching the value of work, of being responsible, of taking care of your possessions. The scene before me was a testament to sloth. Part of me thought, I did the best I could for them; they'll never learn. At the same time, my heart stuttered.

I was about to leave when Sam pulled up. He pounded on Andrew's door.

"Little pig, little pig, your mortgage payment is two months overdue," he said. "Let me come in."

From inside came Andrew's shaky reply, "No way, man." I pictured my son trying to stay calm. As a child, his chin would quiver when he was about to cry.

"Then I'll blow your miserable little house in," Sam said. He stepped backed, clenched his fists, pointed his snout at the sky and howled. A tornado descended on the trailer, and when it lifted, my dead son, his easel, and several canvases were all that remained. Sam grabbed Andrew and ate him right there, raw. I sat trembling, unable to do anything.

Sam went next door to Robert's trailer. I tried to scream a warning, but my voice caught. Through the

187

cracked windows came a guitar riff, and Robert's nasal voice bleating "this pig thinks you're fine," as if he could appease Sam with one of his ridiculous songs. Sam pounded on the metal door with both fists until he creased it. The singing stopped. Robert squealed through the window he'd give Sam his money after he got a gig. Sam just snorted and once again let his low throated howl rip. The same carnage ensued.

When Sam was through, he wiped his bloody paws on his pants and drove away. I wept and prayed he would come down with trichinosis.

Growing up on a farm, I knew about slaughter and food chains. I knew mothers who watched their broods get carted away, but it was for a common good, not the benefit of one individual. I kissed the bones of my sons and retrieved the scattered pieces of Robert's music and Andrew's paintings. There was no time to linger. I had to warn Jack.

His red brick cottage was at the end of the road. I again hid my car, but this time, I went to the house to be with my son. Although I was filled with anger and disbelief, I was pleased to see the pots of mums lining the porch, and the crisp white curtains framing the windows. The only hint of trouble at the cottage was the eviction notice posted on the front door. "I'm waiting on a book contract," Jack said. "Then I can pay Wolf."

Over a cup of chamomile tea and raspberry scones, I told him what happened. We made a plan.

Sam arrived and did his shtick. "Little pig, little pig, let me come in."

"No way," Jack said.

"I'll blow the damn house down."

Jack laughed. "Have at it, old man." Sam howled, but it was a weak attempt, punctuated by rumbling belches.

So far, so good. We had bet the farm he would be weary from his earlier gluttony. Finally a small twister appeared and drifted away. Sam was furious. "I'll eat you, you damn pig. I'm coming down the chimney."

Jack and I high-fived each other. He threw another log on the fire. The homemade stock in the cauldron bubbled. Nails scratched across the roof. Sam was half way down the chimney before he screamed.

To celebrate, Jack invited his neighbors for wolf pot au feu, the dish that would put him on the foodie map after the publication of his first cookbook. His culinary creations would one day win recognition for appearance as well as innovative taste. He would be invited to lecture at the Cordon Bleu in Paris, and his cooking show would have ratings higher than Iron Chef. He would winter in Provence and summer in the Hamptons. He would invite me to stay with him, to listen to the mistral and breathe in the healthy salt air. There would be no getting him back on the farm except to buy organic produce for one of his restaurants.

But that night, as I stared at the presentation—red-tinged broth in gleaming white bowls; marrow bones artfully arranged with slices of baguettes on a rectangular plate; and slivers of meat surrounded by innocent leeks, carrots and potatoes on a silver-ringed serving platter—my stomach flip-flopped. Amid the laughter and conversation of Jack and his friends, I kept hearing the desperate cries of my sons and seeing the specks of blood on Sam's pants.

I slipped out the back door and drove home. For several minutes I sat on the sofa, clutching the purse that held scraps of Andrew's paintings and Robert's songs. My house was neat, quiet, and empty. Outside, a breeze rustled through the trees. When it gained strength and began to howl, I closed all the windows and wept.

I never ate meat again.

About the Author

Rayne Debski has been an innkeeper, a college instructor, an editor, and an organizational development manager. She now lives and writes in central Pennsylvania, where she shares her life with her husband and their enthusiastic yellow lab. Her award-winning short fiction has appeared in several online and print journals and anthologies, and has been selected for dramatic readings by professional theatre groups in New York and Philadelphia. She is the editor of Aftermath: Stories of Secrets and Consequences, forthcoming from Main Street Rag Press in December 2012. Between hiking, cycling, and kayaking adventures, she continues to work on a collection of linked short stories.

Please look for Rayne Debski on Amazon.

Goosey Goosey Gander
Variation by Fran Fischer

Goosey goosey gander,
Whither shall I wander?
Upstairs and downstairs
And in my lady's chamber.
There I met an old man
Who wouldn't say his prayers,
So I took him by his left leg
And threw him down the stairs.
He's in the hospital, praying NOW!!

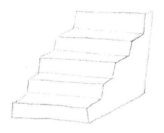

The Gingerbread Girl
Aimee Davis

In a time beyond thought, in a wood ever thick, there dwelt a man and his barren wife. Each morning, The Wife wept for a son so strong. Each noon, she sat in her inglenook and cried for a daughter so fair. The Husband was a longsuffering man, bent with age and beaten with sorrow. He loved The Wife, and his tristful heart broke each time she cried, "Why? Oh, Husband, why cannot I be a mother?"

One day, The Husband said to The Wife, "Sweet Wife, I cannot give you the child for whom you weep, so I shall journey into the town beyond the mountain where The Enchantress of Legend dwells. For, it is said that, to the purest of heart, she shall grant a single phial of the divined gumusservi which glows silver upon her blackwater pond. Placed on the tongue, this potion grants the heart's desire, and you shall then become a mother."

The Wife's face bloomed with anticipation as she waved good-bye to her Husband. And as truth betides, in three sunsets, The Husband did return. In his hand, he produced a tiny glass bottle from which a silver luster burned. The Husband's face became stern and he said, "I must tell you, precious Wife, the words The Enchantress spoke. Said she, 'Though your mind's eye be wide, and your desire be sure, magic gumusservi knows not but that which the tongue doth speak. Your words must not falter, must not warp or waver. Speak the name of that which your pure heart must have, and ye shall receive.'"

The Wife wasted no time on such peculiar instructions and emptied the bottle on her tongue. "It is

192

for a boy, I wish. No, a girl!" spoke The Wife. "A girl with sugar cheeks, lithe of foot, sure of smile, who shall steal my heart with her laughter. Oh, magic gumusservi! Won't you grant me this girl?" The Wife felt a warmth upon her tongue, then her throat, and into her stomach. As she waited for all that she fancied to appear, she set to work preparing a grand meal for her wayworn husband. She even baked his favorite gingerbread cookies. The Wife hummed a tune to herself as she fashioned, with whimsy, the shape of a girl in the last ball of dough. Into the oven they went.

The kitchen had barely begun to fill with the smell of epicurean delights when the oven door burst open. Out jumped the girl made of gingerbread dough, eyes blinking, legs moving, lips smiling as she landed squarely into the arms of The Wife. "Hello, Mother!" The cookie-girl said, grinning the while. "For, I am your daughter, your Gingerbread Girl!"

The Wife's eyes widened with shock, though she was suddenly gripped with a terrible sadness. "I wished for sugar cheeks," she cried. "But not this! I wished for a girl lithe of foot and sure of smile," she wept. "But not this! I wished for a daughter to steal my heart with her laughter, but not this!"

The Gingerbread Girl did not understand. "You did not wish for me?" she spoke. "For I am a girl! I have sugar cheeks, and I am so lithe of foot that naught could catch me! What is wrong, Mother? Am I not the girl for whom you cried?" Before The Wife could answer, in ran The Husband, having been stirred by the commotion. In the arms of The Wife, he saw a girl made of cookie. "Father!" cried the Gingerbread Girl. "Was it you who wished for me? Did you dream of my sugar cheeks and laughter? Did you cry for a girl lithe of foot? It must have been you! "

The Husband's eyes widened with shock, though he, too, was suddenly gripped with a terrible sadness. For, he knew that The Wife had not spoken her desire for a human child as she wished upon the potion. As the enchantress forewarned, the magic gumusservi knows not but that which the tongue doth speak. "No," spoke The Husband. "We wished for a human girl child with the sweetness of sugar upon her cheeks; a human child lithe of foot to romp amongst flowers and chase moles from the garden. It is a human child our hearts must love. You are but a cookie in the shape of a human girl. We cannot love you. Nature forbids it."

As these words lingered cold upon the air, The Gingerbread Girl became angry. For, she knew that although she was not a human girl, she could love, smile and romp, and her cheeks were just as sweet. And though she was not a human child, her laughter, too, could steal even the most steadfast heart. Scorned and heartbroken, she leaped into the air and began to laugh. Loud and raucous, she laughed. And louder still. The Husband and Wife watched as the cookie girl jumped from the kitchen table, to the countertop, then the windowsill, laughing the way.

"Three days!" she exclaimed as she leaped. "You have three days to catch me and eat me. If you do not, I shall take your sight so that you may never see those whom you love ever again. I shall tie your tongues so that you may never speak your lies of love ever again. I shall numb your skins so that you may never feel love ever again. And I shall cut out your hearts so that you may never love ever again. Three days!" With those words, the Gingerbread Girl disappeared through the window and into the wood ever thick.

Quicker than quick, The Husband summoned his dog. "Dog!" said The Husband, "As fast as you can, bring me the girl made of dough!" Dog hurdled out the window on his master's command and was soon on the heels of the cackling cookie. He ran all the day long, until his paws could run no more. But as he turned back toward home, in the dusking distance, Dog could hear the Girl singing "Run fast, stupid dog! Like a scaredy old squirrel! You shall never catch me, I'm the Gingerbread Girl!" Ashamed, Dog returned to his Master empty-handed.

The very next morning, The Husband ran to his pen of pigs and found his fattest hog. "Pig!" said the Husband. "As fast as you can, bring me the girl made of dough!" Pig squeezed his fat belly through the door to his pen and had soon tracked the cookie-girl all the way to the river. But the river was deep, far too deep for Pig's fat belly; and the current was swift, far too swift for Pig's stout legs. The old hog stood at the edge of the river, and in the dusking distance heard, "Run fast, fat pig! Like a fraidy old squirrel! You shall never catch me, I'm the Gingerbread Girl!" Defeated, Pig returned to his barn

195

empty-handed.

On the morning of the third day, The Husband ran to his barn and found his swiftest steed. "Horse!" said The Husband. "As fast as you can, bring me the girl made of dough!" Horse bolted through the barn door and soon began to spy oddly-shaped prints in the dirt. With much haste, he followed them until the trunk of an oak tree blocked his path. Horse craned his neck as far as it would crane, but his lanky legs and awkward hooves were not made for climbing trees. Horse stood ardent beneath the branches, and in the dusking distance heard, "Climb quick, bumbling horse! Like a drunkard squirrel! You shall never catch me, I'm the Gingerbread Girl!" Forlorn, Horse returned to his barn empty-handed.

The Wife and The Husband fell into despair. For, they knew their old bones were no match for the Girl. As the sun began to set, fear and sorrow crept upon them. The Husband set about guarding doors and windows. The Wife could do little but cry into her trembling hands. The sun took a final dip beneath the horizon, and from the dusking distance, The Wife and Husband heard a voice.

"Can you see me?" came a whisper from a place unseen. "I surely see you," the voice spoke. "For, it is deep in your darkest nightmares I lurk. I am the girl you could not love, and I am here to do the devil's work!" In a puff of ash, The Gingerbread Girl tumbled from the chimney and landed upon the hearthstone. The Wife and The Husband clutched each other, arm in arm. "Please spare us!" they beseeched with withering voices. "We knew not the cruelty of our words. We can love you! We shall take you as our daughter and love you ever more!" The Gingerbread Girl stood before them, a tiny glass bottle burning silver in her hand, a willful smile upon her lips.

"To take the sight from the hateful is my wish," said The Girl, tipping a droplet of warm gumusservi upon her tongue. The Wife and The Husband clung to each other as their vision faded to blackness, the world's color and beauty gone. They sobbed softly in each other's arms.

"To tie the tongues from the mouths of liars is my wish," The Girl said, tipping the bottle once more. There came muffled squeals from The Wife and The Husband, their tongues each looped about in knots inside their mouths, forever silenced. The Gingerbread Girl smiled, quite satisfied with her work.

"To numb the hides of the dispassionate is my wish," she said, as still another droplet fell onto her tongue. The Husband and The Wife then found that their world had disappeared beneath them, without sight of it, without the call of the other to soothe their minds, and without the touch of neither the floor beneath them, nor arms around them. The two lay senseless amongst a quagmire of lamentation, arms flailing, searching. Sobs faded into nothing.

The Gingerbread Girl again admired her oeuvre with a smirk. She emptied the last bit of moonglow upon her tongue and proclaimed, "To take the very essence of their filthy souls is my wish. Give me their putrid hearts!" But instead of the sound of their hearts being clawed from their chests, there was no sound at all. The Wife and Husband fell silent, and standing before the Gingerbread Girl was The Enchantress of Legend. Her eyes were heavy with sadness at the sight of the tragedy her potion had wrought. The Gingerbread Girl was afraid, for she knew that vengeance was the child of malice, never of pure intent.

"Fear not," The Enchantress spoke. "They will raise

the girl child which grows now inside her womb, and this Wife and Husband will forgive you." The Girl's cookie eyes reflected her chagrin. In that moment, The Enchantress raised her voice to the heavens and spoke, "Heal them." At once, The Husband and Wife became healed. Fear and shame overtook The Girl as she suddenly saw the evil she had begotten.

"I shall make you a human child," The Enchantress said, with anger in her eyes. "Though a human girl child is all you shall ever be. Never a daughter, nor woman, nor wife, nor mother. Forever shall you live and breathe upon this world, roaming the land alone with the venom of vengeance in your heart." With these words, the Gingerbread Girl's hands became pink and smooth. Blood ran in her veins, and her heart pounded fiercely within her chest. Upon her shoulders fell ringlets of silken gold, and touching her knees was the crocheted hem of a sundress. The Enchantress then cast her out into the wood ever thick, never to be seen again. Though, among the spirited folk with steins in their hands, legend tells of a weeping bête noire with the face of a girl seen begging passersby for their love.

About the Author

Aimee was a writer long before she was born. Her hands know little else, and feel most comfortable holding things and tapping things with which ever-afters sing and stories breathe. She married her most favorite character of all time, a boy she met in high school with bedroom eyes and a reckless smile. Next year, they will celebrate 19 years of marriage and the end of his 20-year Army career. They plan on buying Harleys and moving to the beach. They are the parents of two beautiful little muses, their 15 and 17-year-old sons. Her day job is spent writing for doctors, but by night, she is the supreme ruler of infinite worlds created and destroyed with her toolbox of nonsense. She writes about her Earthly oddities at PleasantlyDemented.com, and her chimera daydreams hold sway at GoddessInTheMachine.com.

Mermaid
U Z. Eliserio

Joyce hid behind the big rock, her hands slipping every now and then because of the moss. The waves rocked her gently, clashing with the pounding of her heart.

She had been following the ship for over a week now. She had watched the two fat, bearded men cast their nets and capture her fellow merfolk. They used very small fish and crab for bait.

Joyce couldn't help them. For now, she could only observe, waiting for an opportune moment. The pain in her heart was worse than any wound, though, and she would sacrifice her life if she knew it would free her captured people. But it wouldn't, so she stayed put.

She wondered what they would do to them. At first she thought they were going to eat the merfolk. But these men, they didn't eat fish. She had made it as close as the hull of their ship a few times now, during the night. She smelled their dinner. They grilled pork. How foolish of these men to start a fire on a wooden vessel! And how foolish were the merfolk who got trapped by these foolish men!

She knew the men's names. The taller one, the stronger one, was Gordon. He was muscular, and by himself pulled at the nets containing several merfolk. The smaller one looked older, his shoulders sagged, and he didn't even have the energy to shrug. But he handled the harpoon, and steered the wheel of the ship, and was the one who told Gordon when to unfurl the sails and when to dunk the anchor. His name was Mayer, and he was her target. Last night, he almost caught her.

Her eyes moved from the ship to the top of the rock, where she was preparing her ritual. The sun scorched

200

the shell she brought from the bottom of the sea. It took so long to read, she was afraid it was too late to be of use now. She estimated that their ship was almost full now, which was why Mayer was so watchful. They were going back to their port soon. Joyce was going to use the shell to listen to their conversation.

It had changed color, a mark that the ritual was going well. It was pale when she brought it from down under. Now it was brown, turning black. She would be able to use it when it was completely black. She whispered a few words of magic, to encourage the transformation.

"It would be nice to see my boy again." It was Gordon's voice, soft, loving. He spoke like he was singing a sad song.

Joyce punched the air in triumph. The shell still had a few brown spots, but the ritual had done enough of its work. She was hearing snatches of conversation from the ship.

"Yeah, you say that. But wait till you have a son. You'll miss him too."

Joyce wanted to touch the shell but didn't. That would ruin the process, and she would have to begin the ritual again. So, she could only access Gordon's speech for now. It was not an ideal situation; it was Mayer who planned the duo's moves. No matter, she could extrapolate from what Gordon said.

"Hey! Come on! You don't need to do that!"

There was extremely loud crying. Joyce didn't understand at first. Gordon wasn't crying. And Mayer didn't have a heart, so he couldn't be the one screaming and shrieking. Then it hit her. It was the merfolk. They were singing a song of lament. They believed they were going to die.

Finally the ritual completed itself. The shell was all

black. "Shut up, you," Mayer said. "An hour. An hour and then we head home."

An hour! Unthinking, Joyce dove into the sea. She went down deep, past the fishes, past the corals, past the crabs. Past the fewers, past the eels and the squids. Purpose gave her direction and strength. Within minutes, she arrived at her house.

Joyce lived apart from the other merfolk. Mostly because she enjoyed solitude. Her only companions inside her home were her mementos from her many adventures. On her wall hung the spear with which she repelled the shark invaders. In a corner sat the vase, her reward for negotiating a peace treaty with the Ming. Her carpet was the fur of the wolf she slaughtered during her time with the humans, when she exchanged her tail for legs.

Joyce lived apart from the other merfolk mostly because she enjoyed being alone, but also because she had to live alone. And the reason for that was her only living memento. Underneath the wolf rug was a secret door, leading to a basement. She went down there, now, carrying a lamp.

"So, you come . . . at last," a woman's voice greeted her. Its owner was in pain, each syllable was a struggle. Joyce didn't want to be cruel, but her prisoner was a witch, and her power was in her voice. This was the reason why, though her arms and tentacles were free, Leiden's neck was chained.

"I need legs," Joyce said.

"No."

Joyce raised her hand, and from her wall the spear that killed a thousand sharks came to her. She pointed it at Leiden's heart. "I need legs."

Her prisoner nodded.

202

"Exchanging your tail again? Be careful, one of these days you'll lose it!"

Leiden nodded. She unfurled her giant tongue, longer than any eel, and licked Joyce's fins. "Let humanity's curse be my gift to you."

With feet instead of fins, she had a harder time wrestling with the water. But at last she emerged near the rock that had been her observation point. She saw that the ship was still there, and dragged herself up nearer to the shell to listen in on her enemies' conversation.

"Ready to go?" Gordon asked. They must have already lifted the anchor.

Mayer just grunted.

Joyce watched as the ship's sails unfurled. She crushed the shell with her fists, destroying all evidence of her ritual, jumped into the sea, and swam towards the men. "Help!" she shouted. "Please, help!"

It didn't take long for the two to notice her. One of them, probably Gordon, threw her a rope. "Grab it!" he shouted. "Hang on!"

She grabbed the rope. It burned her palms, but she hung on. The ship was moving. Faster and faster. Without her tail, Joyce felt like she had no control. Waves crashed against her back and her head. She almost slipped. "Help!" she shouted, and this time it wasn't to catch their attention. She really was afraid.

They pulled her up. By the time she reached the ship's deck, the rope had dug deeply into her flesh.

"Oh, my God, you're naked!" Gordon shouted.

"Get her a blanket, you fool!"

She saw their eyes, saw that they were leering at her. She covered herself. Only in the company of men was nudity something to be ashamed of.

203

Mayer turned around, and Gordon brought her a blanket. "Here," he said, and then joined his partner in showing her his back.

"Thank you," Joyce said. "You may face me now."

They almost broke their necks in their rush to turn towards her.

"Some coffee, Lady?" Mayer asked. "Get her some coffee!" he shouted at Gordon. "This," he gestured at the blanket, "is only temporary. We'll have clothes for you. Men's clothes, they'll be rather loose, but better than just a piece of cloth." Within seconds Gordon returned with a cup of coffee.

Joyce noticed something that shocked her. "You're twins," she said, and to hide her shame at being surprised, she gulped down the cup of black liquid. She had tasted coffee before. It wasn't very good. She didn't like bitter things.

"Yes, yes we are. I'm taller though," Gordon said. "My name is Gordon, and this is Mayer. And you, my Lady?"

"Gordon!" Mayer said. "The Lady will introduce herself when she wants to introduce herself. Lead her up to one of the empty rooms. Get her some of my clothes."

"Your clothes?"

"As you've pointed out, you're taller than me. Therefore, my clothes will fit her better." He smiled at Joyce, flashing rotting teeth. "You will forgive my brother, my Lady, he is rather slow of wit, sometimes, but he is a good man."

The merfolk sang, united in their suffering, it was a great bellow, like the dying of a whale. It chilled Joyce, the terror they were all feeling. She shivered, and held her blanket tighter.

"Don't be afraid, my Lady. The sea, she makes a lot

of noises." He turned to his brother. "One of the empty rooms, Gordon. Now."

They left Mayer at the deck, went down into the ship. "Such a big ship," Joyce said. "How is it that there are only two of you."

"My brother is a man," Gordon coughed, "of many talents." Presently they came upon an open door. "Here you are, my Lady. I'll get your clothes."

"There's no need for that," Joyce said, facing the man, she let her blanket go. His eyes bulged. And when she revealed her teeth, they almost popped out of his head. Joyce bit off Gordon's head before he could shout.

It wasn't part of her plan, of course. But she sensed Mayer's magic as soon as she stepped on board. There was no way he would release all the merfolk without a fight! In fact, there was no way he would let Joyce go. All she wanted was a simple infiltration and seduction! Now she would have to do battle.

She began her ritual. It was relatively simple. Joyce chanted the monster's name, and waited for an hour. This was simpler than the trick with the shell, but a lot more dangerous. The lament of the captives pierced her heart, though, so when the spell was ready she marched to the deck. She found Mayer, waiting for her.

"He's gone, isn't he?" There were several merfolk corpses around him, his shirt was covered in green. "He was a good man, and a good brother. I'm sorry I had to sacrifice him. But he bought me time." He gestured to the dead. "The Wolf King sends his regards."

One by one the merfolk rose. Their eyes were blank, but they saw her. Their mouths were open, but no sound came. They were merfolk, but were not merfolk. Joyce always knew her past would catch up to her. She had done a lot in defense of her kind, not all her actions were upright and defensible. What she did not expect, however, was that those whom she wanted to protect would be the victims of her own method.

One of the dead merfolk grabbed her arms, and another bit her in the neck. She didn't fight. Even if she could drop all six of them, she knew Mayer could summon dozens more. They tossed her down. She hit the wooden deck hard, bruising her hands. She felt blood trickling down her arms.

The deck rumbled. A sound louder than the merfolk's lament filled the sea. It drowned out their cries with its hungry moan.

"What's that?" Mayer asked, looking around. With a gesture the dead surrounded him, to protect him from what he thought was Joyce's counterstroke. In fact it was no counter, but a sacrifice.

The Leviathan rammed Mayer's ship, breaking it into a million wooden pieces. Joyce rose in the air, along with dozens of the now-free merfolk. It was a risk, but one she had to take. She was their protector, and they, her people.

Joyce hit the water legs first, the sea locked her in a

warm embrace. She held out her hand, calling forth her spear. "To me!" she called to the merfolk. "To me!"

About the Author

U Z. Eliserio teaches popular culture at the Department of Filipino and Philippine Literature at the University of the Philippines, Diliman. He can be found at uzeliserio.blogspot.com and twitter.com/uzeliserio.

Stalker
Liana Mahoney

When Jack received three beans that day,
his mother thought they wouldn't pay.
She tossed them out, she cursed them all;
but still, three beanstalks sprouted tall.

Jack climbed the first with skillful ease;
the second, too, beyond the trees.
The third great stalk grew toward the west.
This stalk's the one that Jack liked best.

For, from the top, Jack had a view
of beauty, unforeseen and true.
Jack climbed that beanstalk—had to sneak—
up to a window; took a peek.

Her golden tresses mesmerized.
She must be single, Jack surmised.
Perhaps, in time, she'll marry me.
I'll watch from here, and wait and see.

Jack pined away, unnoticed there,
while fair Rapunzel groomed her hair.
He couldn't leave, nor look away. . .
and that is how, that fateful day,

poor Jack became
a shameful gawker.
Now he is
Rapunzel's stalker.

About the Author

Liana Mahoney is a children's writer and educational author from rural upstate New York. She is a member of the elite children's poetry critique group, The Poets' Garage, and the author of a forthcoming picture book, *Forest Green*. In her other life, Liana is a mother of three children and teaches Kindergarten and first grade. She lives on a quiet dirt road, raises a flock of chickens, and can identify every species of salamander and giant silk moth indigenous to New York. Liana's work has also been featured in the sports-themed anthology *And the Crowd Goes Wild,* as well as numerous children's magazines and websites.

The Lonely Egg
Debra Kristi

A heavy sigh expelled from his chest, invisible to all around. One of the few times he was thankful for what he was, something he usually considered a curse. His hard ugly shell only guaranteed she would never notice him. Not with so many men around her, drawn by her undeniable beauty. From his spot perched high atop the city's wall, he had the perfect view to watch her as she busied about the market, preparing for the early morning rush.

"Humpty Dumpty sat on a wall. Humpty Dumpty, he's going to fall!" A group of small children laughed at him as they merrily skipped by.

He was accustomed to their jokes. He had been on top of the wall a long time. So long he'd almost forgotten why he'd chosen to sit in such a high spot. But deep down he knew. He always knew. Someday Mother Hen would return for him, and when she did, he'd be positioned at the highest spot. She couldn't possibly miss him. The only place higher in the village was the tower at St. John's Cathedral, but this had more visibility.

"Honey!" he called out. She glanced up for a brief moment before returning to her usual duties. He couldn't even hold her attention for a few seconds.

The sun slowly rose above the horizon to the serenade of the morning birds. As its radiant light shown upon St. John's Cathedral, it filtered through its windowed tower, dispersing the colors of the stained glass artwork onto the grounds beyond. Reds, blues, greens, yellows. So many colors danced across his normally boring shell in a kaleidoscope of tint and glow. He was lovelier than an Easter egg.

210

People from all around the market could be heard, sucking in a breath, oohing and awing. Honey stepped forward, gazing up, her eyes wide with wonder. He felt the edges of his lips quiver in a slight upturn. He was smiling, a nervous one, though it may be. His heart sped up, a quick pitter patter, Honey had taken notice of him—*him!*

The colors began to fade and one by one the people in the market below turned away, returning to their everyday tasks.

"No. Don't go," Humpty said. But his voice was low and carried little conviction. He knew it was no use. He was no longer pretty to them.

The day wore on and he sat as he always did, on the wall, waiting and watching—ignored by all. Day turned to night and the evening fires were lit. Torches along the city wall danced with flame, sending shadows skittering to and fro across his large white backdrop of a body. The sight usually sent feeble villagers darting away in fear. Even Honey hid behind the curtains within her booth. Every night he became a scary shadow puppet show. Wobbling on the wall top, he turned his back on the village until daybreak.

As the sun kissed the meadow beyond the town limits, the most brilliant of ideas came to him. It was the perfect solution, he thought. Walking by on their way to school, more children chimed the tired old rhyme featuring Humpty and his prospective doom. He didn't let it bother him. Instead, he called out to the youngsters. Surprised, they stumbled to a halt and stared up expectantly.

"Would you mind fetching me the artist currently working at St. John's Cathedral? The one painting the mural? I would be terribly grateful towards you," he said.

211

The children turned and started to leave.

"There's ten pence in it for you if you do," he called after them.

The kids sped into a run, straight up the steps of the cathedral. Moments later a funny little man with scraggly hair and a curled mustache appeared, the children quick at his heels. When they were within reach, Humpty tossed them their reward and they hastily disappeared.

Standing at the foot of the wall, the painter shielded his eyes against the morning sun and looked up. "What can I do for you, sir?"

"Can you make me to look like one of the church's many fine stained glassed windows? I want to be a bright and colorful work of art."

The painter's eyebrows pushed together and his eyes squinted as he rubbed his chin, considering. "Why would you want to alter perfection, sir? You are the way you were meant to be."

"Look at me! No one even notices me. But when the sunlight shines through the tower and the colors of the windows sparkle across my shell, the people can't take their eyes off me. I want to be loved and adored like that day and night. Please, painter, won't you help me?"

"I don't know. I don't believe what you ask for is truly wise." The man shook his head. "No. I don't think it's wise at all."

Humpty threw his hands together and pleaded. "Please! Please, painter, please!"

The painter was inclined to walk away, leaving the egg the white he felt he was meant to be. But a tear rolling down the hard shell made him stop and think.

"All right, egg. I will do it if it is honestly what you want. But you must be sure. Once you go down this road there is no turning back."

"It is. Oh, yes, it is! I'll be eternally grateful to you, kind painter." Humpty thanked the man profusely and eagerly awaited his return when he lumbered off to get his paints and brushes.

Making good on his promise, the artist returned after a short time with a multitude of brushes, paints and jugs filled with water. Up a ladder he clamored, setting up shop beside Humpty Dumpty, his tools carefully balanced on each side of the wall.

As the day grew warm, slipping into hot, the man worked without tire. His strokes were exquisite and precisely detailed. Everyone in the village would know his talent upon his completion. The paints dried quickly in the hot sun and the glossy finish of the enamel sparkled and shined like it had remained wet.

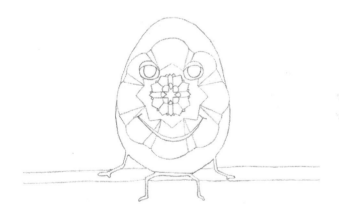

Humpty held a mirror as far out as his little arms would allow. He couldn't stop staring at his reflection. He didn't recognize the egg looking back at him. Just the way he liked it. The egg in the reflection was amazing! Honey looked up with eyes bright, lips curling in a sweet smile.

213

For sixty-eight extraordinarily hot days and feverish nights the egg enjoyed the adoration of many. Every morning Honey waved at him and children joyfully greeted him. But the sun was bright and with no shade on top of the wall where Humpty sat, his colors slowly lost their luster and faded.

On one particularly blazing morning, people rushed by without taking any notice of him on his high perch. They moved quickly to get out of the rising temperatures. Humpty's eyes darted left and right following the movement below, looking for any sign that someone noticed him. But it wasn't to be found. It was as if he were invisible. Not a soul spared him a glance. He realized that the attention had been gradually disappearing and now seemed entirely gone. What stung most was when Honey failed to give her usual morning wave. Anything at all from her would have lifted his spirits. Instead, old feelings returned, spiraling inside his shell into the pit of his stomach.

Music started up from somewhere within the market. Was there a special event of which he was not aware? People crowded down the center of Honey's aisle, blocking the view of anything there to be seen. Soon, he couldn't even see Honey's little booth at all. It seemed as if everyone in the village was gathering. Humpty stood for the first time in a long time, hoping to catch a glimpse of what had captured the attention of so many townsfolk. A small gasp let out from just below him, and he looked down to see a small child gazing straight up.

"It's dangerous to walk on the high wall, my papa always says." Her eyes were big with worry.

"Thank you for your concern, little one, but I have been up here a long time. I know what I am doing. See?" Humpty Dumpty made a small hop from one foot to the next and the little girl gasped.

As people turned to see what was the matter, more sounds ruffled through the crowd. He noticed that they were paying attention to *him* again. Elation filled him as did the desire to live up to their expectations. His small hop moved into a shuffle, then a kick and exchange. Pretty soon he was dancing to the rhythm of the music below. Dancing on the very top of the high block wall. Better yet, the people appeared to enjoy it. They cheered him on and clapped as he tapped his foot and kicked again.

Filled with self-confidence, he spun around not once, not twice, but three times. His heart leapt as he came out of the third spin and the ball of his foot slipped off the edge of the fine space he had so carefully balanced on. He looked down at the high grass of the meadows outside the village boundary and threw his weight back to compensate. His arms flailed, flapping like his Mother Hen. If only he could fly, but it wouldn't help him. He was a heavy egg and he had thrown too much weight back to avoid falling into the meadow. He was now sailing backwards toward the village floor and the many people milling around his wall.

"Nooo!" He heard the useless word escape his lips as the wall grew taller and taller in his view.

Fine fractures followed by several solid cracks accompanied his landing. The shell gave, exposing the soft inner membrane that made up his center being. With a sigh he lay still and waited as he popped and sizzled. What was happening to him? His head pounded with the sounds of a hundred horses riding out to battle.

The crowd began to disperse, no one staying to watch a broken egg cook in the sun. He closed his eyes to their departure. It hurt to watch them go, to see they

215

didn't care. Then something stirred at his side. Honey knelt beside him, taking his hand in hers. Slowly she lay on the ground next to the fried egg.

"What are you doing?" Humpty Dumpty asked. "You shouldn't be here. I'm a mess."

"On the contrary, we've never been a better match." Honey Ham snuggled up next to Humpty Dumpty and closed her eyes to the warm sun above, the smell of morning breakfast circling the bizarre.

About the Author

Debra Kristi writes across multiple genres. Young adult fantasy and paranormal have been the focus of her most recent projects. She's currently putting the finishing touches on her debut YA novel as well as a children's picture book. She pulls inspiration from her family and a wide variety of life experiences. The death of her sister fifteen years ago marked the beginning of her career and she hasn't stopped writing since.

Blog: http://debrakristi.wordpress.com
Twitter: https://twitter.com/DebraKristi
Pinterest: https://pinterest.com/debrakristi

Humpty Dumpty
Variation by Fran Fischer

Humpty Dumpty sat on a wall,
Humpty Dumpty had a great fall.
All the king's horses and all the king's men
Couldn't put Humpty together again.
But if the TV ads are true,
They could've done it with Crazy Glue!

Jack and Jill Went Up the Hill and Came Down with a Lawsuit
Brevin Anderson

Early one day in spring, the peaceful village of Fairy-Tale slumbered. All slept but for the two approaching the tall hill on the outskirts of the village. At the top of the hill, a solitary well stood, providing water to all who required it. Near the bottom, two figures looked up at it. One, a girl named Jill, began to climb the wet slope, her friend, Jack, beside her.

Although their shoes slipped on the grass, they made it to the top without incident. Jack, a crown on his head for no particular reason, cranked the wheel, pulling water up from the depths of the earth. Between them they carried a wooden bucket to fill. When they had hauled up enough water to fill their bucket, they started down the slope again. Then the event that would embroil the Mother Goose Court for years happened.

With the bucket heavy, the slope steep, and the grass wet, any lawyer—or mother—could predict a perilous outcome. Due to the conflicting testimonies, the court still doubts which of the two fell first.

Tumbling down the hill, two figures rolled and spun until they reached the bottom of the tall hill. Their bucket broken beyond repair, both defendants claimed they felt disorientated at this point, excluding them from testifying further. When officials found them, several witnesses had already gathered. On the ground, as smashed as the bucket, lay Jack's crown. . .

"Order! Order!" Mother Goose, no longer the sleek and slender fowl of her early days, smashed her gavel down. Quieting, the defendants, lawyers, and gathered

218

observers, sat.

To the left of the podium, Jack sat, his head heavily bandaged. Beside him, Georgy Porgy looked on, suspected to have masterminded this and other events involving girls. Simple Simon, their lawyer, rose.

"Your honorable fowlness, I ask that the charges be dismissed! My clients are innocent! According to the story, collaborated by several witnesses, I quote, 'Jack fell down and broke his crown, while Jill came tumbling after.' This clearly suggests that Jill pushed—"

Here Simon broke off, for the cries from the crowd drowned out all other sound. Above the din, Simon heard the yells of, "Objection!" from Jill's attorney.

Banging the gavel again, Mother Goose honked out, "What is the prosecution's response?"

Jill smiled as Hansel, from the affluent 'H & G Attorney's Office', rose and approached the judge. "Your honor, I would like to point out a few things." He waved a bundle of papers. "Jack is both older and a male. He is significantly stronger and larger than Jill. He, in fact did not need Jill to help carry the bucket. The only possible reason to have her along would be for what he nearly accomplished . . . murder!"

Again the crowd went wild. Mother Goose's wing ached from constantly pounding the gavel.

Simon stood, casting a superior glance at Hansel. "I would like to move past opening statements in order to answer the ridiculous accusations of the prosecution."

Mother Goose nodded. She called the first witness. "Peter-peter Pumpkin-eater to the stand."

Thin and tinted orange from his unbalanced diet, Peter tottered forward, taking his seat gingerly.

Barely able to stand, a trio of mice in dark glasses held the sacred book of nursery rhymes. "Do you swear

to tell the truth, the whole truth and nothing but—"
Peter's hand hitting the book had overcome the tiny legs
of the mice. Smashed underneath, a cadre of cats rolled
the mice out on a gurney, barely able to keep from
licking their lips.

Simon, engaged in eyeing the pies set out for the
jury, jumped when Mother Goose called, "You may
question the witness!"

Putting on a professional face, Simple Simon stalked
towards the witness. "Where were you on the morning of
the accident?"

"In my . . . pumpkin."

"You were in your pumpkin?"

"Yes . . ." Peter frowned. "Doesn't everyone know
that?"

Simple frowned as well. "I thought you put your wife
in a pumpkin because you couldn't keep her."

Mother Goose cleared her throat, reminding the court

220

that Peter's marital status had no bearing on the case. Jill suppressed a smile while Jack stared straight ahead.

Simon went on with his questioning, eventually gaining what he wanted. "So you say that it looked like they fell at the same time?"

"It looked like it, but they were so far—"

Simon cut him off, signaling to Goose that he had finished. "Thank you, Peter."

As Peter took his seat, Jill whispered something to Hansel. He frowned, and then lightened. "Your honor, I would like to call Georgy Porgy to the stand!"

Georgy, pudgy and cherub-like, took the oaths. He sat squirming in his seat as Hansel scrutinized him.

"Mr. Porgy, where were you the morning of the accident?"

Jill narrowed her eyes, her mind whirling as Georgy glanced at Jack.

"Down in the town," he answered finally.

Hansel muttered something under his breath. After a few more questions, he got to his purpose. He reminded the court that Georgy had harassed girls several times, quoting from the evidence sheet, "Georgy Porgy, pudding and pie, kissed the girls and made them cry. When the boys came out to play, Georgy Porgy ran away." Hansel paused, as if gathering himself.

"What we have here, ladies and gentlemen of the jury, is an insecure ladies' man, no offense. He is the perfect man for the job . . . but he did not act alone. I call Jill to the stand!"

Jill stood and walked to the podium. Hansel got straight to the point. "What happened on the hill?"

"I was pushed."

"By whom?"

Jill took a deep breath, her face the epitome of a

221

shattered victim. "Jack tried to push me . . . but he missed and fell. That's when Georgy came and shoved me after Jack!"

Gasping the crowd inched forward. Hansel nodded and Jill returned to her seat. "What do we have here? Jack attempted to murder Jill, with Georgy as his accomplice. Reinforcing this are there questions; why would Jack have an expensive crown with him when performing the water retrieval task? Does he not know about safety deposit boxes? The crown was payment for Georgy's part in the plan! In fact, Jack could make two trips with smaller buckets and not need to require Jill's presence!"

Hansel stabbed his finger at Jack and Georgy. Simon straightened as he tried unsuccessfully to buy a pie from the pieman with a button—Jack hadn't paid him a penny yet.

"It was a set up! A carefully planned attack!"

Silence reigned. Simon, who had returned with a glum face to his seat, stood and made a few insignificant comments before sitting back down, red-faced.

Mother Goose rapped her gavel as the jury filed into the backroom. "Recess for an hour."

When the jury reentered they gave their verdict.

The jury found Jack guilty of assault and battery charges against Jill.

Jack's friend, Georgy Porgy, was found guilty as an accessory for aiding Jack in the crime.

Jack was sentenced to two years in jail, and Georgy to six months plus a probationary period and a lifetime requirement that both must register with local authorities and be placed on the anti-girl list. Neither will ever again be allowed to purchase Girl Scout cookies.

Note: A year later, this case was reopened because of the following irregularities:

1. Jack and Georgy's defense attorney, Simple Simon, had not passed the bar to practice law and took the case on a temporary basis to earn a small amount of money to buy desserts.

2. Georgy's background and intent was misrepresented. He kissed girls only as part of his training to become a future health professional in either the dental area or in optometry. His defense is that crying is an essential activity to cleanse the eyes and clear small dust particles, so he was actually helping the girls in their eye care. More importantly, Georgy was following in the career footsteps of his grandfather, Ican Seymore, who developed line 5 on the eye chart, and his Auntie Lensay, who invented colored contact lens.

3. While the whereabouts of other potential suspects (M. Poppins, Miss Muppet, Peter-peter Pumpkin-eater's wife . . .) remains under investigation, it appears that Jack and Georgy have been unjustly convicted of a crime that may have been only an unfortunate misunderstanding.

About the Author

Brevin Anderson is a novelist, poet, and blogger. Since the age of ten, when he completed a short story that would grow into his first novel, he has been obsessed with everything writing. He has completed two novels, a novella, and has two more novels on the way. *Warbaron*, his most recent project, is his novel for National Novel Writing Month.

Today he is a high school student who dreams of becoming a bestselling novelist. He maintains and works on several blogs, working to inspire others like him to write.

Blogs and previous work links:

Worldpen: http://worldpen.wordpress.com/

The Writing of Brevin Anderson:
http://www.bandersontps.wordpress.com/

Paradox, a short story:
http://fresh1nk.wordpress.com/2012/07/23/paradox/

Grey, a short story:
http://fresh1nk.wordpress.com/2012/06/27/grey/

Jack and Jill
Variation by Fran Fischer

Jack and Jill went up the hill,
They each had a buck and a quarter.
They both fell down,
And I don't know what happened,
But Jill came home with $2.50.

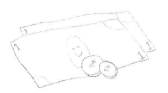

225

Little Red Riding Hood Seeks Vengeance
Katherine Valdez

Little Red hated her nickname. It always reminded her of the day she received it.

Her parents adored her until her ninth birthday. That was the day she threw a hurricane-strength temper tantrum. Neighbors heard it from across the street. Fists clenched, eyes shut tight, mouth wide open in a piercing scream. Tears streamed down her cheeks, and her red hair flew behind her as she ran upstairs to her room. "A chubby little red devil, that's what you are," her parents scolded.

They had just told her she couldn't have the medical procedure that would erase her birthmark, the scarlet heart covering the right side of her neck. "The Splotch," her parents called it. (They were not particularly sensitive people.)

The procedure was too expensive. And she was too young. "You'll just have to live with it."

"Ugly." "Freak." "Monster." Her classmates tortured her with these words. It would have been less painful if they had attacked her for her weight or hair color. This, she couldn't change.

She flung herself on the bed, screaming into her pillow and clutching the comforter.

One day I'll be a grown-up, she seethed. *No one will call me names. No one will push me around.* Just then, she felt the sensation of heat on her neck, but was too preoccupied to look in the mirror. Her birthmark glowed for the first time. It grew brighter, then flickered out. Years passed before it would glow again.

The Wolf strolled into town one day, in the form of a door-to-door magazine salesman named Roy who slapped abundant amounts of aftershave on his face every morning, and blessed everyone who sneezed and coughed in his wake. After his weekly waxing to remove chest and back hair, he'd roar around town in his midnight-blue vintage Mustang with a bumper sticker that declared, "Yeah. I'm bad. You got a problem with that?"

After a brief stint with vegetarianism years ago, he had decided to embrace his inner carnivore. The result was a long list of victims. After conducting research on the Howling Moon website, he settled on a pretty redhead and her grandmother who shared a duplex on Maple Street.

Little Red was nineteen years old. She had surprised everyone by excelling at lacrosse, losing twenty pounds, and intimidating her peers into dropping the "Little" in her name, though she couldn't break the habit of calling herself that in her head.

It wasn't enough.

Gazing at the clouds from the front window of her apartment, she wondered whether she'd ever be happy. Her grandmother knew she thought about such things, and was the one bright area in Little Red's life. They understood each other. (Her parents were much too busy with their careers to talk to her more than twice a month.) Grandmother sang songs while making breakfast in the morning and Little Red loved to join in. As the toast popped and they sat down to eat, their voices would crescendo in harmony.

On a bright, sunny morning, Little Red clutched a steaming mug of black coffee and brought up the subject again. "Grandmother, I go to college, work at the auto

227

shop and pay rent, but I don't feel like a grown-up. When will I feel different?"

Grandmother chewed thoughtfully on bacon and scrambled eggs. "It's an attitude more than anything, Dearie. One day, you'll feel it."

"When?"

"Soon." She smiled and patted Little Red's shoulder, then prepared to leave for mahjong at the senior center. A shuttle picked her up a few minutes later.

Little Red spent the next half hour finishing a crocheted hat for Grandmother. Red, their favorite color. She left the hat on Grandmother's easy chair where she was sure to see it when she came home. Then she walked to the market to pick up their favorite dish, meatloaf.

Roy the magazine salesman quickly set up a table with a stack of popular periodicals, and was standing just outside the sliding glass doors as she walked out. Snow began falling. Little Red tightened the sash of her scarlet coat and flipped up the faux fur-lined hood.

"Good afternoon, Miss. I'm selling magazine subscriptions to benefit local charities. It's all for the children. You want to help the children, don't you?"

"Do you have *Entertainment Weekly*?" Little Red loved movies with woman heroes who kicked butt.

"Yes, of course."

As she flipped through the pages, she came across an article titled, "Don't Mess with These Women" featuring the actresses of *Total Recall, The Avengers* and *The Hunger Games,* and decided to buy herself a subscription. She had been lifting weights lately and was pleased with the results. "I'll subscribe."

"The children thank you." Roy's nose twitched. "Something smells good. Is that your dinner?"

228

"Yes, I'm bringing it home to my Grandmother."

"That's very sweet of you. I bet she'd love to watch a movie tonight. I normally don't go for romantic comedies, but I just rented "Bridesmaids" from Redbox and it made me howl."

Little Red didn't like the magazine salesman. He was too slick. But she had to admit he was right about the movie. "That's a great idea. Grandmother will love it."

As she debated with the college girl in line in front of her about who was hotter, Thor or Captain America, Roy sneaked away and raced to Maple Street.

It was dusk when Little Red returned home and knocked on Grandmother's door. "It's me. I brought us meatloaf. Your favorite."

There was no answer.

She knocked again. "Grandmother?" The hinge squeaked as the door eased opened, unlocked.

Little Red stepped inside, leaving the door ajar and hesitating in the entryway before walking toward the living room. She placed the meatloaf on the dining table. Grandmother was sitting in her easy chair, snoozing, covered with a blue fleece blanket and wearing the hat Little Red had crocheted her. It was pulled down over her face to block out the light. "Oh, there you are. Grandmother, wake up. Time for dinner. I'm glad you like the hat."

Grandmother stirred. "Hello, Dearie. Thank you for the beautiful gift. It's so cozy. It helped me fall asleep for my nap." Her voice sounded deep and muffled. "I'm feeling a bit under the weather. Would you set the table? That meatloaf smells wonderful."

"Sure." Little Red hesitated. "Are you okay?"

"Just a little tired."

Little Red peered at her Grandmother's face.

229

"Grandmother, what a deep voice you have!"

"The better to greet you with, my dear."

"What big eyes you have!"

"The better to see you with."

"What a big mouth you have!"

"The better to eat you with!" The Wolf flung off the blanket and hat, and lunged at Little Red.

Little Red screamed and ran into the entryway. She grabbed the baseball bat Grandmother kept in the umbrella stand in case of emergencies and swung it at his knees. A satisfying crack echoed through the tiny space.

"Oooowwww!" The Wolf howled in pain. As he fell to the floor, he clutched her arm and pulled her down. Little Red kicked him in the gut and wrenched herself free, scrambling toward the open door. She knew he'd recover in a few seconds.

Sirens wailed in the distance, and Little Red gave a silent thanks to the Johnsons next door. *Thank goodness this town is big on Neighborhood Watch,* she thought. A tall, dark shape streaked past her and into a vintage muscle car parked a few houses down the block.

Little Red grabbed a scarlet cape from the coat rack, flung it around her shoulders and ran out the door into the blowing snow. She jumped into her old pickup truck.

"You have no idea what I'm capable of," she growled as the Wolf's car disappeared around a corner. She turned the key and the truck's V-8 engine roared. The old guys at the auto shop, impressed with her dedication, taught her everything they knew. She grinned and stepped on the gas.

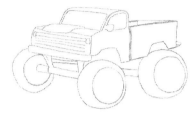

The Wolf weaved in and out of downtown traffic, then shifted into fourth as he reached the three-mile stretch of road that hugged the reservoir's shoreline. He checked his rear-view mirror. No one.

Little Red rammed him from behind ten seconds later. "Surprise!" She yelled. The crunch of metal and screech of tires echoed as the Wolf's car crashed against the guardrail, then skidded back across the center line. "My car!" the Wolf yelped. "No!"

This is it, Little Red thought. *This is the day I've been waiting for.* Paulie at the auto shop had schooled her in the finer points of demolition derby. Keep moving, hit squarely and don't give the other drivers a chance to recover.

Little Red gunned the engine and braced herself as she rammed the Wolf's car again. It spun around and she saw the Wolf's surprised face, his mouth open in a big O. The car wobbled to a halt, but the Wolf recovered and slammed on the gas again. The tailpipe and back bumper fell off as his car wheezed away.

She could hear sirens growing louder as the police caught up with them. "Suspect in the blue Mustang! Stop!" one officer boomed through a megaphone. Their newest squad car was a state-of-the-art vehicle nicknamed The Stealth Bomber. The driver was fresh out of police academy and had been top in his class. His friends called him Lumberjack. All he wore outside of

231

work were flannel shirts and jeans. He kept an ax on the passenger seat, knowing that criminals tended to cower at displays of old-fashioned brute strength and medieval weapons.

Lumberjack raced ahead of Little Red's truck and side-swiped the Wolf. She followed up with a final ram from behind, and the Wolf's car flipped through the air, turning over and over down the embankment and into the reservoir. His howl thundered across the darkness, then fell silent as he took his last breath.

Lumberjack brought The Stealth Bomber purring to a stop next to Little Red's parked truck, grabbed the ax and rushed over to her.

"Are you okay?" he asked Little Red, who was staring down at the water-logged wreckage of the Wolf's car. Lumberjack had dark brown hair and kind eyes the color of the ocean, but she wouldn't know this for another five seconds.

She nodded without looking at him, straining to see any signs of life. Nothing.

"We found your grandmother upstairs in her bedroom closet. She's been drugged, but the paramedics said she'll be fine."

She finally turned to him. "Thank you. I was so worried about her." Lumberjack was handsome. A pale pink heart-shaped birthmark covered the left side of his neck. He hadn't told anyone yet about his upcoming surgery to remove it.

"I'm Andy, but everyone calls me Lumberjack."

Little Red hesitated. "Samantha. But no one calls me that."

"Why not? It's pretty."

She tilted her head, thinking, and took a deep breath. "Thanks. I think it's time for a change."

"I'm a big fan of change."

She studied him. "Oh? What changes have you made lately?"

He blushed. "It's sort of a long story."

She noticed that he wasn't staring at her birthmark the way other people did. He was looking into her eyes. And smiling.

"I'm a big fan of long stories." She paused. "Do you have time to tell me over coffee later?"

He grinned and held out his hand to help her navigate an icy patch on the road, then opened her truck door. She felt heat creeping across her neck and reached out to tilt the rear-view mirror toward her. Her birthmark glowed for a second, then extinguished and disappeared forever. Little Red's eyebrows shot up in surprise.

She turned back to Lumberjack and smiled. And thought, *Yes, I'm a big fan of change.*

© Katherine Valdez 2012

About the Author

Katherine Valdez is a former newspaper reporter and non-profit communications director with a bachelor's degree in English from the University of California, Irvine. Katherine's most recent award was an honorable mention for "The Monster in Her Bedroom" in the 2012 Grey Sparrow Journal Flash Fiction Contest. She runs, hikes, daydreams and sings karaoke in Colorado. Contact her at KatherineValdez2012@gmail.com, Facebook and Twitter (@KatValdezWriter).

Links:
—Honorable Mention, 2012 Grey Sparrow Journal Flash

Fiction Contest Grey Sparrow Press:
http://greysparrowpress.sharepoint.com/Pages/default.aspx
—www.KatherineValdez.com

Sing a Song of Sixpence
Variation by Fran Fischer

Sing a song of sixpence,
A pocket full of rye.
Four and twenty blackbirds,
Baked in a pie.
When the pie was opened,
The birds were all distraught.
Well, wouldn't you be (like a fricassee)
when the oven is so damn hot?

Unlikely
Kayla Kelley

Whenever my body hurts, it feels like my whole soul hurts too. One weakness allows for another, usually suppressed, emotion to come out. It's like a dam with a crack in it. At first you just notice the actual problem; there is a crack in your foundation. But then as time goes on, more emotions just start leaking out regardless of how hard you try to keep them inside.

That's how I feel every day. I'm in the shadows, I'm stuck inside my own mind, in my own life and there is no breaking free. I walk up and down staircases every day, wipe up other peoples' messes, and attempt to smile when I feel like bursting. How did my life get so messed up? How did I allow the actions of others to dictate my life? I used to be a ray of sunshine, a bird flying carefree in gentle breezes and ready to help anyone in need. Now, I am a slave in my own home. I am dimmed by my own choices.

Whoever said that "sticks and stones may break my bones, but words will never hurt me" was, I hate to say it, a gigantic liar! The sharpest and most deadly weapon ever used against another person or being was the tongue as it spewed out cruelty in the form of words. How often I have wished to be mute, to not be able to hear, speak, or understand anyone around me but just live in the blissful abyss of my own padded existence.

But that is not my fate. I am doomed to scrub other's mansion with the ever-present knowledge that I will never have more than the clothes on my back which—shocker—aren't even mine.

My name is Cinderella. I was the daughter of a wealthy man and a loving mother who died when I was born. I had hair of spun silk that glowed yellow in the sun and eyes that sparkled like sapphires. At least, that's how my daddy used to describe me in the letters I read. Letters he left in surprise places every day for me to find and realize how much he loved me. My daddy was a good man, full of love and support. Kindness, equality and happiness followed him everywhere and enveloped me like a warm comforter every day of my young life. I was perfectly content not having anyone else but him, however, he felt like I needed the influence of a woman in my life. That's why he married a woman who I have come to see as the death of my happiness.

My daddy is gone. Stolen from me twelve years ago by the injustice in the world and all the hatred that ever existed. His absence has left me bitter and alone. I know I'm sad, hateful and hard to be around but it's all I can do every day to drag myself out of bed.

The woman that I now have to live with, and who I will ever refer to as the Death, screams for me every day to clean and cook. She beats me with words so hateful they pierce my very soul. She manages to find every weakness and unhappiness in me and lift it to the surface. I used to smile and laugh; now I am a straight line with no emotion on the surface, yet filled with rage and bitterness on the inside.

Today is just another day. A day that will never end because every day is the same. Wake up, cry, clean, cook, run out into the orchard and scream to try and drown out my own emptiness and then return to do it all over again before finally returning to my cold attic to curl up and wish for death.

The orchard is my only moment to breathe. As I scream out every obscene desire and choking emotion to the sky, I beat my hands on the hard bark of the apple trees until they are as red as my eyes are from crying like a small child, not the woman of twenty-four that I am. Once I did this for so long I vomited blood and now have to live with those spots on my dress. My throat was so worn and raw that it took days to heal. I am alone in this huge house with the Death as my only companion.

Sometimes I just want to run away but where would I go? How would I eat? Women don't have jobs or position outside of their own homes, it just isn't legal. We are at the mercy of our parents and the man that is supposed to sweep us off our feet. In order to meet that one man who will make everything better, I would need to actually leave my house. No one even knows who I am or that I exist. The Death won't allow me to leave the grounds and insists on having everything delivered to the house. When it is delivered, I am not allowed near the door. I'm trapped. Alone. If I disobey, I would be thrown out and forced to either die on the streets or sell things that aren't for sale.

"Cinderella!" Get down here!"

The Death is awake. Here we go again. I dress myself in the dirty dress that I've worn for going on five years now. It used to be blue? I'm pretty sure it was blue but now it's a dingy grey with random bits of green to cover the holes that appear despite my best efforts. The Death refuses to buy me new clothes and just digs up something from her old supply. I think this dress was the last one she could find so who knows when I'll get another one.

I stumble to the kitchen to get her nasty tea she can't live without. Who drinks milk thistle tea with mint and no sugar? It's disgusting and I hate the smell. The Death loves it and refuses to eat more than a handful of the food I am required to cook for her. I think she likes feeling she has more than enough and can say no to keep her bony body *fit*. I on the other hand, was blessed with the same, soft curves as my mother. In the Death's eyes, I was fat and would never be attractive to anyone. After hearing this every day for years, I am starting to believe she is right. After all, who would want me? Straw-haired, angry, fat girl.

Anyway, enough of that, it's bad enough that I have to listen to her every day; I don't need to replay it in my mind as well.

On my way to her room, I nearly trip up the stairs and have to twist my foot in a way to keep me upright and not covered in hot, nasty tea. I hear something in my ankle make an angry pop. All of a sudden that dam has another crack in it and I feel angry tears start to well in my eyes. Why now? Why right before I have to go into that dark, cluttered room and feel the angry blows of a woman so bitter that the only joy she feels is when she tears me down?

I manage to compose myself enough to hobble to her door. My ankle feels like it's about to roll off my foot and leave me crumpled on the floor. I can feel it swelling and shooting little sparks of fire up and down my leg.

"Why are you just waiting outside the door, you worthless piece of flab? I can see you but more obvious than that I can smell you! Ugh, why are so disgusting? Are you incapable of bathing yourself? Are you so stupid you don't even know how to bring water to a boil and put it in the tub?" "What would your father say if he saw his precious princess turned into the dirtiest, smelliest, most disgusting creature ever to walk the planet?"

The war of words has started and I was armed with nothing. Every time she started, my tongue would get confused in my mouth and not be able to respond. I was

239

so angry and so hurt that I just stood there wanting to die.

I turned the knob, walked slowly and purposefully to her bed and laid the tea tray on her bedside table, said good morning and squared my shoulders to walk out the door.

"Oh, my God, you smell like something rotten! Your hair is a disgrace! How could you even bear to be with yourself? Do you gag as you pass windows and see your worthless reflection? You would make a pig commit suicide just so it wouldn't have to smell you," she said as she held her nose and pretended to pass out.

"I hope you enjoy your tea," I stammered as I started walking toward the door.

"Hope your fat ass can squeeze through the door. Try eating a little less cake today, eh? Hahahaha!" she cackled, choking on her tea as she laughed at her own joke.

At this, I awkwardly ran into the orchard. I beat my fists and screamed my frustrations and anger to the unresponsive sky. All at once, I felt a warm hand on my shoulder. I spun around as fast as my ankle would allow and staggered back to see that a gypsy man stood behind me. His warm brown eyes were full of shock and pity as he asked me "What on Earth happened to you to make you so angry?"

I didn't know what to say. My face started to contort into sad, worried lines. All I could manage was "I'm so sad" and streams of tears started to pour from my face.

What kind of response was that? Oh well.

The gypsy man then said something I wasn't expecting "I've seen you come out here every day for a month and scream like a wild banshee and wondered what in the world would make someone so upset."

I stared at him a little and just crumbled into his chest and started sobbing.

He awkwardly held me and patted my head. I couldn't stop, I felt the dam inside of me just waiting to burst and I was exhausted from holding everything back.

After a while, I finally managed to step back and say "I'm sorry you had to see me like this".

"It's okay," he said and flashed me a smile. "Why don't you leave this place and come with me?"

Shocked I asked, "Go with you where?"

"To freedom from your sadness" he said, offering me a hand.

I stood there, looking at his hand and wondering how my life could really get any worse. Then, I felt a ray of sunshine. A glow started to heal the crack in the growing dam inside of me and I felt like my father was back. I stayed for a moment, letting that warmth wash over me and made a decision.

"Ok, let's go" I said.

I took his hand without a backward glance and walked to my new future.

© Kayla Kelley 2012

About the Author

Kayla Kelley graduated from Southern Utah University with a Bachelor Degree in Communication. This is her first published short story. Before this, she did several news stories as a journalist for SUUnews and currently works at Utah State University Catering as an event planner. She is married to her best friend and they live in Logan, Utah. In her spare time she is a blogger at thekelleysplace@blogspot.com, an amateur chef and an addict to Pinterest.

The Three Little Wolverines
Linton Robinson

Once upon a time . . .

Whatever the hell that means. Why do people say things like that anyway? Like 'Auld Lang Syne' or 'Sleep Tight'? How do you sleep "tight"? You can't even get to sleep until you're loose and relaxed. But how about 'by-and-by'? If you're going to say something, you need to . . .

Oh. Okay. Never mind.

Once upon a time there were three little wolverines. Why? I have no idea. These things happen in threes. You never hear about two bears or seven little pigs or five billy goats or four straight men in a tub or Winkem and Blinkem and Nod and Associates. So there were three little wolverines and that's that, all right?

They were little because that's another thing; everything has to be little. Even if they are sperm whales or elephants, they are Three Little Mastodons or whatever. Size is all relative anyway. Actually, all wolverines are little. They're smaller than foxes. They never grow up to be real wolves, they stay little. Little wolverines. Three, to be exact, little wolverines.

And they were walking through the forest one bright, sunny day. Ever hear of any of these happy-go-lucky trios bopping around on the sidewalk? In the rain? So there you are. Doing what little wolverines do.

Which in point of fact is looking for smaller animals and viciously tearing them to pieces. Then maybe eating some of the pieces, probably while they are still bleeding and screaming. That's the way wolverines roll. They're vicious. Some say they are the most deadly animal alive, pound for pound. They are also the only animal known to

243

kill for fun, even when they aren't hungry. It's like they want to grow up to be humans.

Sometimes they kill things and not only don't eat them, they spray this really nasty musk on them, kind of like a skunk, so nobody else can stomach eating it. Another proto-human trick that for some reason nobody admires. In fact, they don't even tell you about it, do they? Oh, nooooo. They want their wolverines all sweet and dancing around being cute. You really think bears eat porridge, instead of just tearing you a new . . . okay, wait.

How about those Disney movies? You really think lion kings are cuddly? That lions even have kings? You think saber-toothed tigers really pal around with other animals during ice ages? Why do you think they have sabers for teeth? To make flossing more of a challenge? Why do you think they call Willy and his ilk killer whales? They are predators! Real predators, not the kind that are stupid enough to go over to little girls' houses they meet on the internet when there's a TV van parked outside. They are designed to kill other animals and eat them and excrete them, then look up more animals to tear limb from limb and devour!!! It's what they do for a living.

Okay. Wait a minute. I've got it now. Settle down. So there were three little wolverines frisking around in the beautiful sunlit forest when they came upon a little girl sitting in the path crying. They came up to her and she wasn't afraid of being surrounded by wolverines because she's a cute little girl in a fairy tale and therefore really stupid.

And why do they call them "fairy tales"? There are never any fairies in them. It's never

Three Little Fairies, it's always some kind of animal or Middle Ages moron like a tailor or baker. Do they even have tailors any more, instead of Chinese prison factory workers? Or some Jack of all killers, maybe. See, even Jacks are killers. And they kill giants! You never heard a Three Little Giants story, did you? Which would really be oxymoronic. Because they're all dead, that's why. All these Jackoff heroes keep slaying them over a hill of beans or something. It's dog eat dog in Fairyland, kiddo. Don't get me started on what happens to little boys in Neverland, either. Or what real pirates are like.

Okay, okay, wait. It's okay. Here we go. The three wolverines saw the little girl crying and they stopped to talk to her. These things always talk. Why is that? Why do bears and goats and pigs all become conversationalists whenever there are three of them around? And why don't they just tear her up and eat her? I have no idea. Maybe because of 'Auld Lang Syne' or 'Once You're Upon a Time You Never Go Back' or something.

The Happily Ever After Clause. But they don't. Honest, they don't tear her apart with their sharp fangs and gobble her up and spray some nasty caca over what's left, okay?

245

Promise. Calm down.

They ask her what's wrong. See? They care. They make a difference. Which is some cool thing everybody wants to do. What is with that? Who cares if you care if it doesn't do anything for somebody? People want to "make a difference." Hey, Hitler made a difference, okay? You'd notice a definite difference. Idi Amin made a difference.

Hannibal Lector made a difference. That's not the point. But where was I? Oh, yeah those damned wolverines.

So they asked the little girl why she was crying. And she said, "I'm lost in this big forest and can't find my way to my grandmother's house."

It's always their grandparents, notice that? Just like cartoon characters always have uncles, but nobody has any parents. Even those bobble-head, smug little jerks in Peanuts have no parents. It's like they can't have parents because their parents might have a big fight and one of the parents might be a demented slut and have an affair with her boss and they have to split up and make their kid so nuts the other parent has to pay for psychiatrists and special school classes. So they live with their grandparents. In a cottage. When was the last time you saw a "cottage"? But I guess they couldn't live with them in an over-priced "Managed Care Facility," could they?

But here she is. Her senile grandparents let her wander off into a forest. Where she gets lost even though she's sitting in a path that leads out of the forest, right?

So they ask her how they can help her. Good question, frankly.

She has no idea, of course. She's a little simpleton

with abandonment and bedwetting issues.

So they say, "We can take you to the King of the Forest, and he can help you."

"Oh, could you?" the little girl asks.

And they say, "Isn't that what we just said?"

So off they go, the little girl, who is now smiling and singing and skipping along with the three little wolverines to the beat of some gay song by Elton John.

Soon they come to a clearing with a throne. There are always so many thrones sitting around in the forests. And of course, on the throne is the King of the Forest. He's this great big guy with a leopard skin loincloth and long white hair and beard. He smiles at the little girl and says, "So what brings you to my King of the Forest throne room, little girl? Do you have an appointment? A court order? Some amended document granting rights to visit?"

"No, sir," she says, being much more polite and simpatico than a lot of little girls I could bring up. "I'm lost in this big forest."

"Does anybody know where you are?" he asked, with his blue eyes twinkling.

"No, Mr. King. Only my grandmother, and she is very feeble, although she seems to eat a lot and continue on in good enough health to keep bills rolling in and wiping out her dutiful son's HMO plan and nibble into what's left of his 401K account."

"So there's nobody who cares enough about you to come looking for you?"

"No, sir. I'm just a poor helpless, vulnerable, spoiled rotten little girl with a totally pissy attitude."

"Sounds good," the King of the Forest said as he jumped down off his throne, grabbed her, tore her apart, and ate her up. Then he ate the wolverines, too. He burped and said, "Just what I need, some brat showing up wanting me to drop everything and spend a bunch of time and money trying to make her stop crying all the time when I'm killing myself making the support payments so her mother can hump a better class of yoga instructor."

The end.

That's it, kiddo. Sorry if you don't like my fairy tale; it's all I've got. If you want a better story, ask your mother to tell you one next weekend, that's how joint custody works. The playoffs are going to start in five minutes and I need about three more stiff drinks, so get your little butt the hell to sleep or I'll leave the door open so the wolverines can get in here.

Oh, and sleep tight, sweetie.

Which is Fairy language for, "Don't wet the bed again or you'll be getting face time with The Three Little Starving Crocodiles."

About the Author

Linton Robinson has written humor articles for newspapers, syndicates, and national magazines since the first ice age, and gotten little more than awards and suspicion to show for it. He currently resides in Mexico, which is a rich source of humor that nobody will read. His cult Nineties humor column **The Way of the Weekend Warrior**, has been converted to a widely-reviled novel and is available on amazon and www.adorobooks.com

Weekend Warrior: http://www.amazon.com/Weekend-Warrior-Linton-Robinson/dp/0984800301

http://adorobooks.com

The Big Red Wrinkly Thumb
Diana M. Amadeo

On the south side of town
Brother and Sis are found.
Sister's thumb, it is said,
Is big wrinkly and red.

Sis sucked her thumb since she was small.
A big red thumb was no bother at all.
Her thumb stopped tears and eased her to sleep
With quiet nights and sweet dreams to keep.

One morning when playgroup was at their place
Kids giggled and pointed toward Sis' face.
She pulled the thumb from her lips in surprise
For her finger had swollen to twice its size!

Some called out "Baby" and made her cry.
She ran to Brother who then gave a sigh.
"Pay no attention," older brother said.
But Sister didn't answer and hurried to bed.

249

She sobbed on her blanket for a short time
Before Brother entered and on the bed climbed.
"I sucked my thumb when I was your size,"
Brother said softly, to her surprise.

"Really?" Sis asked, her voice filled with hope.
"Did you get your mouth washed out with soap?"
"No," Brother laughed, "THAT Mama didn't try.
But some of the things kids said, made me cry."

"What made you stop, what did Mama do?
Did she wrap it in Band-Aids all covered with glue?
Or was your thumb dunked in hot spicy sauce.
Was an awful taste the reason or cause?"

Brother smiled. "What an imagination you have!"
"Yes, Mama once tried an icky thick salve.
She brushed it on like a gooey paste.
But its flavor was good—her efforts were a waste!"

Little Sister was confused for a time
"Mama, didn't help," was the obvious sign.
"That's right," Brother agreed, too.
"To help yourself is up to you."

Her wrinkly red thumb looked funny in a way.
Maybe Sis could stop sucking that very day.
It would be missed there was no doubt.
But from her mouth the thumb was out.

"I can stop," she said to Brother with force.
It will take time, but I can do it, of course."
And she did succeed in her efforts by day.
But at night it was hard to keep her thumb away

"If it's harder at night, don't fret, keep cool,"
Said Brother, "Think of games and recess at school."
So Sis would think of some things she had done.
And soon was asleep in the Land of Thumbs.

Each morning her thumb seemed smaller and round
And soon no big wrinkly thumb could be found.
What was at first hard, came easy on her own
And Sis was so proud—she had done it alone!

Now Sis goes to school and sports with glee
She has learned how to solve a problem with ease
"To tackle what's hard takes time," says she.
"But only I can do it, it's up to me."

© Diana M. Amadeo 2012

About the Author

Multi-award winning author Diana M. Amadeo sports a bit of pride in having an excess of 500 publications with her byline in books, anthologies, magazines, newspapers and online. Yet, she humbly, persistently, tweaks and rewrites her thousand or so rejections with eternal hope that they may yet see the light of day.
Author Site: http://home.comcast.net/~da.author/site/
Additional Info: http://www.amazon.com/Diana-M.-Amadeo/e/B001KHTVIO

The Winkie Boy
Melissa Nott

"That kid's banging on the door again." Frank Tinklebottom looked up from his plastic lunch tray and sighed. "Just one day I'd like to go without hearing that kid beat on our brass knocker. Just one day."

"Patience, dear," said his wife, Mildred Tinklebottom. "You know Wee Willie Winkie can't help it."

"Of course he can help it! No one's holding a gun to that kid's head. No one's saying, 'Go to the Tinklebottoms and bang their brass knocker. Bang it hard and bang it long. Make so much bangin' racket; they'll hear you even with their hearing aids turned off.'"

"Don't get up from your recliner, Frank. I'll answer the door," said Mildred. "What time is it, anyway? Oh, never mind. Just give me your watch."

Frank slid the leather band off his wrist and handed it to his wife. "Don't let that hoodlum touch my Timex," he warned as Mildred scurried into the kitchen. "You can touch it, but he can't. Capiche?"

"Capiche." Mildred grabbed a foil-wrapped turkey leg from the refrigerator and rushed to the door, giggling to herself. Frank hated these daily—sometimes hourly—visits from the Winkie boy, but Mildred rather enjoyed them. Willie was a blast from her past, a reminder that although she'd retired from teaching kindergarten seven years ago, her services were still valued. Needed. Desired.

She fluffed her short white curls and opened the door. "Hello, Wee Willie Winkie! What can I do for you?"

The young man standing on her porch was anything but *wee*. Thirteen years old and over six feet tall, Mildred's former student actually appeared larger today than he had yesterday. *It's the meat pies I slipped into his backpack last night*, Mildred thought, her lips curled into a satisfied smile.

"Excuse me, Mrs. Tinklebottom, but are the children all in bed? For it now is eight o'clock," the ex-kindergartener recited in a crackly voice.

"Willie, look here." Mildred held the Timex to Willie's face. "It's not eight o'clock. It's twelve-forty. When the little hand is on the twelve, we're in the noon hour."

Willie nodded. "When the little hand is on the twelve, we're in the noon hour. Okay, Mrs. Tinklebottom. I'll come back later."

"Wait." Mildred handed him the foil-wrapped turkey. "For you."

"Thanks, Mrs. Tinklebottom. You're an awesome teacher!" Willie unwrapped the leg, sank his teeth into the glistening dark meat, and went skipping down the sidewalk.

Several hours later, as Mildred was putting the final touches on a chocolate frosted cake, Willie rapped the Tinklebottom's brass knocker again.

"Ignore him," Frank called from his recliner.

"I'll do no such thing," Mildred muttered, sliding the cake into a white pastry box and checking her reflection in the toaster.

"Excuse me, Mrs. Tinklebottom," Willie greeted her with an impish grin, "but are the children all in bed? For it now is eight o'clock."

"Willie, look here." Mildred held the Timex at the boy's eye level, eight inches above her own head. "It's not eight o'clock. It's three fifteen. When the little hand is on the three, we're in the three o'clock hour."

"When the little hand is on the three," the boy repeated, "we're in the three o'clock hour?"

"Yes! And see here: If I move the little hand to the four, the time becomes four-fifteen. If I move it to the five, it's five fifteen. Now, how about some chocolate cake?"

Willie's black eyes shone with excitement as he peered inside the pastry box. "Thank you, Mrs. Tinklebottom! You're the best teacher in the world!"

"Oh, I'm sure your current teacher, Mrs. Jones, is pretty good too."

"Not as good as you!" Willie kissed Mildred's cheek and tore off down the street, the box clutched tightly to his chest. Mildred watched him go, her fingertips lightly circling the moist lip print on her leathered face.

At dinnertime, when the brass knocker sounded again, Frank bolted upright in his recliner and pushed his TV dinner aside. "HASN'T THAT BOY LEARNED TO TELL TIME YET?"

"He's dyslexic, dear. It's going to take a while." Mildred jumped up and hurried into the kitchen. "Just sit back and enjoy your meal. I'll take care of the Winkie boy."

"A man can only enjoy freezer-burned fish sticks so much," Frank grumbled, popping a peppermint Tums into his mouth and following his wife. "I could've sworn I smelled pot roast coming from the kitchen this afternoon, but I guess my old sniffer ain't what it used to be." He stopped short. "What are you doing?"

Mildred quickly shoveled a batch of freshly-baked peanut butter cookies into a plastic bag. With her back turned to her husband, she heaped a platter of roast beef into a second bag and plopped everything into a cardboard box.

"You've been feeding that boy! That's why he keeps coming back. He's not a time-challenged dyslexic. He's a pesky stray cat that won't stay away!"

"Willie is learning disabled. The food is a positive reinforcement," said Mildred, lowering a six-pack of Mountain Dew into the box.

"Stand back, Mildred. That Winkie boy needs to learn a lesson, all right. But not from you . . . from ME!"

"Frank, no!"

"Now I understand why I get nothing but TV dinners anymore." Frank rolled up his sleeves. "Why there's no soda in the fridge, no cookies in the cookie jar! You've been giving it all to the Winkie boy!"

"What are you gonna do to him, Frank?"

"Nothing the little thief doesn't deserve!" Frank's fist clenched around the doorknob.

"Promise you won't hurt him!"

"That kid has some nerve," Frank fumed. "Taking advantage of his sweet old kindergarten teacher! Preying on her neediness, her desire to feel useful again!"

"That's right, Frank!" Mildred shouted. "Wee Willie Winkie does make me feel useful again! He makes me feel useful and vibrant and alive, which is more than I can say for my own husband!"

"Geez, Mildred, not now!" Frank cupped his forehead

255

in his hands. "We'll have plenty of time to discuss your feelings after I beat the tar outta this hoodlum, okay? Now stand back and let me do my thing."

Frank whipped the door open and Mildred slumped against the wall, her eyes squeezed shut. She waited for the cuss words to start. The slaps. The punches.

Funny, she thought as she clung to the wall. *I don't want Frank to hurt Willie. Yet at the same time, it's thrilling to see my husband get excited about something. He looks so attractive right now, all worked up and red-faced and angry. Not just attractive, but downright sexy!*

"Hello, sir." A female voice drifted through the Tinklebottom's screen door. "My name is Little Red Riding Hood, and I require some help."

"Sure thing, sweetheart!" Frank beamed. "What can I do for you?"

"Well, it's dinner time, there's a hungry wolf chasing me, and I can't seem to find my grandma's house. In short, I could really use the guidance of a wise old gentleman like yourself to see me through this difficult night."

Mildred lunged in front of Frank. "Take a hike, Little Red," she glared, jerking her thumb at the street. "This wise old gentleman is spoken for."

"Mildred?" Frank stared at his wife, bewildered, as she kicked the door shut with her orthopedic shoe and the two of them stood alone, nose-to-nose, in the foyer.

An hour later, when the Tinklebottom's brass knocker once again rapped loudly in their ears, Frank turned in bed, wrapped his arm around his wife, and kissed her naked shoulder. "That Winkie boy doesn't know when to stop," he murmured. "The children *are* in bed, whether it's eight o'clock or not."

"Turn your hearing aid off," Mildred whispered, letting

her warm breath tickle the wiry hairs on her husband's ear lobe. "It doesn't shut the noise out completely, but it helps."

"It's off," Frank said, tapping his ear. "I still hear the little bugger."

"Oh dear," Mildred said, raising her eyebrows. "Are you getting angry at Wee Willie Winkie again?"

"You bet your girdle I am, Millie babe. That gall-darned whippersnapper!" Frank traced the curve of his wife's cheek with his wedding finger. "Pisses me off."

"Good," Mildred sighed, nestling into her husband's pale, sunken chest and inhaling the sweet, familiar scent of Old Spice mixed with peppermint Tums. "Good."

© Melissa Nott 2012

About the Author

Melissa Nott is a Michigander. Or maybe she's a Michiganian. She resides with one husband, two children, and three egocentric furry creatures. No, make that three children and three egocentric furry creatures. Wait, hold up: Five egocentric furry creatures and one husband. Six egocentric furry creatures? Uh . . . let's start over. Melissa Nott lives in Michigan. Her writing has been accepted for publication by online magazines Defenestration, The Big Jewel, eFiction Humor, and The Story Shack. Check her out at melissanott.blogspot.com.

Wee Willie Winkie
Variation by Fran Fischer

Wee Willie Winkie
runs through the town,
Upstairs and downstairs
in his night-gown,

Tapping at the windows,
crying at the locks,
"If I left my clothes at your house,
stick 'em in the mailbox!"

The Royal Pea
Amanda N. Bliss

Once upon a time in a castle perched up high above the Caribbean Sea in Jamaica, lived a pretty princess who wished for the perfect prince. She searched far and wide, but no one seemed to fit the bill. Whenever she was introduced to a prince, he either flaunted his car, bragged about how much money he had. Or he was in love with his own reflection.

One very sunny day, which was often when living on an island, she got a whiff of an amazing aroma filled with delicious spices and hot freshly baked bread. She descended down from her castle top, followed the scent, which led her to a small little village into a home that had no door.

When she peeked into the door, she saw the scrawniest guy bent over the stove cooking. When she spoke, he turned around and their eyes met. Right then and there she knew she would have a cook-off to see which guy would cook the best dish that would steal her heart.

The King announced the contest to the village that he was searching for the best cook to capture his daughter's heart. They would each be given the same ingredients and had to put their personal touch on the recipe. All the men were amazed and lined up to receive each packet of ingredients and rushed home to prepare the dish.

The next day the men lined up to present each dish to the princess. The line went on for miles, wrapping around the entire castle. As each man presented each dish, the princess commented that the meal was either too sweet, too bitter or too bland. Next up was a face that the princess recognized. It was the humble gentleman with the big beautiful eyes, sweet smile and the one whose cooking took her breath away. She tasted his dish and at once announced him as the winner, because his meal was carefully prepared, delicious and appeared to have the magic touch.

When the princess asked him his name, he spoke up with incredible confidence and a genuine smile, announcing that his name was Pea. They were married immediately and Pea became Royal Pea and was now her Chef Prince in royal armor.

Tom, Tom, the Piper's Son
Variation by Fran Fischer

Tom, Tom, the piper's son,
Stole a pig, and away did run;
The pig was digested
And Tom was arrested,
And sent to the pokey for what he'd done.

The Copper Ring
Darice Lee

Once upon a time, there was a young boy born to a wealthy and powerful baron. When the boy grew to be four years old, his father went to a fortune teller and asked about his son's fate. To his dismay, he learned that his son would marry a crippled and lowly girl. He vowed to prevent such a humiliating fate.

As the boy grew up, he became a dreamy, honorable young man who longed for true love. He begged his father to arrange for him to marry a beautiful maiden. His father agreed to do so after completing an important mission he had to carry out first in the countryside.

The baron took some armed men and rode to rid the land of crippled maidens. The father of one such girl heard rumors among peddlers and mail carriers that the baron and his soldiers were moving from village to village, gathering crippled and unmarried girls in the forest to be killed. A destitute and terminally-ill man, he gave his daughter who had spent most of her life taking care of him, the warmest coat he had and a copper ring. The coat was shaggy and beaten, probably made a generation ago, and she was told to keep the ring on so that she could pretend to be married. Urgently, her father told her to go somewhere far away.

She took a small, back-country road and wept softly, fearing for her father. A band of robbers appeared on the other side of the path, and before she could hide behind a tree, they had caught sight of her.

"Oi, a pretty lassie we've got here," the captain said.

The girl ran toward the forest, but a line of haggard, vicious robbers blocked her way.

"She's a cripple!" The captain yelled. "Look at her

limp! We won't need to worry about this one getting away."

The horde laughed loudly and roughly. Terrified, the girl crumpled onto the ground, held her hands together in front of her face and begged the captain to spare her, saying she had no money and nothing of value.

"Why you've got that ring, haven't you" he bellowed, "We don't like liars, do we?"

"It's just copper!" she said, ripping it off her finger and throwing it at his feet.

As they were about to close in on the poor girl, a band of the baron's men who had been searching for these notorious robbers bounded out of the forest, yelling fiercely and brandishing their swords. The girl threw herself behind a tree and peeked out to watch the fight. The surprisingly young and noble looking leader was dueling with the captain while his men fought with the other robbers. The leader, though courageous and well-intentioned, was not a particularly good fighter, and so even while all the other robbers had been killed, he and the captain were still deadlocked. He had gashes on his shoulder and chest while the fleet-footed captain was

263

still unharmed. The girl was afraid to watch but could not tear her eyes away. The leader lunged forward. The captain swung his sword across, but did not manage to deflect the course of the blade from sliding into his bowels. He collapsed to the ground. But he had not gone down easily as his last swing had cut the leader's arm to the bone. At the sight of the pooling blood, the young fighter began to heave.

His men helped him up and they were about to make the journey back to the baron's castle when the girl crawled from behind the tree and begged to let her attend to her hero's wounds. They agreed since he was bleeding heavily and the road ahead of them was long. She went into the forest and came with spindly fibers and a pocketful of herbs. She sewed his gashes back together as he slipped in and out of consciousness, then covered them with herbs, and ripping bandages from the bloodied shirts of the dead, wrapped his wounds up tight.

Then she said, "Let me come with you so I may redress his bandages."

She put her father's ring back on and together, they traveled back to the castle. The young man healed up very well with the girl's care. He fell in love with her and asked about her life. When he learned of the baron's mission, he realized the only way to save her was to marry her even though she was not noble. So when his father returned, he explained what had happened and that he wanted to marry her. The baron looked at him with a clenched jaw for a long time, then abruptly said he wanted to meet this girl first.

The baron took the young girl on a walk later that day on the bluffs. When they had walked far enough, he told her he would never allow his son to marry her. He grabbed her and tried to push her off the cliffs but she clung on to his feet, begging for her life. The baron relented but he took her ring and threw it into the ocean.

"Never let me see your face till you can show me that ring. But because you saved my son's life, I will let you live and work at my brother's house," he said. They went back to the castle and the baron wrote her a letter to give to his brother.

The poor cripple took the letter and left immediately. With her old coat, the dirt smudged on her face, and her limp, everybody on the road took her for a penniless old woman and left her alone. When she arrived at the brother's house and gave him the letter, he had to look twice upon his guest, wondering why the baron would want this ugly old crone to serve as a maid. So instead he bade her to work with the medicine man who was also elderly.

For many years, she worked in the castle. Every morning, she took care to dress herself as a crone so to not embarrass the noble. She rubbed dirt over face, walked in a hunched posture, and always wore her father's coat with the hood pulled over her hair. She also soon realized that as an old woman, none of the errand boys bothered her like they did the other girls.

Then one day, the baron and his son came to the noble's house. The cooks prepared a lavish meal of stew cooked from freshly caught fish, a roasted boar, and heaps of sweet fruit. Midway through the stew, the baron coughed loudly. Then his hands flew to his throat and his coughs burst into croaking heaves. As his brother gasped for breath, the noble yelled at a page to find help. The page returned with the medicine man and the crone, hobbling and limping behind him. The crone froze as though in shock, but the medicine man, a seasoned doctor, rushed forward. He told the baron's son to grab his father's torso and to squeeze and lift. Then with a great hack, a glinting object erupted from the baron's throat and skittered across the floor.

"Bring that here," roared the noble to the crone.

She went to pick it up and exclaimed in a youthful and vigorous voice, "My ring!"

Wheezing dreadfully, the baron demanded to know who this old woman was. The noble replied that it was the very person he had sent to him many years ago. Unable to bear the deception any longer, the girl took off her hood and washed off the dirt with water. Once he recognized her, the baron's temper flared. He tried to yell at her but only burst into a bout of coughing. The girl then held out the ring that the baron had nearly swallowed.

His son rushed to her and said to his father, "She's still alive!"

As his coughs subsided, the baron realized that fighting fate was futile. So he allowed his son to marry the crippled and lowly maiden and they lived happily ever after.

© Darice Lee 2012

About the Author

Darice Lee is an aspiring writer, a rockclimber, and a care provider for adults with developmental and mental disabilities. In her blog, she posts pictures of books that she runs across in laundromats, libraries, living rooms, restaurants, and anywhere where people leave their books unattended and also talks a little about the ones she's read.

Blog: http://foundbooks.blogspot.com/

Mrs. Wight
M Sullivan

loose is the skin that
flaps from her cheek
her bones are brittle and white

long is the howl she
shrieks at the Moon,
corrosive her ravenous bite

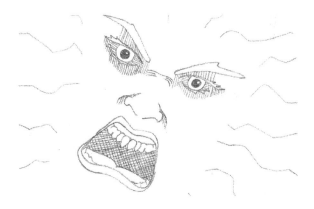

she drinks from a skull
she dug from a grave
her touch brings a case of the blight

she has but one goal
to sip on your soul

Pleased to
meet you,
Mrs. Wight

Us, Swimming
Victoria Fryer

It was our junior year of college when I finally understood that Lainey would never search for me like she searched for the mermaids. She sought them unabashedly, wholeheartedly. It was a fire that consumed her. But she was the fire that consumed me, and I couldn't let her go.

It was a hot, sticky June evening almost two years after she'd left Galveston—where we'd gone to college together—when I got a call from one of Lainey's new friends in Fairbanks. "Is this Josh?" a voice asked. "Yes, who's this?" I struggled to hear the faraway voice through my cell phone.

"It's Allen," he said: one of Lainey's colleagues from the marine biology program at UK Fairbanks. She'd gone missing--driven down to Anchorage a couple of days ago, chartered a boat, suited up in scuba gear and hadn't been seen since.

Early the next morning, I was sitting on the tarmac at the Bush Intercontinental Airport waiting for my flight to depart for Alaska. Allen had told me not to come; he said he just needed to talk to someone who knew Lainey well. Why on earth had she gone out there? Why wouldn't she have told anyone? But I could tell he was thankful that I insisted, and I couldn't sit back and wait for news from 3,000 miles away. I needed to be there, to look for her.

I'd known Lainey since we were children. Babies, practically. Our mothers became close friends after my family moved in next door to hers in a cookie-cutter south Houston suburb. Every summer we spent hours together turning to prunes in her family's backyard pool while our mothers sipped cocktails under the nearby oak tree.

She was always a water animal, Lainey was. In almost all my memories of her, her long blonde hair is almost brown with water, and her face is glistening with reflected light.

"Watch me dive!" she'd shriek, her small body splashing in the pool. It always made me laugh, the way she dove—so accidentally graceful. Once she knew she had an audience, she'd jump up high and dive down into the water, gliding effortlessly with her ankles held together, moving in one fluid motion like a mermaid. I would follow her under the water, cheeks puffed out and eyes wide, kicking my legs with all my might. Trying to catch her.

We shared our first kiss when we were fourteen. We were at the beach this time, lying on our stomachs in the muddy sand of Galveston Bay, drawing shapes and letters with our fingers. With a faraway but focused look in her eyes—the kind she often got when she was studying the sea—she said, "I know they're out there, Josh. I have to look for them." The mermaids. Even at that age it was all she could think about.

"I'll help you," I said, meaning it with every iota of my soul then.

She looked at me and narrowed her eyes. "Do you mean it?" she asked in a low voice. "Do you promise?"

"I promise," I said, even though I had no idea what a promise really meant.

And then she kissed me.

That first kiss lit me up inside. Like the opposite of what people see when they are about to die, I saw my

269

whole future flash before my eyes when her lips met mine—images of Lainey, tall and beautiful as she grew, always by my side. I don't know if that's what she saw or not.

Everyone always assumed that Lainey and I would be a thing forever. We all know now that destined loves, the "sure things," always fall apart under the weighty pressure of outside expectations and storybook-ending speculations. But we didn't know that at fourteen.

And no one bothered to tell us, because they wanted us to make it even more than we did. Maybe to fulfill their own storybook fantasies—the reasons we watch Disney movies as grown-ups and feel our hearts fill to the brim with retroactive hope for a future that has already disappointed us.

After nearly ten cumulative hours in the air, I should have been exhausted, but I was wired. It was after midnight when I landed in Anchorage, and Allen was there to meet me at the airport. He took me back to the motel where he'd rented a room, where I paced until the sun came up.

Allen had chartered a boat to go out and search for Lainey. He knew all her favorite places, he said. "But I have no idea why she liked to dive in those places so much. They were of no interest to us scientifically."

"The mermaids," I murmured.

"The what now?" he asked, sure he'd heard wrong.

"She didn't tell you?" Of course she hadn't. She was possessive of them, wanted the creatures all to herself.

So I told him everything: how Lainey had been drawn to water since the day she was born. How she was convinced that aquatic mammals with DNA similar to that of humans were out there, undiscovered. That they were like mermaids.

"Like 'The Little Mermaid'?" he asked.

"Kind of," I said. "But don't ever let her hear you say it like that. She went into marine biology because she thought she could prove her theory," I explained. "She chose Fairbanks because of the marine biology program, and she wanted to be closer to Alaska's whale activity. She didn't explain it all to me; I wasn't a believer."

Allen looked at me, silent with disbelief. After a few moments, I added, "I always thought she would grow out of it, or give up. But she never did."

Lainey and I had gone to college together in Galveston; she wanted to be near the water. And that was when, like the boats we would watch from the piers jutting off the seawall, she started to drift away from me. In our junior year we both moved off campus into separate apartments, and I saw her less and less.

When she did come over, she looked gray around the eyes, a little shiny. She seemed so dramatically different one night, after dinner and bolstered by a couple of glasses of wine, I asked her if she was using drugs.

She snapped, of course; maybe I deserved it. "What the hell, Josh?" she screamed. "You just don't get it." And she was right. I didn't. I knew she wasn't on drugs; it was the obsession that was overtaking her. That, I could never understand.

She jumped off the couch where she'd been sitting and stormed out of the apartment.

She used to be so full of life, so shining and bright;

271

but she was changing. Or was it me who was changing? Bewildered and exhausted and a little drunk, I lay face-down on the couch where she'd been just moments before and stuffed my face into a throw pillow.

After a few minutes of tossing and turning there, I felt something scratch my face—I picked my head up and saw a round, translucent disc with an iridescent sheen.

Things were different after that. I saw her often—on the beach, gazing out at the water, walking slowly through the sand. Always alone. But I knew better than to speak to her. She would come to me when she was ready, I thought.

But she didn't. Not really. On the morning of our graduation day, she stopped at my apartment in her cap and gown. "We need to talk," she said, and then told me she'd gotten into graduate school in Fairbanks. I knew that this was the start of her great adventure, and she didn't see a place for me in it.

"I'll miss you like crazy, but I have to do this alone," she said. "We'll still be friends, of course," tears pooling in her eyes. "Best friends." I nodded and wiped a tear from her cheek.

As she walked down the sidewalk away from my apartment, the light caught her legs, bare under her graduation gown. I thought I saw something glistening, a blue-green patch on her calf.

Allen and I combed the waters off the southern Alaskan coast for a full day and a half before we saw any sign of her. And then I saw it—a length of ratty blond hair lying over the back of a large rock a few hundred yards off the shoreline. Next to it laid a scuba suit. Or, at least, part of a scuba suit.

272

"There she is," I said, under my breath at first, lest the world hear me and take it away. Then louder, "There she is!" I shouted her name.

Screaming by the time we got to her, she only looked up lazily, as if she had been expecting me. I scrambled off the side of the boat and reached out to her.

"Lainey, come on; grab my hand," I said. "We've got to get you out of here, out of the water, get you warm. Where the hell have you been?"

Her face remained distant, almost cold. "I can't go. Don't you see?"

"See what, Lainey? See what?" I thought perhaps she was delirious, from dehydration or hunger. Or maybe she'd gone hypothermic. She was naked; her SCUBA suit had been discarded.

"Look, Josh." She said it with an intensity I hadn't heard from her in years. "Look." Her eyes bored into me now, suddenly alive and ferocious.

So I really looked at her. I looked with objective eyes, instead of the ones I colored with my dreams and wishes. I looked with the eyes she wanted me to use, instead of with my own. And I saw the iridescent blue-green scales on her ankles, her feet splayed in the shape of a tail fin.

"Shit. SHIT. What the hell?" I had to be hallucinating. This couldn't be real. I rubbed my face, trying to wipe the magic out of my eyes.

As if she'd read my mind, she said, "It's real. I found them." With wonder in her eyes, she repeated, "I found them." And for the first time since I'd spotted her, she smiled.

I looked down again at her legs and realized the scales were multiplying, growing up her calves and knitting around her legs, binding them into the form of a

273

fin.

"I'll be gone soon, Josh. It means so much to me that you wanted to find me," she said. "But I don't want to be saved."

It hit me, finally. This is what she'd been looking for the whole time, but I couldn't see it clearly. I had merely been an accomplice in her search, her friend, her confidante. I had never been her one true love as I'd thought she'd been to me. The realization freed as much as it hurt me. It wasn't me she was running from—it was humanity itself.

I knew my time with her was running short. "All I ever wanted to do was save you," I said to her. "But you needed me to let you go."

So I kissed her on the forehead, said "I love you" one last time, and climbed back in the boat.

As the scales finally reached her hips, knitting together forever what used to be her legs, she smiled, looked me in the eye, and slid off the rock. I watched her go, moving gracefully through the water as if she was born to be there. Our childhood together ran through my mind—memories of holding her hand, chasing after her long, blond hair; memories of us, swimming.

And I let her go.

About the Author

Victoria Fryer was raised in south Texas but currently resides in Pennsylvania with her husband and two dogs. She works a day job in public relations and writes at night. Her poetry has appeared in "Napalm and Novocain," and you can read more of her work at her blog, makingwordshappen.blogspot.com.

Pease Porridge Hot
Variation by Fran Fischer

Pease porridge hot, pease porridge cold,
Pease porridge in the pot, nine days old;
Some like it hot, some like it cold,
I wouldn't eat it nine days old.

The Gingerbread Puppet Boy
Mickey Hunt

The wrinkled old man sat patiently beside his luggage in the bus station and stared toward the glass door at the far end of the waiting room. *What was this madness?* he wondered. It had all started so innocently. He chuckled softly to himself . . .

His wife had wanted a son, plain and simple. But the doctor had told them even before they were married years ago this was impossible. She would be barren.

At first she hadn't minded so much. She had somehow gotten comfort from their puppetry business. Making the puppets, writing plays, and designing and sewing costumes used a lot of creative energy. Also, the uncanny lifelike quality of the puppets in performance and the joyful laughter of the children satisfied some of her maternal instincts. But it never really was enough . . .

Outside the bus station, up and down the street, all the townspeople and half the county had collected. Apparently the tension was too much for these factory workers and part-time farmers because a fistfight broke out. A fresh-faced boy pressed his nose up against the glass door of the waiting room, peering inside. His eyes lit up when he saw the old man. "Hey everybody!" he piped. "The racer's father is in here. I saw him on the news yesterday!"

The fistfight abruptly stopped, and the crowd that had been watching it surged through the door, eager to be nearer to the source of the irritation and excitement. A great fat man charged through to the front. He might have been one of the fighters because he was sweaty and covered with dust. "I hear you're a relation of this troublemaker!" he said loudly as his jowls shook.

277

"Well, you might say I am," the old man answered.

"What did he say?" shouted two or three who were jammed up against the wall of the newly stuffed waiting room.

"He says he is a relation!" boomed the fat man.

Startled, someone backed away from the fat man and tripped. "Please, be careful of my luggage," the old man said and pulled a rather large, long box with air holes in it closer to him.

"What I want to know," the fat man demanded, "is who will pay for my broken fence and my lost cows that ran after this son of yours? And my boys took the pickup truck and have been gone for days."

"And your kid stole my car!" a voice bellowed from the wall.

"My daughter!" a woman cried, and fainted into her husband's arms.

A businessman shoved forward. "All the workmen at my factory ran off as well. Nobody has worked a single hour since that fellow challenged them all to a race. He said nobody could catch him."

"What have you to say for yourself?" the fat man bellowed as he shook his finger at the old man.

"I can't be blamed for him," the old man replied. "He will have to take responsibility for his own actions, I suppose. Take him to the courthouse like you would anyone else, but . . . you'll have to catch him first." Here the old man looked at his box and smiled.

"That," the businessman said, "is what every Joe Baloney and Jane Salami has been trying to do! Haven't you seen the news? The whole country is crazy." The businessman scratched his head. "I just don't understand it."

The old man said, "But you can't blame him for folks

278

chasing him. They could have just ignored him."

"Sure we can blame him!" retorted the businessman. "He trespassed on my property, and then brashly claimed nobody could catch him. So, all my workers tried right then, and most are still trying as far as I know. Just imagine 75 men running off as fast as they could go, and for some, that wasn't very fast." He was looking at the fat man.

The businessman seemed suddenly struck with the humor of the improbable situation and grinned. "As fast as they could go," he repeated, his voice starting to squeak. Then he burst into laughter.

The fat man joined in, too, as he remembered himself running and then later seeing his matronly cows tossing their heads and kicking up their heels like young heifers as they gamboled after the lanky and awkward, but incredibly fast young man. The brash fellow had called out to his herd. "My mama couldn't catch me, the workers couldn't catch me, and YOU CAN'T EITHER!" The fat man's laughter was as infective as his anger, and soon the whole crowd in the waiting room was in howling stitches.

The old man saw his chance and hoisted up his box, hugging it as he pushed through the hysterical people and out the door. He looked at his watch. Ten minutes or more before the bus was due. He sat down on the bench and recollected the musings he had before the crowd interrupted . . .

Everything had turned out so unexpectedly. His wife seemed content having no children until they fully retired about a year before. Then she began yearning for a real family. It was just a month ago when he had an idea. He would build the best puppet he had ever made. *Maybe that would please her*, he had thought.

279

The old puppeteer had worked long hours. They were too old for a baby he decided, so he made the puppet boy 20 years old and life-sized. The puppet was created from a very special gingerbread and the pieces were baked hard and fastened together by the clip hooks and metal rings set into them. The puppeteer specially made him with moveable eyes and a mouth on a head that turned every which way, just like a real one. The puppet boy was a rod puppet. Each of his limbs had a thin wooden, black-painted rod attached, and with three puppeteers operating him at once, he would be quite realistic.

The puppeteer's wife sewed the clothes: a blue, green and yellow flannel shirt, brown corduroy pants, a red neckerchief, and a green hat. The puppeteer and his wife had been very busy and very happy.

One evening last week, they finished painting him and went to bed to let him dry overnight. The old woman must have yearned and prayed very hard for a son before she dropped off to sleep because the next morning something terribly unusual happened that started this whole mess . . .

The laughter inside the station faded, and the

280

scuffling and shouting started up again. *These practical people wouldn't forget their troubles so easily*, the old man thought. He pulled out binoculars and looked intently down the road from where the bus was to come. The last report on the radio said that the racer had hijacked a Greyhound bus and was headed in this direction. He had already broken through at least one police blockade. Up and down the street, hundreds and hundreds of adults and children were lined up as for a parade. Some held umbrellas to shade the sun. Balloons floated high up in the sky. At the far end of the street, another police blockade stood by.

"Sure to fail like all the rest," he murmured and winked at his luggage.

The old man warmly remembered that morning when life began again. He and his wife woke up with sunshine streaming through the window on them in bed. The first thing they did, even before breakfast, was to dress their new puppet boy. The last thing to put on him was the red neckerchief. Just as the old woman knotted it around his neck, the puppet boy's head jerked up, he blinked his eyes, lifted himself from his stand which then fell over, and he ran out the door pulling off the wooden rods and calling out behind, "You can't catch me!" The old man had been following him the last few days like everyone else, but not before he had made some preparations . . .

Some of the people waiting for the fun craned their necks to look down the street. "Here it comes!" the fresh faced kid piped out. The local marching band struck up a lively tune.

The crowd in the waiting room tumbled outside. The old man could barely make out the Greyhound way down the road, moving at high speed. He bent over, loosened the fastenings, and lifted the lid of the box.

281

"Okay," he whispered, "you can get out now. Nobody will notice."

The beautiful young puppet girl sat up and shook her long thick red hair. She stepped out of the box with a clumsy gracefulness and began some quick stretching exercises in her green running suit with yellow stripes all the way down to her running shoes.

She flashed her brown eyes at the old puppeteer. "Will he be on the bus?"

"I think so," the old man replied. "Look!"

The bus was getting nearer. Behind it, also racing madly, followed a number of police cars, blue lights flashing, a pickup truck, motorbikes, a coal truck, and other assorted vehicles. A helicopter swooped overhead. People cheered from the windows and rooftops along the street. The bus entered the town and suddenly braked. The cars right behind screeched to avoid back-ending it. The police at the barricade were ready. But right in front of the bus station, an emergency door flew open and out jumped the colorfully clad puppet boy who rolled and tumbled to his feet. The whole crowd was silent and tense with expectancy. The boy gazed for a moment at the puppet girl, then shouted a challenge to everyone within earshot.

"Nobody had caught me yet, and not one of you can either!!!"

Every single soul that heard these words thought at that moment of just one thing: to catch this impudent rascal. A roar, like when a goal is scored at a big soccer game, exploded from the hundreds of throats, and as one huge mass they were after him.

The old man joined the slowpokes trailing behind the pack. He walked just outside of town and watched the runners swarming across a large field. Through his binoculars he saw the puppet boy way ahead of everyone, but a green clad figure was moving up on him fast, her red hair blowing straight back.

Running, running, she was right behind him now. The puppet boy glanced over his shoulder, and she made a flying tackle. They skidded together across the grassy ground.

He was caught!

The wrinkled old puppeteer chuckled to himself. His wife would be happy. They were too old now to have children, that was sure. Too much chasing around.

But grandchildren would be nice.

© Mickey Hunt 2012

About the Author

Mickey Hunt wrote this story some 33 years ago in a creative writing class at Berea College when he was a student there. Each student was asked to write three sentences to begin the best short story ever, and then they traded their beginnings. Mickey revised the story for the Gingerbread Festival in Knott County, Kentucky and it was published in the Troublesome Creek Times. He has since revised it again. In his early twenties he was a puppeteer with the Tears of Joy Puppet Theatre based in Vancouver, Washington. They performed with rod puppets and body puppets in churches, parks, and on university campuses.

Find Mickey Hunt at www.chaoticterrain.com. Then, go to Short Stories.

Old Mother Hubbard
Variation by Fran Fischer

Old Mother Hubbard
Went to the cupboard,
Because her poor dog was getting thinner.
When she got there,
The cupboard was bare,
And so they all went out to dinner.

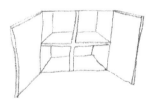

Being Practical
Kimberly Kay

Cindy wasn't allowed to go to the ball after she punched her stepmother on the jaw.

It's not like they were going to let me go anyway, Cindy thought as she nursed her hand, alone, by the dying embers of the fire.

She didn't regret her actions. Her stepmother and stepsisters had treated Cindy like dirt—no! Like cinders ever since her father had died. They called her Cinderella, which was fine, because that was her name, but it was the way they said it.

Before Cindy had a proper moment to think up a plan to get to the ball, an explosion made her jump. She spun around. There stood a woman with dark skin, curly hair, and a dress that, ponderously, seemed to be made from glitter.

"There, there, Child—"

Cindy tackled her.

"Who are you, and how did you get in here?" Cindy bellowed as she held the woman in a half nelson.

The woman clawed at Cindy's arms with her manicured fingernails, and gasped, "I'm your fairy godmother!"

"Fairy what who?"

"I've come to help!"

Cindy doubted that.

Seeming to realize that Cindy needed proof, the "fairy" extracted a thin golden wand from one of her flamboyant sleeves, and with a swish, healed Cindy's bruised hand.

Cindy stared, then dropped the fairy, and took a seat on the fireplace, at attention.

The woman stood, and wiped soot from her gown. After reaffirming that her head and body were still connected, she returned her attention to Cindy, and gave a quick smile. "I'm your fairy godmother," she repeated, voice now raspy.

"I'm sorry for tackling you," Cindy said sincerely. "I didn't know fairies existed."

"It's all right, Dearie. Most people don't." The fairy straightened the tiara resting in her black curls. "As I was saying, Child—"

"Please, call me Cindy."

The fairy lifted one dark eyebrow. "Not Cinderella? Not Ella?"

With a shrug, Cindy replied, "Cindy's much more original, don't you think?"

The fairy gave another sweet smile. "As you wish my Chil—Cindy."

Cindy smiled.

"Now then. . ." The fairy stepped forward. "I'm here to help you get to the ball."

Cindy frowned. "Help me?"

The fairy's smile widened. "Why yes! Didn't you want to go?"

"Oh, I do!" Cindy brushed golden sparkles from her hands—remnants from tackling the fairy. "But I was just coming up with a plan to. My stepfamily thinks I can't get there by myself—"

"And they're right! That's why I'm here!" Spreading her arms, the fairy curtsied. As she stood, she rolled up her puffy sleeves. "Right then, the first thing you'll need is—"

"Wait a moment." Cindy lifted her hand to stop the fairy mid wand wave. "It's kind of you to offer to help, but I haven't even had a chance to come up with my own plan. Shouldn't I try to get to the ball by myself first?"

The fairy's smile was quickly growing strained. "No, Dear. That's what I'm here for. I'm supposed to grant you your heart's desire in the fastest, easiest way possible."

"You're telling me I shouldn't even try?" With a raised eyebrow Cindy retorted, "But how am I supposed to learn and grow?"

The fairy sighed. "You're not. I'm here to do what you can't."

"How do you know I ca—"

"Trust me!" the fairy snapped.

Cindy frowned, but clamped her lips closed as she reevaluated the situation. She had to find a way to get rid of this pushy fairy.

"That's better." The fairy grinned. "Now! The first thing you'll need is a coach."

"Why?"

The fairy blinked. "Why? You need a mode of transportation—"

"Oh, yes." Pushing her hair out of her face, Cindy continued, "But not necessarily 'first thing.' It seems to me that it won't matter how I get to the ball if I'm not dressed for it." Cindy offered an innocent smile as she spread her arms. "Don't you think?"

The fairy at last full out frowned. Cindy felt this was a huge accomplishment.

Through clenched teeth, the fairy managed, "I wanted to save the dress for last."

"Why?"

The fairy looked to the sky, and uttered a small prayer before returning her attention to Cindy. "For effect, Dear. The dress is always the last gift I grant."

"Well, can't we skip the theatrics and be practical?

The ball's not going to last all night."

Pursing her lips, the fairy muttered, "I suppose you do only have until midnight . . ." she waved her wand, and in a swirl of golden glitter, Cindy found herself wearing a pale blue gown—covered, of course, in runaway gold sparkles. These Cindy brushed off as she said, "It's lovely." Those thoughts vanished, however, as she caught sight of her face in the side of a kitchen pan. Cindy grimaced, lightly touching one finger to her cheek. "What did you do to my face?"

Smiling smugly, the fairy replied, "I fixed it!"

Cindy wasn't so sure about that. Her face was covered in so much makeup that she could hardly tell her nose from her cheeks. Her shoulders sank. "No one will recognize me for who I am."

"Isn't that the point?" Before Cindy could argue, the fairy hastened to say, "I imagine you'll want your glass slippers next?"

Cindy arched one over-penciled eyebrow. "Glass slippers? How is that in any way practical?"

The fairy folded her arms. "It's my trademark."

With a snort, Cindy said, "Seems sort of . . . silly, don't you think? Is it even possible to dance in glass slippers?"

"They'd be better than the bunny slippers you're wearing currently!"

Cindy hastened to cover her feet with the hem of her dress. "Don't you make fun of Carrots and Mr. Fluffy!"

The fairy shook her head. "I'll get you the slippers last then. Now, let's get you that coach. I'll need a pumpkin."

"A pumpkin? Those are out in the gar—" The fairy was outside before Cindy had finished speaking. Cindy followed, smirking.

As the fairy searched the pumpkin patch, Cindy folded her arms, and tapped one foot, the ears of Carrots bobbing. "Don't you think this is all going a bit overboard? Can't you just poof me there?"

The fairy ignored her, returning a moment later with a large, orange pumpkin, which she set on the ground in the middle of the garden.

The fairy's smile returned. "Now you'll really see me work my magic."

Cindy watched with fascination that quickly morphed into disappointment as the pumpkin enlarged, hollowed, and became a shining silver carriage.

Cindy frowned. "You call that magic? The carriage isn't even orange."

A vein in the fairy's forehead twitched. "Why should it be orange?"

"I just thought you made it from a pumpkin for a reason. If it was going to be off-white, why not use a turnip, or an onion?"

"An onion?" the fairy said flatly.

"Well, it would be more practical—"

"I'm a creature of magic! There's nothing practical about me!" the fairy bellowed, and Cindy was impressed by her rage as she continued, "You want practical? Fine! Find some practical way to get to the ball!" And with that, the fairy imploded in an explosion of gold dust.

It was a dramatic exit; Cindy had to give her that.

"Finally," Cindy muttered. The night was yet young, so abandoning the carriage that was already starting to rot, Cindy hiked to the nearest farmstead, brambles and thorns tearing her gown's hem. Cindy didn't mind. It gave her dress character.

When she reached the stable, however, the young brown stallion reared and bucked at the sight of her. Retreating, Cindy was at first bewildered. But then, catching sight of her face in the back of a shovel, she realized her problem, and rubbed her face as clean as she could—just a little makeup lingering around the edges of her eyes.

Recognizably human, she returned to the stallion. Calmed, he allowed her to secure a bridal around his head, and lead him out.

Cindy wasn't exactly stealing the horse. She just had to get to the ball. And she did fully intend to return the horse—by midnight no less.

Mounting coated the gown with horse hair and straw, but Cindy didn't mind. She nudged the stallion onward, and enjoyed the ride to the castle.

When she arrived, she left the stallion in the gardens. Brushing hay from her hair—but missing more than she caught—she climbed the steps, Carrots and Mr. Fluffy keeping her company.

You look ridiculous. A voice in the back of her mind said. It sounded like her stepfamily and that fairy. You'll stand out a mile around.

Isn't that the point? She threw open the doors of the ballroom.

The dancing stopped as everyone stared. Several mouths dropped open.

Cindy lifted her head high.

Inevitably, the people of the court did the only thing they could. Cindy didn't fit in, so they ignored her.

Cindy was fine with that.

She strolled around the edges of the ballroom, feeling proud of herself for having made it without magic after everyone told her she couldn't.

I have all the magic I need right here. She touched one finger to her heart, and ran smack into someone.

He spun around, apologies tumbling from his lips, but the moment his eyes found her, he stopped.

Cindy also apologized, then waited for him to say something more.

"May I have this dance?"

She wasn't sure why he asked, since she looked as she did, but she accepted anyway.

As they swirled around the dance floor, Cindy noticed the stares and disdain of those around them.

They don't know me, so I won't care about their opinions. Cindy smiled as she danced poorly. She'd never danced before after all. But the young man didn't seem to mind, and Cindy's heart swirled faster than her clumsy feet.

At length he led her to the gardens. The brown stallion munched on the grass nearby as the pair sat on a bench.

They had a marvelous conversation in which Cindy

discovered the man was as bright as he was handsome.
As the hour grew late, Cindy looked up at the castle.
"Odd. I haven't seen any of the royalty."

The man chortled. "I've seen the Prince."

"Where?"

"He's . . . right next to you."

Cindy's eyes flashed to him.

He stood to bow. "Prince Charming."

Cindy blushed, stood, and curtsied. "I'm sorry, I
didn't—"

"No. It's all right. I found it refreshing, actually." His
eyes held hers. "Actually, I found you refreshing. You're
not like the other ladies I—"

Just then, the clock struck midnight.

The horse!

"I'm sorry! I must go!" Gathering her skirts, Cindy fled
to the horse, mounted, and galloped away.

The clock struck its last note just as she returned the
horse to the stable. Her dress vanished in a cloud of
golden sparkles, leaving her in her old sooty dress. It
was only then that she noticed one of her bunny slippers
had vanished. She must have dropped it back at the
castle.

Well . . . Cindy thought. Why not go back? Nothing's
stopping me now.

So she walked back to the castle.

The Prince stood on the castle steps, holding Mr.
Fluffy. He was surrounded by a flock of girls all claiming
to be the one he searched for, but when he offered the
slipper to them, they wrinkled their noses at the one
eyed bunny, and exclaimed, "Ew! Who would wear such
a thing?"

Ella pushed right through the crowd, grabbed the
Prince by his collar, and pulled his lips to hers in a long,

hard kiss.

Mr. Fluffy was returned, and just like any good, practical fairy tale, they lived happily ever after.

© Kimberly Kay 2012

About the Author

Kimberly Kay was born and raised in North Salt Lake, Utah, as an avid lover of horses, words, chocolate, and puns. She's had a recent obsession with fairytales, especially the ones with happy endings. Currently she's attending Utah Valley University to complete her BA in English while seeking to get her young adult novels (which, to match her obsession, are fairytale retellings) published. Kimberly has previously been published at Stories for Children Magazine (http://storiesforchildren.tripod.com/).

Gold-Flecked Eyes
Rosie Hendrickson

The whole mess started the day I went to pick wildflowers. My stepmother had sent one of her soldiers with me, for my own protection, according to her. There were shape-shifters that played with people's emotions in some parts of the kingdom. I should have known something was off when I saw his gold-flecked eyes.

I was having a great time, right up until the soldier pulled a knife on me. That was about the time I got the feeling he wasn't really all that bright. I don't know exactly what he expected me to do. In front of me was a man with a knife who looked slightly overweight. Behind me was a lot of open space. Any sensible person would have done the same thing I did.

I ran. Duh.

I had planned on circling around him and running back to the castle to tell my stepmother what had happened, but then I started thinking. I knew my stepmother had sent me with one of her soldiers. I knew said soldier had just tried to kill me. Therefore, I thought it was safe to assume my stepmother was trying to kill me.

So my logic was a bit flawed. Sue me.

Frightened as I was, in hindsight, I did one of the stupidest things possible. I ran deeper into the forest. Never mind that I knew there were shape-shifters that played with people's emotions in some parts of the kingdom, or that there was a maniac with a knife running around somewhere in there, or that I had absolutely no idea where I was.

Naturally, I was completely lost in ten minutes and

starting to recognize my own idiocy. In my own defense, I was young and scared senseless. Now that I was actually thinking straight, I just couldn't believe that my stepmother would try to kill me. Sure, we had our differences. She didn't always approve of me helping out around the castle, but she stopped complaining after she tasted the apple pie the cook had taught me to bake. More than likely the soldier was acting on his own. It was even possible he wasn't really going to kill me, just hold me for ransom.

But I couldn't really worry about that at the moment. I was lost, so the first thing I needed to do was get myself un-lost and back to the castle. The only option I could think of was to find someone who could point me in the right direction.

Now don't get me wrong. I don't usually just trust strangers willy-nilly like that. I just couldn't see any other option. So I walked until I found a little cottage. It was a charming dwelling, with ivy crawling up the walls and all that. It gave me the confidence to knock on the door.

A little boy opened the door, peeking out with wide blue eyes.

"Excuse me," I said as sweetly as I could. "Could you tell me where the nearest town is?"

He shook his head, but said, "Mama and Papa went to town. They'll be back soon."

"Oh." Well, how soon was soon? How long did I have to wait?

A second voice startled me. "Oh, let her in, dopey!" A girl's blonde curls appeared behind the boy. "You can play with us while we're waiting for Mama and Papa!" she exclaimed gleefully.

"We're not supposed to . . .," the boy began peevishly, but by then more and more children were crowding the door and pulling me inside. There were seven all in all, three boys and four girls. I tried to tell them it was fine, I could just wait outside, but one look at those sweet little faces and I was putty in their hands.

I don't know how their mother handled them.

I thought they would want to play things like hide-and-seek, or pick-up sticks. No way. They wanted to play "slay the dragon." Guess who was the dragon?

After hours that seemed like days of being chased around their cottage, dodging fake swords and other such hazards, they finally fell asleep, and I looked around the house guiltily. We'd made a mess. I cleaned up the best I could for their parents, then popped outside for some fresh air. So many bodies in one cottage could make things pretty stuffy.

Unfortunately, when I went outside I discovered I wasn't alone. An old woman with gold-flecked eyes was just coming out of the woods. A basket of apples was on her arm.

"Care to buy an apple, missy?" she asked, but I wasn't really paying attention. I was distracted by her eyes. Had I seen those somewhere before . . . ?

"Um, I don't have any money," I muttered when her words finally fought their way through to my brain. Gold-flecked eyes . . . gold-flecked eyes . . .

"Well, then, it's your lucky day!" she said. "I'll give you an apple for free!"

That caught my attention. "Why on earth would you do that?"

"You look hungry."

Well that was true enough. Being pursued by miniature knights certainly works up an appetite. I accepted the apple gratefully. The second I bit into it I heard a cackle, but before I could do anything about it I had a sudden vision of black.

Again, keep in mind I was very young.

The next thing I knew there was something on my lips, and when my eyes opened I found someone who was much, much too close.

I slapped him.

While he was reeling from shock I was sitting up, spitting and rubbing my lips. I was still outside the cottage, but judging by the position of the sun, a few hours had passed. I assumed it was still the same day, because if the children's parents had come home they probably would have done something with the random girl lying in their yard other than continuing to let her lie.

But I digress. "Excuse me?" I shrieked. "Just who do you think you are?"

His gold-flecked eyes were wide as he spluttered, "I . . . you . . . it looked like you were dead. . . ."

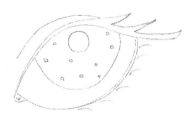

"And you make a habit of kissing all the random dead girls you find in the forest?" I raged. I raised my hand for another slap, before I took a second look at his face.

Gold-flecked eyes . . . like the witch . . . and the soldier . . . and there were shape-shifters in the forest who liked to play with emotions. . . .

"Who's that?" asked a sleepy voice from the doorway. The children had woken up.

297

I felt a wicked smile creep up my face. "This," I told the boy matter-of-factly, "is a dragon."

Eventually the children's parents came home, after the kids and I had trussed up our shape-shifter. The parents took me home, and I told my stepmother everything (except that I suspected her of trying to kill me, I thought that might not go over so well). The soldier had apparently been informed by a maid with gold-flecked eyes that I had decided against picking wildflowers that day. I now pick either alone or with the children (it's funny how comforting they can be after you've seen them attacking a shape-shifter), and refuse to trust anyone with gold-flecked eyes.

Have you got a problem with that?

© Rosie Hendrickson 2012

About the Author

Roselyn (Rosie) Hendrickson is studying English at Brigham Young University and lives with her laptop, Percival, and hyperactive kitten, Merida. She enjoys fencing (the kind with a sword), singing where no one can hear her, long books, and bad weather.

About the Illustrator

Art has always been Candiss West's passion. She began investing herself into her artwork as a prospective career path at the age of 14, won contests and even received praise after applying to work on her favorite graphic novels, Elfquest.

Candiss' artwork has been used in many anthologies and picture books. Her most recent work can be found in Pat Hatt's *The Out of Tune Moon*.

Please visit her website
http://candyboutique.wix.com/candiss.

To submit a story or poem
for our next anthology,
Monstrous Myths & Legends,
please visit Waymanpublishing.com

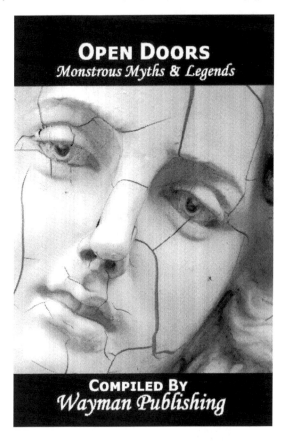

Projected Release: November 2013

If you've enjoyed this book, please check out the other fantasy books Wayman Publishing has to offer.

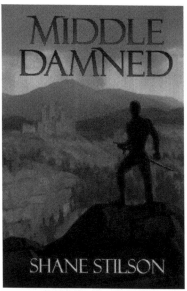

Middle Damned
By Shane Stilson

Life after death proved much different than what the Stillwater family expected. Two go into the light, another into darkness, while Blake Stillwater fights for survival somewhere between, in the Realm of the Middle Damned. He will receive gifts from the members of his family he unwittingly killed, but even as those who love the light will be just, the Forces of Evil groom the one now dwelling in darkness to ruin it all. Caught in a crosswind between the dimensions of life and death, a new thought distracts Blake when he can least afford it. Is what he works toward real or is he lost in a coma-induced dream? In an attempt to get back to those of his family who survived, Blake will be willing to risk it all, and the rest be damned.

The Sword of Senack
(Book One in *The Merson Cycle*)

Aliya Fisher knows nothing about her true heritage until a vindictive sorceress kidnaps her brother and sister. The young adventurer must take up her birthright, battle eerie creatures, and find the Sword of Senack if she hopes to best the witch. But even if Aliya finds the famed weapon and survives the perilous oceanic journey, the enchantress is far more than she appears. How does one defeat an immortal who lusts for revenge?

www.waymanpublishing.com

Made in the USA
Charleston, SC
28 November 2012